IT CALLS FROM THE FOREST
VOLUME ONE

AN EERIE RIVER PUBLISHING ANTHOLOGY

IT CALLS FROM THE FOREST
VOLUME ONE

Paperback ISBN: 978-1-7770410-7-6
Hardcover ISBN: 978-1-7770410-8-3
Digital ISBN: 978-1-7770410-1-4

Edited by Alanna Robertson-Webb
Cover design by Michelle River
Book Formatting by Michelle River
Title page art by Sebastian Zunino

When you are finished reading this collection of stories please take a moment and review it on Amazon, Goodreads, and/or BookBub.

**AVAILABLE NOW FROM
EERIE RIVER PUBLISHING**

Storming Area 51: Horror At the Gate
Don't Look: 12 Stories of Bite Sized Horror

COMING SOON: 2020

Forgotten Ones: Drabbles of Myth and Legend
It Calls From The Forest
It Calls From The Forest: Volume II
It Calls From The Sky
It Calls From The Sea
The Spaces In Between

Dedicated to all our families and friends. Those that have stood beside us, and often behind us while we type away, bringing us coffee and listening to us talk about our characters as if they were real; because they are.

Thank you for believing in us.

Contents

Foreword

We want to take a moment and thank you for purchasing this book, for supporting Eerie River Publishing and for experiencing the talented authors we've featured.

It is in our nature to seek the wild. We yearn for it, we crave it within the essence of our souls. We clamour out of cities to search it out, this fleeting promise of peace and solitude within nature.

There are dangers that lurk within the boundaries of trees and soil, where fresh air and meandering streams are not the only things that whisper our names.

Inside this anthology of the dark and twisted, you will read original stories over from award-winning authors that have dared to take this journey. Let them weave you tales of the hidden, secrets within plain sight. Stories of beasts, both human and not, and of unspeakable horrors dwelling amid the trees.

May you be forever entertained,
Eerie River Publishing

A Wail of a Tail
Emma K. Leadley

Bill's stomach grumbled loudly enough that his dog, Jasper, turned to see what the noise was. They had spent a long, fruitless day together, and now dusk was setting. No damned animal had stayed long enough in the groundsman's sights for him to aim, and even his traps had been disappointingly empty of potential dinner. Not even a tasteless, bony squirrel. Vegetable stew and stale bread it would have to be.

Taking one last look around before heading for the cabin, his heart leapt. Deep-brown fur flashed between the trunks only a short distance away. Bill estimated it to be the size of a very large cat — enough to eat like a king for a week. He pulled up his rifle and breathed deeply to steady his shoulders. Taking aim a single shot rang out, followed by a shrill, piercing scream. "Come on, lad," he called to Jasper whilst running towards the kill. "Dinner for us!"

On the ground, where the creature should have been, was a tail. It was thick, meaty, and covered in coarse fur. Yet here was no body and, even more puzzling to Bill, no blood — not even a drop. He scratched his head whilst he looked around, perhaps it was getting too dark? Jasper circled, whining in excitement, but couldn't find a scent trail to follow. It was as though the creature had just... disappeared...

Bill hefted the tail; it was definitely enough to add to the stew pot. Back at the cabin he sat on the stoop and skinned it, hanging the pelt on the rafters to dry. He cut round the bones, and finding them too small for Jasper, threw them into the woods for something else to enjoy. Taking up his knife again he sliced the remaining meat, thinking how sweet it smelt, not earthy like the plentiful squirrels or occasional deer that were his usual fare. Stirring together his foraged selection of herbs and bartered vegetables with the meat, he left the stew to cook over the open fire.

As it bubbled away the cabin filled with a mouth-watering smell. It was exotic and intoxicating, unlike anything Bill had ever experienced before. It promised a satisfying meal and, when staring into the smoke from the fire, he saw strange shapes form: hints of adventure and riches, the woman of his dreams...No, not just those, but all his hopes and aspirations coming to pass?

He shook his head, clearing his sight and his mind. Something wasn't right. Had he put the wrong kind of mushrooms in the cooking pot? Jasper didn't even seem to smell anything — he should be whining and pacing by now. But, Bill thought, the meat was tender, and he was ravenous.

He spooned a large portion into his bowl and dug straight in. His lips and tongue blistered with the heat as he ate, but he didn't care. It tasted too good. He continued eating, spoon after spoon, topping up from the pot and shovelling it into his mouth as though in a trance. He mopped up every last drop with bread.

"Sorry, lad," he said, turning to Jasper as he realised what he'd done. "There's just biscuits left for you tonight." Bill's eyelids drooped, and even speech was an effort. It felt as though his face was disconnected from the rest of his body, and the room swam. Stumbling to his bed, like a drunkard, he sprawled flat out on the mattress fully clothed. "Must be coming down with something," he muttered.

Moments later he was snoring. The visions that had started earlier in the wood smoke invaded his dreams, flickering faster and faster. They became darker as he tossed and turned and, even asleep, he screamed. He was desperate to run from these nightmares.

He felt his limbs being ripped from his body as though they were twigs. He heard the wet pull of muscles and sinew as sharp claws shredded his torso, inch by inch. When he screamed his tongue was torn out, and he passed out from the virtual pain. He bled out, left for dead, until the cycle started over again. All the while brown fur flashed in his peripheral vision, the words "Give me my tail," repeating like a mantra.

Bill awoke with a start, gulping in a great lungful of air as he sat bolt upright. He was dripping in sweat, and he shook as the remnants of his dreams faded from memory. The embers of the fire were still burning, a candle guttering in its holder as it cast long, flickering shadows. He swung his legs out of bed, wanting to take a good swig of brandy, but something was rustling in the cabin that didn't sound like Jasper. Claws scraped and scratched along the floor, and Bill pulled himself back into bed, gripping the blanket as he stared into the shadows.

He couldn't see anything, but the noise got louder. Closer. With a final grunt whatever it was stopped, and Bill came face-to-face with orange, glowing eyes. The bright eyes were peering out from coarse, matted fur as it landed on his chest. It stank. Bill choked on the smell, eyes watering as he tried to wriggle out from under the fetid creature. Its sharp teeth and claws glinted in the dancing light, pointed ears silhouetted against the cabin.

"Give me my tail," it said, mouth working hard to make the right shapes to talk.

Bill blinked and rubbed his eyes. Surely this was another layer of dreams? Jasper paced round, hackles raised, teeth bared as he rumbled a low, warning growl.

"Sleep until the morning, my friend," soothed the creature. "I have no fight with you." Jasper sank to the floor, breathing deeply.

"Your dog will be fine, and tomorrow will be rewarded with a fine feast. Now! Give me my tail." the creature tapped its claws on Bill's chest. The sound boomed, vibrating through him as though the ground were shaking. His heart beat nineteen to the dozen.

"I c — c — an't," he said. "I ate it."

"Give me my tail!"

"How? I ate it!"

The creature jumped down from the bed and began marching round the cabin in circles. "Oh, oh, how I wail. Oh, oh, I want my tail," it sang in a melancholy lament, its voice pounding inside Bill's head. Every time its foot struck the floor the ground shook, and the beast appeared to grow larger. The sky filled with thunder, and rain hammered down on the roof, but all Bill could hear was the creature's song and a distant stamp, stamp, stamp, as though the thing was far away.

Bill swung out of bed with slow, gentle movements and inched towards the door. His gun was there, and he wanted the safety of its wood and metal. He needed a barrier to put between himself, and whatever that creature was. Perhaps, if the threat of the gun wasn't enough to scare it off, then he'd have to shoot it. He'd have to steady his hands first though.

Before he could reach the door the creature loomed over him, even larger than before. It was grinning, a too-human expression. "I want my tail." It reached out a claw-tipped limb and pushed against the man, sending him sprawling to the floor.

Bill scrambled backwards, eyes darting back and forth as he calculated the distance to the door. Not much further...

The creature jumped, landing on his chest. The iron-like weight forced the air out of Bill's lungs, and he struggled against it. The creature weighed too much, and it pinned his entire body down. Bill's vision flickered and blurred with the lack of oxygen. He screamed, emptying his lungs, and just like in his nightmares the creature grabbed his tongue and pulled. He passed out as agonizing pain overwhelmed his body, not hearing the loud 'snap' that would have rung through his ears as his jaw dislocated.

The creature forced a limb down Bill's throat, claws scratching and gouging, shredding the windpipe and lungs as it worked its way down. "Oh, oh, how I wail. Oh, oh, I can't reach my tail," it sang as it pulled the limb back.

It jumped off Bill's chest and dug its claws lower down into his torso, a wet, ripping sound filling the cabin as muscle and sinew was torn from bone. Sharp cracks rang out as the creature broke through the man's ribs, and soon lengths of intestine filled the floor as the creature piled up semi-digested chunks of meat.

It slipped and slithered through the eviscerated remains to the door, returning a short time later with the discarded tail bones and pelt. Piling everything up together it started singing again, this time happy and upbeat. "Oh, oh, I no longer flail. Oh, oh, I have my tail,"

It pieced together the pelt, flesh and bone, hydrating it with fresh blood from Bill's corpse. With a quick, sharp toss the tail arced through the air, the creature jumping and wiggling excitedly below until the tail reattached. With a swish of its rebuiltd tail the creature left the cabin. It shrunk back to it's normal size, and gleefully jumped and leapt its way into the woods.

* * *

A few hours later, at dawn, Jasper awoke. He licked his lips at the smell of blood and raw intestines, saliva drooling from his mouth. After too many meals of dried bread and biscuits this truly was a fine feast. Out the open door of the cabin, a flash of chestnut-colored fur caught his eye, but Jasper didn't care. He was hungry. Squatting down, he had his fill.

Emma K. Leadley
About the Author

Emma K. Leadley (she/her) is a UK-based writer, creative geek, and devourer of words, images and ideas. She began writing both fiction and creative non-fiction as an outlet for her busy brain, and quickly realised scrawling words on a page is wired into her DNA.

Emma has always had a love of putting words together but only more recently developed the confidence for those words to reach further than gathering cyber-dust on her hard drive. Since early 2019, she's had multiple fiction stories published (or are upcoming) online, in eBook and in print, ranging from 100 words to 2000 words. They're mainly speculative tales: fantasy or horror with some science-fiction thrown in.

The biggest surprise to Emma was a new-found love of writing horror: she is a total wimp when it comes to watching anything with even the vaguest hint of horror — yes, that includes Doctor Who, Stranger Things and Buffy the Vampire Slayer — unless it's animated or in book form and consumed in daylight with the curtains open.

Visit her online at her blog where she talks about writing, books and other topics: autoerraticism.com; her author website for new and upcoming publications, emmaleadley.co.uk; or on Twitter @autoerraticism.

THE THING IN THE WOODS
D. R. SMITH

We found it in the woods behind my house. My friends and I were playing hide-and-seek when Austin tripped over it, doing a faceplant in the mud. It sat under a birch tree, black and steaming like some weird, volcanic rock belched out of the earth.

It fascinated us.

All its surfaces were smooth, flat, and gleaming. Yet it shimmered, it stirred, even as it sat motionless amid the weeds. It warned us away, yet tempted us to touch it. It was everything boys like us dreamt of finding in their treasure-hunting forays into the woods, all of the wonders of the world in one odd thing. And it was a nightmare. A strange, beckoning nightmare, a horror for which we had no response except to stare at it.

"What is it?" Justin asked, wandering over from his hiding spot.

I glanced at my friend. "I don't..." I started to answer, but my throat dried up. "HellifIknow," I spat out as a single word.

Austin brushed the leaves and mud off his clothes. "Why does it look like that?" he said.

"Is it alive?" Justin asked.

We crept up to it for a closer look.

The rock, for I had no better word to call it, seemed to shrink and expand imperceptibly, as though it drew quick, shallow breaths. Its angles and lines morphed into curves and corners almost at once, like a weird trick of the light. But that didn't make sense, because the sun was hidden behind the clouds. There was no wind to speak of either.

Something else, then.

The rock stared back at us, though it hadn't the eyes of a living thing. Yet living it was, living and watching, as if it had been waiting patiently to be found for a thousand years.

Waiting for us.

"What do we do with it?" Justin asked.

"What can we do?" Austin replied. He reached out to poke it and then jerked his hand away. "It's hot!"

Justin stuck his own hand out and touched it. "Freezing," he said matter-of-factly. "Like ice."

Both of them turned to look at me.

It was my turn. I slowly reached out and brushed my fingertips along its unexpectedly silky surface. "Warm," I told them. I was about to add that they were both crazy, but how could I? The rock was crazy. It shouldn't have been there. It belonged on another planet somewhere.

I was convinced of that fact, but not enough yet to share my theory with my friends.

"What do we do with it, Mike?" Austin sucked his burning fingers and looked at me.

It was a fair question. My family owned the woods, so the rock was on my land. It made sense that it fell to me to decide. Only I wanted no part of it. No part of the thing, the rock, or whatever the Hell it was. No part of this whole weird day. My stomach hurt and bile bubbled up my throat as my eyes strained to focus on the thing's constantly churning surface.

"Kill it," I heard myself say.

We stared at the rock.

Austin had his slingshot with him. We all did when we played in the woods. We called them our peacemakers, but we were really just looking for squirrels to target.

He pulled back on it now and launched a sharp-edged stone at the rock from only three feet away. He shouldn't have missed, but the missile sliced harmlessly into the tall grass behind the rock, which had shifted in the weeds in the blink of an eye to avoid the projectile.

Austin took a step back, startled. "Did you see that? It moved!"

We saw it, Christ Almighty.

Justin fired a shot; same result. The rock jigged to the side again. The thing was now six inches from the spot where we'd originally found it, quivering, gleaming, smirking at us. Somehow I knew the rock was mocking us. Daring us.

"It won't work," I said, sighing. "It's been waiting too long, and now it has what it wants."

"What's that?" Justin asked.

"Us."

A sudden urge told me to pick it up. I was twelve; how could I resist? Boys our age have urges coursing through their bodies all the time, usually about girls, but this one was different.

This one was coming from the rock.

"Let's take it with us."

Austin looked at me like I was insane. "What do you mean, 'take it with us?'" He was almost in hysterics. "What for!? Why? C'mon, Mike, what are you going to do with it? I mean, it freaks me out."

"I don't know yet." I walked up to it and placed both hands on it. I felt a thrumming vibration deep below the surface of the thing, as though energy cells were heating up.

"Help me," I called over my shoulder. I tried lifting it myself, but the bitch was heavy. Though the rock was only a little bigger than a bowling ball it was incredibly dense. My back muscles protested as all three of us carried it to my house.

"Let's take it inside," I said, as we struggled to climb the steps of the back deck.

Fortunately no one was home. My mother had taken Cody, my four-year-old brother, to the park and Dad was at work. We lugged the rock into the living room and set it down slowly, making sure it wouldn't crash through the floor. Then we all sat around it, cross-legged, like three chiefs planning their battle strategy. My heart roared in my chest. I couldn't tear my eyes away from the rock, from the subtle and ever-changing patterns of faint luminescence on its surface.

MMMiiiiikkkeee, the thing taunted. But it was only my imagination.

Or so I told myself.

"How much do you think we can get for it?" Austin asked. I looked at him. When you're a kid you ask dumb questions, dream stupid dreams, and wish for things that can never happen.

"Who the Hell would pay for something like this?" I asked him.

"A collector of some sort," he mumbled, shaking his head.

"Of some sort," Justin mocked, smacking him on the arm.

The rock, still breathing, waited.

I felt I had to ask the question that I knew was on all of our minds. "I wonder what it can do."

Austin perked up. "You mean, like, its powers or something?"

"I'll bet it has some," I said. "I felt something inside the rock while I was carrying it in. Energy waves, or something."

"Me too," Austin said.

"Maybe it's a meteorite," Justin replied. His dad was an astronomer at the local university, so he was always talking about space.

I smiled. This wasn't just a piece of cosmic scrap metal that fell from outer space. It was…intelligent. I didn't sense a complex brain, however, but rather a desire to live, to feed. Yes, that's what it was. A spike of fear drove through my body. I immediately put a stop to my thoughts before they led me to a place I didn't want to go.

"It's no meteorite," I declared. "But I don't think it came from here, either."

"You mean the woods?"

I glanced at Justin. "I meant Earth."

Time passed. The surface of the rock, the thing, whatever you want to call it, flowed in waves of dreamy color, entrancing us completely. Suddenly a cold, wet touch on the back of my neck made me jump. Our tabby cat, Mewler, was curiously nosing around us. She stopped in mid-stride when she saw the rock. She froze, the tip of her tail twitching curiously.

"I wonder what it can do," Justin whispered to himself when he, too, noticed the cat.

Then he lunged with incredible speed and scooped up Mewler before I could stop him.

I must not have been the only one the thing was communicating with. Justin dropped the cat on top of the rock. At first, nothing happened. Mewler lowered her head and sniffed at the thing, pawed at it lightly, and issued a few warning sounds in the back of her throat. We remained still, gawping at the cat. I should've snatched her away immediately. Why didn't I? It was Cody's cat for Chrissakes, but what would happen if…

Suddenly a small opening at the top of the rock sprang open with a metallic clank, and Mewler got sucked inside. Bent and twisted at sickening angles, her joints popped and her leg bones splintered as she cried like a human baby for us to rescue her. The cat got drawn down into the rock in stages, like a python gulping its prey, and after about twenty seconds, she was gone. The rock made a series of disgusting slurping sounds and gaseous exhales as the last few inches of tail disappeared into its maw.

Then a horrific fount of gore erupted into the air, splattering all of us in the face. It flowed over the sides of the rock like an erupting volcano, and when I looked back on it later I didn't think the cat suffered too much beyond the first few seconds. It was lights out for Mewler before she ever really knew what happened.

I must have blacked out, because when I regained my senses both of my friends were screaming and practically sitting on top of me. The thing was still in the middle of the living room floor, except that it had changed.

Mewler was back, only it wasn't Cody's cat anymore.

The lifeforce in the rock stared at us from behind those imperious, feline eyes. Not a cat, but something alien.

And hungry.

Mewler watched us with an icy gaze. Those crazy, geometric patterns from the rock were swarming all over her body, changing colors, shapes and sizes. They made her silky coat ripple, as though invisible fingers stroked it in haphazard directions.

"We have to kill it," I sobbed. I loved that damn cat, but now I was thinking about my family. We had to kill it before they got home.

Before it grew large enough to swallow us whole.

But just as I thought it the cat leaped forward and dashed from the room. Her legs made grinding sounds, like rusty gears, as she fled down the hallway with all of us in close pursuit. She headed for Cody's bedroom where Miranda, our labradoodle, slept during the day.

The cat was lightning quick, and it pounced on Miranda while she slept at the foot of the bed. We had no chance to stop what happened next. The cat's mouth cranked wide open just as the rock's hole had, the top of her head falling backward until she stared upside down at us with glassy eyes. A series of mechanical whirrings and buzzings emanated from her chest as it sprang open, revealing a menacing row of razor-sharp teeth.

I stared in horror as the teeth began chugging and spinning, just like a circular saw. They sank into the dog's squishy middle, and gouts of blood erupted in thick waves that painted the walls and ceiling with gore. Clanks and clunks echoed in the thing's belly, like a lawn mower running over fallen branches. The dog was devoured, bones and all, in greedy, wet gulps. Mewler, the rock, whatever you want to call it, sat astride it now, sucking down the last sinewy bits of dog meat until nothing remained but a crimson stain on the floor.

Miranda didn't even have time to bark. The cat, now

so engorged and fattened with meat that it looked once again like a rock with stubby legs, rolled over and let out a belch that filled the room with a fetid, greasy stink.

Then, horrifically, its stomach broke open.

Watching Miranda ooze out of the gash in Mewler's belly was like watching a baby calf be born. Miranda, smothered in sticky pink viscera, shook the cat's guts off its matted fur and stood before us on unsteady legs. Our adorable little Labradoodle was now a monstrosity, her mawing showing off teeth that packed its mouth like razor blades. It glared at us wetly and barked, only it didn't sound like Miranda's bark anymore. No, there was nothing about it that sounded like a dog anymore. It was almost like it was trying to utter a word.

It was almost like it was trying to say my name.

Beside me Austin puked all over his shoes, and Justin had the shakes so bad I actually heard his teeth chatter.

"Get back!" I screamed, herding us all out into the hallway. I slammed the bedroom door shut. Clutching the knob I braced for the impact of the thing, but nothing happened. Except for my own ragged breathing, and the muffled sobs of my friends, all was eerily quiet. It could have broken through the flimsy door any time that it wanted. What was it waiting for?

I'm waiting for you, the rock's voice hissed in my head. Though it added nothing more of value I had the distinct impression it couldn't attack again because it was sated.

For now.

I dragged Austin and Justin downstairs with me to look for weapons. The basement was large and overflowing with boxes of crap my parents refused to throw away, most of it stacked into towers resembling a cardboard metropolis of forgotten memories.

What was I searching for? A gun? Unlikely I'd find one. My father wasn't a hunter; he didn't believe in it. He told me once that he believed in a universe of kindness and order. He couldn't accept chaos as a functional part of life.

Neither could I, until I found the thing in the woods.

Austin paced around, not looking for a weapon but wandering aimlessly. He was scratching his head and waving his arms around.

"Calm down," I commanded, but I only agitated him more.

"Did you see what that fucker did up there?" Fucker. Now it was out in the open. We were talking about a living thing.

"Of course we did," Justin said.

"It ate his cat, man, and his fucking labradoodle!"

"So it did," I said calmly. For the first time since we found the rock I felt myself gain control of my emotions. I kicked over a few more boxes. Where the Hell did my dad keep his old golf clubs?

"I guess we know it's power." Justin slumped against the wall, exhausted. He looked green, like he was going to be sick.

"We don't know shit," I pointed out. A couple more

boxes tumbled over, disgorging Christmas memorabilia.

"It needs to fucking die," Justin pointed out uselessly.

"That's why we're here," I said. "We're looking for a weapon."

"It needs to die," Justin repeated, only not to us. He was saying it to himself now, like a mantra, something his mind could hold on to so it wouldn't slip away into infinite madness.

"We'll kill it," I assured him.

Austin came up to me and grabbed my shirt. His gamey breath wafted into my face. "How, smart guy? How do you kill a fucking, whatever the fuck it is? It's a goddamn robot or something, a monster. That's it — a fucking robot monster."

"Dude, get a grip!" I shouted, shoving him off me. Austin must have seen something he didn't like in my eyes, because he sank to the floor next to Justin and shied away.

"It'll be alright," I said, with all the conviction I could muster. "It has to be alright. That thing can't be allowed to leave Cody's room. Alive, that is."

"We need help," Justin said, his face crumpling into tears.

"Yeah, from who?" I shouted. "The cops? You think they'll believe us? Austin here has been busted twice in school for marijuana possession, and last year got caught slashing school bus tires. They'll assume we made the whole story up to cover our asses. Wouldn't you? Then, when they find the blood all over the walls in the living room and Cody's bedroom, they'll drag us to juvie for killing the animals. And what'll happen to that thing if we're gone, huh? It'll keep on killing, that's what, and the taste it got for cat and dog won't last for long."

"Did you see it grow?" Justin muttered. His voice sounded distant and detached. "After it ate Mewler? It got bigger."

"And it took her shape," Austin added. He shook his head like he didn't believe his own words. "It's a fucking shape-shifter, dude."

We were silent after that for a few minutes, each of us catching our breaths and thinking. I couldn't say I was thinking about much though; by then my mind was a total blank, but the silence was a blessing. It gave me a chance to scan the basement and continue looking for weapons. Could we beat the thing to a pulp while it was still small, wound it enough so that we could carry it out of the house? When we got it outside I knew exactly where I wanted to dump it: in the pond my parents installed last year. We found the rock on dry land, so maybe it hated water. Maybe we could drown it. It was worth a try, but first we needed a weapon.

"It doesn't belong here." Justin's dreamy voice and glazed eyes were starting to spook me. He seemed to be in deep shock.

"What do you mean?" Austin croaked.

"My dad makes me read science fiction sometimes," he said. "He told me it'll make me like science class better, but I still hate it. Anyway, did you ever read War of the Worlds?"

"Saw the movie," I said.

"The machines that woke up and started destroying everything were already here, buried in the ground for thousands of years. Put there by some race of aliens a long time ago. Then one day they just flipped the switch when it was time to annihilate us all."

"Armafuckingeddon," Austin added unhelpfully. I didn't like what I heard in his voice.

"Bullshit," I said.

He shrugged. "Then where the Hell did that rock come from? What is it? No person built a thing like that."

"We don't know that," I said. "We don't know anything about it."

"My dad says the more science teaches us the less we actually know," Justin said vaguely.

"Wow, that's deep Mr. Professor," I said, "but not very helpful. Do you have any more insights, Einstein?"

"It talked to me," Justin continued. "It told me to pick up Mewler."

I believed him. I heard the voice too. Besides, there's no way Justin would murder my cat without good reason, not with knowing I'd kick his ass for it.

I glanced at Austin. "Has it talked to you?"

Austin looked away, and said in a small voice, "Yes. It wanted me to pick it up."

"The rock?"

"Yes," he growled, "and smash it on your head!"

I swallowed hard. It was only a matter of time before one of us snapped. We were close to it already. Justin was spacing out, and Austin had a look to him like one of those meth heads in those scared-straight videos they showed us in health class. Like he could murder someone. We had to go back up there, take care of business, and do it quick. But not empty-handed.

Goddammit, where are those golf clubs?

Then I noticed the furnace, and the dark space behind it. I hurried over to investigate and broke out in a grin. Wedged back in there, moldy and forgotten, were my dad's old clubs from his college days. I started pulling them out, one-by-one, discarding the wooden ones immediately. I settled on three of the irons, giving the five-iron to Justin and the six-iron to Austin. I kept the nine-iron for myself. Thus armed we faced each other solemnly one last time.

"Anyone got anything to say?" I looked them both in the eyes. "It's now or never."

"Let's waste the motherfucker," Austin snarled.

I couldn't agree more, and without another word we marched up the stairs to finish the deed. As we neared the top of the stairs I heard a sound. A muffled scrape, like a chair being pulled back on linoleum. Then footsteps thumping around hollowly in the house. My heart jackhammered in my throat. I bounded up the remaining stairs and burst through the door — and found my mother standing in the kitchen, chopping carrots and singing softly to herself.

"Hello, Michael," she said cheerfully. "Are your friends staying for dinner?" Her eyes narrowed when she noticed the golf clubs in our hands. "Thinking of taking up the sport? Your father would be so proud. He thinks you spend too much time playing video games."

"Jesus, Mom!" I cried, shaking violently. "Where's Cody?"

"Language, young man! He's in his room, of course. He couldn't wait to get home and play with Miranda. What's gotten into you?"

Once when I was five a hornet stung me on the ass. I was sitting in the middle of a clump of clover, watching my mom pull weeds, when the goddamn thing came out of nowhere and plunged its stinger right in my crack. I howled in agony for a good half hour and had to sit on bags of frozen peas for the rest of the afternoon. An existential moment, I guess you could say, when I learned the universe could give two shits about my personal welfare.

But I never realized until now how cruel the universe could actually be.

I shot off toward Cody's room, Justin and Austin at my heels with my mother's frantic voice floating in the air behind us.

When I reached Cody's door I stopped and listened. A scuffling sound came from the room, then a low, lilting hum, like a little boy singing to himself. My head buzzed as relief flooded through me. The voice was Cody's. I swallowed a lump in my throat and handed my golf club over to Justin. I didn't want my little brother to be spooked when he saw me, and I didn't want to set that thing off and make it feel threatened either. It must have still been digesting.

What must Cody be thinking about all the blood in his room? He wasn't crying, which was good. I decided I was going to calmly get my little brother out of there. I was going to do it quickly and quietly, and then I was going to buy him the biggest goddamn ice cream cone he'd ever seen. After we drowned the Miranda-thing in the pond, of course.

I twisted the knob and pushed the door open, only to feel the universe sting me in the ass again.

Cody stood in the middle of the floor, arms at his sides, head cocked slightly to the left. His expression was serene, his skin shiny and swirling with those perfectly alien colors. A wet ring of sticky blood encircled his mouth, and more stained the front of his Curious George T-shirt. His eyes lit up with recognition when he saw me. Miranda was gone, and the room stunk like a morgue.

Cody lifted his hand and gave me a little wave.

I braced myself for what I had to do. I had my friends; I had my mission. There are no answers sometimes for the mysteries of life, but there comes a time when the questions don't matter anymore. Sometimes all you need to do is finish the job.

Justin came up behind me and slipped the cool steel of the nine-iron into my hand, and whispered, "I'll distract your mom."

D.R. Smith
About the Author

D. R. Smith lives in Livonia, NY with his wife and two children. He is a special education teacher in the Canandaigua City School District in Upstate New York. Ever since he was a boy, his haunted dreams have spurred him to write about the macabre. He loves a good horror story, especially ones that leave you wondering what horrors even the author was afraid to write. His favorite authors include Stephen King, Clive Barker, Ray Bradbury, and Neil Gaiman. He's published numerous short stories in Ezines and local magazines. He is the author of over a dozen books for teens and young readers, both horror and fantasy, and three writing guides for people of all ages. His latest horror novel, Curse of the Witch, is available on Amazon.

Check out his work at his website http://www.davidrsmith-books.com or visit him on twitter @DavidRSmith20.

THE HIKE
E.E.W. CHRISTMAN

The morning's gray. The air is cold and dry, and I wriggle deeper into the nest of blankets I've made. I'm briefly alarmed when I see Becca's gone, but then a sleep-muddled memory reminds me: it was dark. Early in the morning. Becca was shaking me, saying my name: "Steph. Steph, wake up."

"Mmhmm. What?"

"I'm going for a hike. I'll be back later, okay?"

"Mhm."

"I love you."

"Loveyoutoobye."

She'd looked so sad. She was probably still upset about the fight…

The fight. I had almost forgotten about it in the brain-fog of early morning. I groan as it comes rushing back, pulling the blankets over my face as if I could hide from the memories. I couldn't, so I try running from them. I jump out of bed, dragging the blankets with me through our cold cabin. The stove, which was the only source of heat, had gone out in the night. I ignite it again, then make a cup of breakfast tea, wishing I could go out for coffee. We were miles from anything, and hours from anything good. Out here, in the Oregon woods during the chill of January, it was just Becca and me. Or just me, it seemed. Becca hadn't come back from her hike yet. I check the clock. Nine in the morning. When had she gone out? It had still been dark. When did the sun rise in January? Becca would've known.

I don't know how Becca can even think about physical activity. After yesterday's excursion, I never want to move again. Every muscle aches, and my bones creak from the cold. She was like a mountain lion, I guess. Powerful, wild, strong. I was more like a housecat that had accidentally wandered outside, coming home damp and grumpy, desperately wanting to curl up in a warm, comfy spot by the window.

Ten minutes pass. I finish my tea, and feel warmer. I pace the cabin, glance out the window up the winding trail, see no one, then continue pacing. She's punishing me, sulking outside because she knows I'll sulk in here. That's the angry part of my brain as it fizzes with emotional conspiracies. The anxious part of my brain is whirling with body-horror fantasies of Becca's beautiful face mangled at the bottom of some trail, or her strong calves broken and bloody, trapped under a rock or a tree.

I groan. The housecat was going to have to check on

the mountain lion.

Outside the wind rips at my coat. There are only a few paths leading away from our cabin: the road we drove to get here and two trails, one of which we hiked yesterday. I take the other one. "Sunrise Trail," the sign reads. This path is rougher than the other. It leads up the foothill, narrow and overgrown, barely keeping the forest at bay. I'm panting by the time I reach the top, leaning on my thighs, sweat dripping onto the forest floor. In front of me is a sheer rock face, and at first it seems the trail ends here. However, as I look more closely, I see steps carved into the stone, leading upwards to a plateau. The perfect spot to watch the sunrise.

There's an alarming yellow sign nearby: DANGER–ROCKSLIDES. Next to it is a smaller, wooden sign: "Sunrise Trail: Warning! Falls have resulted in death. Stay on the trail. Be alert." The anxiety rises in my throat again, like thick bile. I imagine Becca. Beautiful, superwoman Becca, who ran marathons and chased goats up mountains. Climbing to the top, watching the sun rise over the naked trees, briefly transforming the gray landscape into a forest of warm honey. I imagine her foot slipping. She falls down the other side, her body a mangled mess on the ground somewhere I couldn't see.

The steps are difficult to navigate. They're littered with pebbles, still slick with morning dew. Some instinctive, panicked part of my reptilian brain tells me to run up them as quickly as possible, but I take each step carefully, my hands clinging to the rockface. My progress is slow, and as I near the top I'm practically crawling. But I reach the top. Up ahead there's a clear, wide horizon. The sun is obscured by slate-colored clouds now, but it must be quite a sight on a clear, summer day. Becca would definitely want to watch the sunrise here, regardless of the weather. After a moment of looking around, I find proof.

At the edge of the cliff I find Becca's clothes. They're not strewn across the stone, but carefully folded into a neat pile. Her pants, jacket, sweater, t-shirt, bra and underwear, all meticulously left with care. Her socks are even gently tucked into her boots. I look over the edge, but the only thing below me is more rocks. I spin around, but the only obvious way down is the way I'd come.

"BECCA!!!"

My voice echoes across the treetops. A few birds squawk unhappily and fly from their perches, and they're my only response.

The ranger station. I'd seen it on our way in. It was at the entrance to the camping area, inside the park. It was only five miles or so. I'd get in Becca's truck. I'd drive there. And tell the ranger…

The words are there, hovering in the forefront of my mind. I can taste them, can feel the pressure of them in my mouth. But when I try to say them, they dissolve into nonsense. My girlfriend went for a hike. She took off all her clothes, and disappeared into the woods. I'd have to say it. It was true. I start to bring Becca's clothes with me, but what if she came back for them? I refuse to think about her not coming back — I push thoughts like the cold and the weather, and words like "exposure", out of my mind. I compromise and take her coat and boots, leaving everything else in their neat, cold piles on the plateau.

The walk back seems shorter. Easier. I barely register my movements at all. Adrenaline? Fear? The woods are barely on my radar. I keep thinking about Becca, and how she'd looked this morning when she'd woken me up. Out of focus, eyebrows furrowed, her eyes so sad...had there been tears? I didn't want that to be my last memory of her. Sleep-fuzzy, upset, possibly crying before disappearing into the forest. That couldn't be how we ended. It just couldn't.

I reach our cabin, panting. Had I been running? I am suddenly aware of the sheen of sweat stinging my face in the frigid air and the burning in my lungs. I chuck Becca's clothes into the bed of the truck, thankful she'd given me a spare key 'for emergencies'. More like when she was at my apartment and was too lazy to get out of bed to move her car. As active as Becca was, she loathed putting her clothes on after sex...

And I have to force happy memories down. They're too sad now. Maybe. I didn't know yet, I remind myself. This could all still be some misunderstanding. I cling to that feeling as my stomach twists into a grieving knot. I get in the truck. The engine lurches, gives a heaving, oily whimper, and dies. I turn the key again, refusing to believe that the truck wasn't going to start when I most needed it to. It sputters again before fizzling away.

"Why is my life a goddamn movie!?" I punch the

wheel and the horn goes off, scaring some nearby squirrels.

What do you need, Truck? Gas, oil, a new battery, a hug? What? I pop open the hood, but even my unmechanical eyes can spot the problem. Some very important-looking wires and tubes have been cut. Not broken, not chewed. There's no fraying. Someone came here, and opened up Becca's truck...

I turn slowly toward the woods, but nothing moves. There's only the unflinching, unending gray of barren, wintry trees. My girlfriend went for a hike. She disappeared, leaving her clothes...

Or someone left them for me to find. Maybe the same someone who messed with the truck. Maybe they were still here, watching me. I turn back to the cabin. Had I locked it in my haste? The windows were dark, and there was no movement from inside.

I run. The rest is a blur of nightmarish shadows rushing around me, darting through the trees, matching my pace. Never catching me, and never letting me out of sight. I imagine a dark creature running low through the bushes. I think I see yellow eyes, but when I turn there's nothing. When I reach the ranger station it's raining again. I pound up the stairs to the cabin, gasping for breath and choking on raindrops. I scan the woods, looking for someone lurking in the brush and undergrowth, but I appear to be alone.

The ranger station squats above the ground on stilts, with stairs leading to a narrow porch that wraps around the entire cabin. The door is at the other side, and it's open. No, it's not just open, it's broken. The door hangs off a single hinge, and the wood has been torn in places. Fluffs of splinters dangle from its edges and fall onto the floor of the cabin, which is now damp with rain.

Claw marks. The ruined door and doorframe are covered in long gashes.

Looks like claw marks, Steph. I think it very loudly, trying to keep my heart from breaking my ribcage. Run. Runrunrunrunrunrun. My brain's shrieking at me. Get the Hell out of here! I want to listen, I really do. I'm terrified. I've never been so utterly, horribly, completely scared in my entire life. But before I can decide not to go in I find myself inside the cabin, taking tentative steps, making my feet hit the floor as softly as possible. The ranger could still be here. Then again, so could the thing that destroyed the door. A bear, I guess? What else could be powerful enough to do that? And even if the ranger...well, there would still be a landline here. I could call for help.

There's a smell that sends my "fight or flight" instinct into overdrive. A pungent odor that warns other prey: stay away. It grows stronger the more steps I take. The marks that only remind me of claws, but are not necessarily claw marks, run across the floor in harsh, jagged gouges. I almost imagine I can see glimmers of the thing, running and skidding across the floorboards. The lacerations in the wood seem much, much too long. I listen, but there's only the patter of rain against the roof and window panes. Whatever was here seems to be gone, so I follow the gashes. The door opens up into a large communal area. I can see a kitchenette to the left, and the rest is a general living space. The couch is overturned. The thing leapt onto it. I can see tufts of stuffing popping out from the rips like pale cotton candy.

There's blood everywhere.

The ranger must've been sitting on his couch. There's a magazine on the floor, alongside a broken mug and a soggy teabag. Reading his magazine, drinking his tea. Then digging claws and teeth shoving him down so hard the impact sent him forward and destroyed his coffee table. That's where I find him, amidst the splinters and broken glass. I can still make out some of his uniform underneath the blood. But as for him…

He's torn apart. Open, bits of him spilling out. Things you're not supposed to see: ribs, organs, intestines, fluids, all stained a burning red. The smell is intolerable now; hot and rotten and filling my nostrils until my eyes burn. His eyes are blue. They stick out in that sea of bodily fluids. They're wide open.

I run outside, chased away by the sight and the smell. I throw up on the wet porch, my vomit slowly sliding away in the rain. I cough up a couple of sobs, too. For the ranger, for Becca. For me. The last place I want to be is inside this cabin. But after a few minutes, I make myself go back in. I need to find the phone. I make a point of not looking at the ranger. In the narrow hallway leading to the other rooms, there's an old rotary style phone on an end table. Frantic, I pick it up and start dialing 9-1-1.

The line's dead. I'm almost too petrified to look. The phone line's been neatly snipped in half, just like the truck's inner workings. I check the other rooms, but only find a dark bathroom and a bedroom. Just as I worked up the courage to check the dead man's pockets for his cellphone, I see a smartphone on the floor. Smashed into little pieces, tiny circuits and plastic crushed into useless bits. That's when the rising alarm coiling up inside of me finally snaps. I curl up on the bed and hyperventilate for at least ten minutes. But it's hard to keep track of time during a panic attack, when every second seems to draw out into an eternity of anxiety and dread.

I'm gonna die, I'm gonna die, I'm gonna die…

I force myself to take long, deep breaths. It helps a little, and eventually my heart no longer feels like it's going to tear apart my chest like the poor ranger's. I sit up, and I think.

Something was in the woods. A bear, or a cougar maybe.

And Becca was out there. Naked, confused, cold…

I needed to get out of here and find help, before Becca ended up like the ranger. I didn't want to believe she was already like the ranger. I grab two bottles of water from the fridge, drinking one right there. I put the other one in my pocket. I don't look in the living room. Outside there's a green Jeep, and the door's unlocked. Before I go looking for a key on the mangled corpse inside, I pop the hood. Someone's snipped this engine up, too. No surprise there. That left walking. The sky is illuminated by the dim ashen light of late afternoon. The sun sets early in January, so it will be dark soon.

I stick to the dirt road. It must be so easy to watch me from the trees, but I don't trust myself to try and navigate off-trail. My calves and thighs throb in protest. My feet ache. They beg me to stop. Just sit down by the side of the road, take a break, it won't matter anyway… I just keep walking. I keep looking over my shoulder. I watch the trees, expecting to see eyes. I don't know if they'll be human or not. Sometimes a twig snaps, or an owl hoots, and I break into a brief, frantic run before I calm down.

The sun is setting faster than I thought. The sky is a grisly shade of red. I try not to look at it; it reminds me of flesh. When the visceral sky finally darkens, I stop. I'm tired. There's no panic left, no adrenaline remaining in my tanks. I can't be far from the road, though. I have to keep going. I turn on the little flashlight I keep on my keychain as the woods grow dark. Every shadow looks like a monster.

Snap.

I stiffen. There is a low growl from the bushes. My blood is ice, and I can't breathe. But slowly, I swivel the light to my left. There is the glint of bright yellow eyes, the glimmer of drooling teeth embedded in a maw the size of my forearm, fur so dark I couldn't distinguish it from the night.

There's no scream, just running. The light from my phone casts an erratic silhouette into the trees and across the road as my arms move back and forth. There's the sound of paws padding behind me, gently hitting the dirt. It's much too close.

"Steph?"

I stop so fast I almost fall flat on my ass. I turn, and there she is in the harsh white light of my flashlight. Becca. Naked, caked in filth, and alive. I make a noise because there aren't words for the immense wave of relief that I feel. I take her in my arms, kissing and crying into her neck.

"Becca, Becca, oh my God…!" I wrap my coat around her, although she doesn't appear to be shivering. "We have to get out of here right now! There's…"

Nothing. Behind Becca, there's nothing in the beam of light. Where did it go? I stumble behind her, drunk on adrenal fluids and confusion. There are its tracks. God, it's enormous. Bigger than any normal wolf or bear. But are they getting smaller? My eyes are playing tricks on me. Now they're a different shape. My head is swimming. They end at Becca's bare feet, and she watches me carefully as I fumble with this information.

"The hike was beautiful this morning," she says casually, shrugging off my jacket. "I mean, you saw the ridge, didn't you? When you came looking for me? Imagine all that stone turning gold, and the trees below are every shade of red and orange and yellow…like the entire forest is burning." She turns. She's between me and the road now. Like I had any hope of outrunning her, anyway.

"I wanted us to come here together as a…kind of test," she continues, taking light, slow steps toward me.

I stumble backwards and fall, and the keys slip from my hand. The flashlight shoots out a cone of light, casting horrible shadows across Becca's body. It makes her look longer, taller, more monstrous. Or maybe she'd always been that way.

"I'm...sorry," I blurt out. "About last night. I don't even know what that was about."

This stops her. Becca cocks her head, as if she was assessing me. Then she sighs.

"You told me I was trying to shame you into changing. That hurt."

"I know. I shouldn't have said that. It's just...this isn't me." I gesture to the woods. To her. "I'm not like you."

Her face twists. She looks like she might cry. She sniffs sadly, covering her bare breasts with her arms. "I know. But I love you anyway."

"I love you, too."

"Then it doesn't matter, does it? I was so mad...until I saw you trying to save me today. You were trying so hard to get help. How can I let you go now? After all that?"

"Becca," I murmur, pushing my tired body across the ground, but it's too late. The shadows take over her body. I hear the snapping of bones as my girlfriend elongates. Is it the light? Her nose is now a hideous snout, her skin covered in nightmare fur. I can't tell if she's still smiling or snarling. Her eyes are slivers of topaz in the dark.

"I have something for you," she growls.

"P-please, Becca..."

"Don't worry, babe." Her hands — paws? — scoop

me off the ground easily. She cradles me. I try to fight, I struggle against a grip I can't break away from. I scream into a wilderness devoid of anyone who can help me.

But I'm so tired.

"It'll only hurt for a little bit," she snarls into my ear. I can feel her hot breath as she pants against my face. A long tongue flicks against my shoulder, and now I'm whimpering quietly against her. When the teeth break the skin, it's like a hot poker against my flesh, and I can't tell if I'm crying or screaming.

"We'll be so wonderful, Steph." Becca's voice fills my head as everything else fades away, consciousness dissipating. Her bite is a catalyst, I know that. My body is changing as I pass out. The last thing I hear is Becca whispering in my ear:

"We belong together now."

E.E.W. Christman
About the Author

E.E.W. Christman is a word witch who lives on Lake Sammamish near Seattle where she strings nonsense words together. She received her Bachelor's in Creative Writing and her Master's in Creative Nonfiction from Ohio University before moving to the west coast. Her work has been featured in several anthologies of fiction and in magazines, including Unwinnable Magazine, The Bronzeville Bee, & PULP Magazine. You can find more of her work on her website:

eewchristmanwriter.wordpress.com.

You can also follow her on Twitter for vague ramblings and bad jokes: @eew_christman.

Only Snow
Clint Foster

"Can you hear it?" Nils' breath heaved from his chest to his shoulders, and he was staggering against the bole of the pine upon which he leaned so heavily. He urged, "Can you?"

"No. No." Sera leaned her head against the tree. "No, only snow."

"Only snow?"

She nodded, and Nils relaxed as well. Their breath formed crystals as it slowed, in time, and they shivered as the sweat on their brows cooled. The sun had only set ten minutes ago, but it seemed like a lifetime.

Sera and Nils lived in Whitlin, where the darkness meant danger, and the days began at noon. Nestled into the foothills of the White Mountains, which were so enormous that they dominated the eastern half of the sky, Whitlin was a tough town that raised hard souls. Crops were thin, taxes were high, and no one went outside from the time the sun was gone behind the horizon to when it peaked out from the mountaintops at noon.

For decades Whitlin had run several lumber yards in the mountains, never growing beyond a small village. The people took care of one another, and had little need for bartering, or even for money at all. Most born in Whitlin never leave, because to do so would mean staying the night in the White Wood.

Miles of conifers isolated Whitlin from the rest of the world, and the only way in or out was the single road that was only passable in the summer. Hunting parties kept the city in sight when they entered the woods, and many tied ropes around their waists to anchor themselves to the rest of their group. The White Wood was not an innocent forest in which creatures thrived and frolicked. It was a dark place, contrary to its name, where ill will seemed to hang like a fog among the low boughs of the close trees. In the woods the wolves were king, not the humans.

"Only snow?" Nils repeated one last time as they both caught their breath.

"Only snow." Sera repeated. A mantra that meant safety, for now at least. A prayer to cling to in the woods.

Both of them had hunted before, and every child in Whitlin knew the rules about the White Wood. When the sun goes away, the wolves come to play, just like the rhyme said. Unfortunately, there was no helpful information on how to deal with the wolves when they came, and no one had ever brought a body back to town with them.

At his nod Nils curled around the tree and crouch-walked silently back east, toward Whitlin. His steps were soft and close, and Sera followed suit, stepping in his footprints and brushing their trail with needles. Every precaution had to be taken in the woods, since many hunters had become prey there.

A harsh gust of wind, blown down from the mountainside, brought with it a lone howl, long and low. They did not stop, pressing on and only hoping that the wolves had not yet found their trail. Sera glanced over her shoulder and could see the sun dimly through the canopy. It was low in the west, lower than she would like, and she had to focus to keep her breathing under control.

Like a thunderbolt, a cracking twig ahead of them froze the pair midstep. "Probably just the ice," Nils muttered, mostly to himself.

"Trees branches fall all the time. Besides, that howl was at least a mile away."

They nodded to one another, hands twitching as their eyes seemed to catch every flake of falling snow, every needle and cone upon the trees, every hint of movement that might betray their enemy. They found no fallen bough, but saw several freshly cracked trunks, and both breathed deeply for the first time in what seemed ages.

"How far do you think?" Sera was nervous. The shadows were getting long, and she could see no more than fifty feet ahead.

"To Whitlin?"

"No, to the sun."

Nils grunted, "Shouldn't be more than another mile."

"It'll be dark by then, Nils." Her voice quavered with her courage, and she slowed, glancing back over her shoulder. "We can't go fast enough, Nils."

"Shhhh, we're fine," he said, more confidently than he felt. In truth his heart was in his throat, and his stomach knotted to see the sun falling so low. He ran now, urging Sera to do the same. They no longer pretended to be stealthy. In both of their minds this was a race for their lives, and they flew across the snow with their feet scarcely touching the ground.

They both heard it, the betraying crunch of old, frozen snow beneath a foot too heavy to hit it softly. A growl shook the trees and air around them. Neither dared look for fear it would slow them, and they ran harder than they ever had, pouring out the last of their energy into cold, tired limbs. The sunlight failed, and the shadows gaped in front of them, threatening to hide tripping roots and holes. Sera heard Nils swear as he fell, kicking up a cloud of snow and profanity. A part of her felt she should stop and help him, but that small part was easily overpowered by the fear that dominated her motivation. She had to run, and he did not resent that her pace never slowed.

After a few moments Sera expected to hear screams. She thought she would hear tearing flesh, breaking bones, and the sounds of the wolf feasting, but it did not come. She slowed when she heard Nils' laughter break the silence, "It was just the snow!" His voice was jubilant with relief, and he laughed loudly once more.

Sera shouted back, "Then hurry!" Her voice echoed

among the trees, but there was no reply.

He was silent, and the only response was an awful crunch. She thought to run, and tried to move her legs, but they were frozen in place. As she turned the crimson maw, filled with dagger-like teeth and fresh flesh, engulfed her vision. She did not even the time to scream before the wolf's jaws clamped down on her throat, silencing her forever.

A stormy winter night in Whitlin followed, and soon enough the red patches were buried by drifting, white snow. Invisible, as though they never lived at all. Returned in the end to that which made them feel safe, and there was only snow.

Clint Foster
About the Author

Clint Foster published his first novel, Pawns of the Shadow, in 2017. In 2019, he began submitting shorter pieces to anthologies, and in that short time has received 25+ publications, and the list continues to grow. His work can be found in the upcoming and already released anthologies, Love, Hate, Oceans, Apocalypse, Pride, and Lust by Black Hare Press, Fall into Fantasy 2019 by Cloaked Press LLC, Organic Ink Volume 2, and Reign of Queens by Dragon Soul Press, and It Calls From the Forest by Eerie River Publishing. His first professionally published solo piece, the epic poem, The Lay of Thorriman, is set to be published by Dragon Soul Press in September of 2020. He loves telling stories as much as he does reading them, and hopes to create pieces that bring enjoyment and maybe a little terror. He lives with his herd of four cats, beloved Basset Hound, Zero, and wonderful wife, Nik, in Iowa. www.facebook.com/clintfosterauthor

CARHAZE
DALE DRAKE

Benny Matheson turned up the radio, perhaps a little too loud. If Marsha noticed, she didn't mention it. He was pissed, but trying hard not to show it. This was, after all, a special weekend, and Benny had big plans. He had been dating Marsha for a little over two months now and, apart from a horny almost-tryst on the sofa, he had gotten no further than a wild night fumbling at her bra. His erection had pushed at his jeans like an insane Jack-in-the-box before she had shoved him away, a maddening little laugh chasing him.

Once she had gone home he had masturbated, almost angrily, then gone to bed. His dreams had been no better; she pranced naked as a nymph through his subconscious mind. He had awoken the next day, sandy-headed and more than a little moody. He was just grabbing his first cup of coffee when the phone let out a shrill ring.

"Hold on," he said, setting down his cup and hurrying across the room. "Just hold your God-damn horses." He scooped up the phone, growling an ungracious "Yes?" into the line before plonking himself down on a nearby sofa. Marsha's voice floated through like a soothing balm. Pissed as he was he was still glad to hear from her.

• • •

He had known her ever since high school. She had walked the hallowed halls like a blonde goddess, ignorant of Benny's existence as he watched her breeze by, hanging off the arm of a muscle-bound jock. After secondary school Benny had left for university, leaving Marsha and her circle of golden friends behind. He majored in business studies and, even surprisingly to himself, sports and physical education. It was here that Benny found a new passion sculpting and building up his scrawny body. The passion soon became an obsession. When his final year at college was over Benny left with a degree in both majors, and a body the jocks at his old school would have killed for. In all aspects he was a new man.

The only thing that ruined that year was the death of his beloved grandmother, an old widow with a sharp mind. She must have made some wise investments in her younger days, because when she died she left Benny and his family a small fortune. Benny had thought for some time about what to do with his newfound wealth before deciding, much to his mother and father's chagrin, to open a new gym in his hometown of Mevagissey. It was here, after a very successful opening year, that he once again ran into Marsha.

It had been late on a Tuesday night. It was about an hour before closing, and Benny was working out when she had first breezed in. She was a blonde, spandex-covered goddess, her hair up in a simple ponytail and her gym bag tossed casually over a smooth shoulder. Benny's mouth had gone dry, and his heart had skipped a beat. He had said nothing, just watched her reflection as he secured his bag and headed over to the treadmill. The rest of his workout consisted of trying hard not to watch the fine contours of her body as she stretched and exercised with a vigour only matched by his own.

He was just getting ready to leave when he finally caught her attention. There was a momentary look of confusion in her eye, then a slow dawning recognition.

"Benny Matheson," she said. "I haven't seen you in forever!" 'Did you ever see me?' the old Benny wanted to say, rearing his ugly head. Benny squashed that side of him quickly. The past, with all its old bitter memories, was behind him now. He had wanted her to notice him, and now she had.

"Hi, Marsha," he replied, his palms starting to sweat. "How've you been?"

"Same as always," she giggled. "But look at you! You've certainly changed. You must live at the gym," she said, running her eyes over the muscly contours of his body. "Of course, it always helps when you own one, I suppose."

"How do you know I own the place?" he said, perhaps a little too quickly. She only smiled.

"Your name is right outside the door, Benny. I just didn't connect the dots until now."

"Oh," he smiled, somewhat whimsically. "I suppose it is."

"Listen," she said, drawing closer, her perfume surrounding him in an intoxicating cloud. "How about we go out and have a drink later? Catch up on old times." That was how it had all begun.

• • •

"Forest?"

"What?" Benny said, wrenching himself back into the present.

"Carhaze Forest, doofus," she chuckled into the phone. "Do you want to go, just you me and a tent full of booze? Should be great, since the nights are nice and warm now. What do you say?"

"Just you and me?" he hurriedly repeated. "Sure, that sounds great."

"Okay," she replied. "Pick me up Friday. Oh, and Benny? Don't bother with a sleeping bag. I have a double." She hung up on his grinning face, leaving him to count the days until Friday.

When Friday had finally rolled around he had packed the car with a four person tent - plenty of room to manoeuvre - and he had also packed a crate of booze before slamming the door of his new Bronco shut. He hurried to Marsha's house, but of course she wasn't ready. In fact he had to wait for another two hours, his temper starting to fray as she fixed her hair for the fourteenth time and touched up her makeup yet again.

"Jesus, Marsha!" he said. "We're going camping, not to the fucking Paris catwalk."

"Oh hush! Don't be so cross, Benny. Some things are worth waiting for."

Now they were driving through the country lanes, heading to Carhaze Forest with the radio playing too loud. If only she would have hurried the Hell up. His thoughts were suddenly broken by a warm hand softly caressing the front of his jeans.

"Damn, Marsha," he said, quickly glancing over at her smiling face, trying to concentrate on his driving as she gently squeezed and caressed his rapidly-growing bulge.

"Sorry," she said, in a throaty whisper. "Just trying out the merchandise."

"God," he groaned as she gave him one last squeeze before retreating back to her side of the car.

"You still mad at me?"

"Shit, no," Benny grinned, rolling his eyes. She laughed at that and everything was alright between them again.

They parked at Carhaze carpark just as the sun was starting to set. They quickly shouldered their packs, grabbing their equipment and heading into the forest. The interior was heavily wooded, adding to the general gloom. They walked for some time, the sun a dying glow in the west.

"Did you hear that?" Benny said, suddenly coming to a stop.

"What?" Marsha asked quickly, glancing around.

"Exactly," Benny said, also glancing around. "Nothing. There's no noise, no bird song, no insects. Nothing."

"So?" Marsha shrugged. "It's twilight, Benny. All the creatures go to bed early."

"Right," he laughed, a little nervously. "Just like the Wind and the Willows."

"Come on," she said, heading up the trail. "It will be full dark soon. That's when the fun really begins."

"Really?" Benny said, hurrying after her. "I can't wait."

Moments later they came to a nice, leaf-strewn clearing next to a shallow brook. Benny dropped his gear and immediately began setting up their tent while Marsha sat on a nearby log, drinking expensive wine straight from the bottle. And, just as promised, Marsha produced a double sleeping bag from her pack. Benny set up various battery-operated lamps around the clearing and got a small fire lit, carefully brushing away the surrounding leaves in a fussy way that made Marsha laugh.

"Safety first," Benny chuckled. "Always safety first."

"Talking about safety," Marsha said, licking the rim of the bottle seductively. "Did you bring any?"

"Shit!" Benny said, despairingly. "I didn't think."

"Well," she said, standing up and drawing him closer. "Good job I did." She crushed a pack of condoms into his hand as she kissed him deeply. Her mouth was warm and tasted sweetly of wine, their tongues clashing as Benny's hands found the firmness of her breasts. She pulled away then, but there was a promise in her eyes.

"Build up the fire, Benny. It's a beautiful night," she said, gazing up at the first stars that had just started to appear in the night sky. "Let's have a drink and enjoy it."

When he had the fire roaring they sat huddled together, passing a bottle back and forth and smoking the occasional cigarette.

"Tell me," she said, a slight slur in her voice as she cracked open another bottle, the flickering firelight dancing in her eyes. "What do you know about this forest?"

"Oh God, here we go, another ghost story round the campfire." Benny knew from dating Marsha for the past couple of months that she had a fondness for horror movies and books. "Is that why you dragged me here? To seduce me, then scare me half to death?" Benny laughed.

"No," she gave him a nudge, "but this forest does have a history to it."

"You mean those old stories about people disappearing, and ghoulies and witchcraft," he said, taking a long drink.

"Yes," she said, lighting up a cigarette.

"Oh, do go on," Benny said, taking a seat on a fallen log beside her. The night was drawing in now, the darkness swallowing the light. Benny was suddenly aware of the looming trees that seemed to bend toward them, their rough bark almost creeping in the flickering firelight. "Fill me with tales of terror and fairy stories around the campfire."

"It's no fairy tale."

"Sure," Benny said. He had a good buzz on now, and he liked the sound of her voice and the shape of her lips as she spoke.

"Okay then. Where to start?"

"I usually start at the beginning," Benny said, tossing another branch on the fire. "Let me guess, your friend's cousin's grandma told you something creepy."

"No, actually. I read all about it on the internet."

"Ha," Benny laughed. "A great source of information!"

"Do you want to hear this or not?"

"Sure, sure," Benny said, raising his hands in mock surrender. "Knock yourself out."

"Okay," she said, taking another drink. Benny was surprised to see they had nearly finished off another bottle. "Here's what I know. The first accounts start way back, around the times of the Puritans. They came to the area to settle the place. They built themselves a small village on the fringes of the great forest, no more than twenty families. They were hounded for their beliefs as Separatists, coming to Cornwall to escape persecution at the hands of the church they had so recently broken away from."

"Sounds like a good deal," Benny chuckled.

"At first it was," she went on. "They built themselves a modest village and lived off the land. It was a cold, Christmas Eve when the first screams came from the forest, followed by monstrous howling and bubbling laughter that woke up the entire village. Nobody dared to go outside. They barred their windows and doors, staying huddled together with their families as they prayed loudly for the Lord God to protect them. After what seemed like an eternity the screaming, laughter and guttural howling faded with the first rays of the coming dawn. It was then, when the villagers had finally built up enough courage to go outside, that they witnessed first-hand the terrible devastation."

"What did they see?" Benny asked, becoming even more aware of the shadowy trees looming above them.

"Dead animals," Marsha whispered. "Dead animals everywhere. Squirrels, rabbits, foxes, deer. Even the birds had fallen from the sky and they were torn up. Guts and blood were everywhere. The entire village stank like copper, and like shit from the ruptured entrails. The villagers checked their own livestock, but the village animals were all fine, showing little concern for the night's events. It was decided by the village elders that these dead, wretched creatures were to be dragged away and burned."

She paused, taking a breath.

"It was said that one man, somewhat poorer than his neighbours and a known wastrel, kept a brace of rabbits for himself. They say he died an agonising death after partaking of the tainted flesh. That evening, the villagers went to bed early, their doors and windows barred. Some even nailed crucifixes to the doors but nothing else happened that night. In fact, nothing else happened for the next few weeks. Then the first child was found dead. A village woman woke one morning to find her new-born baby, or what was left of it anyway, the poor thing, torn to shreds. Its flesh was all clawed up, its eyes bulging with terror and its mouth wrenched open in a silent scream."

Just then a branch snapped off to Benny's right, causing him to jump up and cry out.

"What the Hell was that?" Benny gasped, squinting into the growing shadows, his heart beating hard, but Marsha only laughed.

"Town boy. Sit down Benny, it's probably a fox or a lone deer looking for a date. Now do you want to hear the rest of this story, or not?"

"I am not too sure," Benny said nervously, sitting back down and taking a long drink.

"Pussy," Marsha laughed. "Now, where was I?"

"The baby," Benny said, somewhat reluctantly.

"Ah, yes, the baby. It was dead, torn to pieces. The doors and windows were all still locked tight, but the baby had been mutilated."

"What did they do?"

"What would you do?" Marsha replied, gazing deep into the fire. "The mother lost her fucking mind. She was in such a state. She was given over to the village clergyman, but he had to have her confined to the church basement for her own safety. Her husband, a village woodcutter, led a small party of brave men into the forest, but they never returned. The next morning the grieving mother was also dead. She had gouged her own eyes out with ragged fingernails, then gnawed at her own wrists."

"Jesus," Benny breathed, an image of tooth-marked wrists seared into his head. Marsha started talking again, her voice almost lullaby-like in the silence.

"Things started to happen quickly after that. First the children started to disappear, then the women, until only the men folk remained. They were angry, frightened and confused. It seemed whatever entity haunted the forest wanted nothing to do with the menfolk of the village. Soon after the men started to hear their children weeping in the forest, and the voices of their wives calling to them through the darkness. A few foolish ones entered the forest to chase after the phantom voices, but none ever returned. Ever since then this forest has had a reputation among the locals for strange occurrences. Not that you would ever know it. The summer tourists flock here in their droves, knowing nothing of its terrible history."

Another branch snapped loudly, interrupting Marsha, but this time the sound came from off to Benny's left. He leapt up with a curse. He had a sense that something was watching them, stalking them, circling the camp as if trying to catch them unawares.

"Jesus," Marsha said, pulling him back down. "Will you relax? It's probably just a badger, grubbing for some worms."

"Pretty big fucking badger," Benny said, snapping nervous glances over his shoulder.

"Here," Marsha said, going to her knees before him and fumbling at his jeans. "Let me take your mind off it." Before Benny could reply she had his cock in her hand, working it up and down before slipping it into her mouth with delicious slowness, engulfing him in the wet warmness of her mouth. It was soon stiff, the forest noises momentarily forgotten as Benny enjoyed the blowjob.

"Shit," Benny groaned, running his fingers through her silken, blonde hair as she cradled his balls with her free hand.

"Still afraid?" she taunted, coming up for air.

"Hell yes," Benny said. "Afraid I'll cum too soon."

"Well, we can't have that," she said, giving him a last lick before rising to her feet. "I think I may have something you want to see, Benny, perhaps even two things." She laughed as she pulled her heavy coat over her head, blouse and all, before Benny's face. She deftly unhooked her bra, releasing her ample breasts. He nearly fainted as her nipples grew hard in the chilly air.

"They're perfect," he said, wiping at his mouth and tottering to his feet. "I mean, you're perfect."

"You haven't seen the best part yet," she said, running her finger seductively under the lip of her jeans. "But if you want it," she laughed, running past him, her breasts bouncing deliciously as she scooped up a nearby lantern, "You're going to have to catch me first! Come on, Benny," she said, disappearing into the tree line. "Let's see if there's really anything to be afraid of in this forest."

"Oh, there is," Benny laughed, scooping up his own

lantern as he chased after her. "And it's right here in my pants."

"Come on then," she called over her shoulder, disappearing behind a large spruce. "Catch me, and I'll let you fuck me right here on the forest floor."

"Shit," Benny cursed, slipping on a pile of damp leaves. He was insanely horny now. Quickly he righted himself. She was pulling further ahead now, her lantern bobbing as it cast eerie shadows on the trees. "Wait up," Benny yelled. "Hey Marsha, wait up! You don't want to get lost out here."

"Bennnnyyy," her voice floated back to him. "Come find me, Bennnyyy."

"Fuck," he cursed again, pushing through a clinging privet and scratching the Hell out of his jeans on a thorny scrub. It was like chasing a goddamn jack rabbit. "Marsha," he called again, starting to get a little pissed with her silly games. His hands still ached to touch her, to run his fingers all over that glorious body, so he kept going. Her light was almost completely gone now. He picked up his pace, mindful of low hanging branches.

He was gaining on her now, cutting the distance between them. Breathing hard he pushed his way through a couple of low-hanging branches, their wet leaves slapping at his face. That was when he noticed her lantern had stopped its insane bobbing. She was close now, hiding behind the trunk of a large oak, waiting for him, perhaps naked and brazen on the forest floor.

"Gotcha," he laughed, quickly rounding the tree. She

wasn't there, only her glowing lantern remained. From behind him came the sound of heavy footfalls and the snapping of twigs. Benny whirled, his lantern held high. A woman stood before him, but it didn't look like Marsha. She was naked, tall and impossibly thin. She leapt forward, hissing through blackened teeth. Her teeth gnashed as she pulled him in, locking her mouth over his. Benny tasted her terrible breath as she forced her tongue down his throat, spilling a bitter tasting liquid into his mouth, before casting him away. He fell to his knees, clawing at his constricting throat, retching and heaving, unable to breathe. He tried to climb to his feet, but black blooms filled his eyes. His vision was turning red. He was falling, floating, and her terrible laughter followed him down into darkness.

When he awoke he was being dragged into some kind of clearing, his head lolling to and fro. There were people here, hundreds of them, dressed in black robes. Their flickering torches filled the air with the acrid smell of smoke. As Benny was dragged past it seemed that he heard someone call out his name. His head rolled in that direction. There was something tied to a tree. Wet, raw and glistening, something that seemed to call for him over and over again. But his head was filled with a thousand buzzing insects, and his ears rang deafeningly as he slipped back down into darkness.

He awoke a few moments later, his body laying upon a rough, wooden altar. The smell of smoke was everywhere, and the sound of a hundred chanting voices filled the night. A naked Marsha loomed above him, straddling his unclothed torso.

"Marsha," he tried to focus through the fog. "What's happening?"

"Be still, my love. Drink this," she said, leaning forward to offer him a wooden chalice. "It'll make a new man out of you."

"What," he tried to ask again, but the cup was already at his lips. Its fiery liquid poured down his throat, spilling over his face and down the side of his neck. The liquid hit his stomach and sent waves of heat burning through his body. He was suddenly aware of the naked woman before him like never before. "Ha," she crooned, wriggling against his hardness. "He is finally awake!" Benny groaned as he slid into her wetness. Finally they would be together.

"Marsha," he gasped, as she rode him back and forth.

"Fuck me, Benny," she laughed. "Fuck me, the Goddess commands it." Benny did as he was bid, thrusting hard into her, his brain a red fog. "Yes," she screamed. "Fuck me! Bring the master forth." Benny barely heard her. He could feel his orgasm building as he reached up to grasp her glorious breasts, but his hand found only flattened skin flaps.

"What?" he cried, scrabbling at her waist. "What's happening?" he screamed, clawing at her back until his twisting fingers found the rough stitching. They became entangled as he tried to pull away, and the woman above him shrieked with laughter as the torn skin ripped off of her. Benny started to scream as Marsha's flesh fell away, revealing the hag from the forest.

"No," he screamed weakly, pawing at her face, pulling as the flesh that had once belonged to Marsha slid from the woman. A bloody mask landed on his chest, glistening in the moonlight. And yet she still rode him, grinding at his unwilling flesh as Benny tried to pull away from her, out of her. She pinned him down, her thighs clamping down hard by his side. She chuckled obscenely, running a sharp fingernail down Benny's chest and drawing blood.

"Cum for me," she intoned. "Spray your seed into me. Bring forth He Who Walks the Darkened Forest. Bring forth the God of the Wild Hunt, our Devourer of Small Children."

"No," Benny screamed. "Get off me!" But he had come too far, betrayed by his treacherous flesh and the magic that grew heavy all about him. He cried out, spurting into her molten core. The hag above him wailed in triumph, leering down at him.

"We thank you for your service," she grinned. "But now you must d…" But that was as far as she got. Suddenly her eyes widened, and blood shot from her mouth in a great glut. It covered Benny's chest as she doubled over, falling down onto the forest floor. She began to jerk and convulse, black smoke pouring from her screaming mouth, from her ears and even her bulbous eyes. As Benny watched on in horror her stomach began to stretch and grow, bulging and pulsating, her skin stretched tight. "He comes," she moaned, reaching out, twisting her fingers towards the sky. She let out an ear-piercing shriek as her stomach erupted in a shower of steaming blood and gore.

Benny tried to get up, to run as far away as he could, but he was unable to move. He watched the horror that slid from the woman's ruined remains onto the forest floor, where the thing lay mewling and glistening in the moonlight. The surrounding people stopped their Hellish chanting. They began to writhe and claw at themselves, tearing at their eyes and ripping at one another's flesh in an orgy of blood and sex. The creature had started to grow now, its bone and sinew forming as it grew bigger, its antler-like horns gouging the forest floor as it cried out in pain.

At last the terrible transformation was complete. It staggered to its feet on crooked legs, its lidless eyes glowing like hot coals in the darkness. It had become a great, hulking beast, its body covered in patches of brown fur. Its muzzle wrinkled back in a terrible smile as it watched the humans writhe and bleed on the forest floor.

"God save me," Benny gasped, rolling naked from the altar. He staggered to his feet before falling down onto the damp ground. At the sound of his voice the creature's head swivelled towards him, great antlers gleaming like bone in the moonlight.

"Father," it said. Benny began to scream. The creature smiled, reaching out with a cloven hand.

"Father!"

DALE DRAKE
ABOUT THE AUTHOR

Dale Drake was born in Lancashire, England in 1975 and now resides in Cornwall with his wife and three children. After his career in the army, Dale moved to Hertfordshire to train to become a chef but his real love and passion has always been writing. Dale's first book, Blood Heritage, was written whilst he was still attending college and is a high fantasy book full of sword wielding heroes, dark magic and blood thirsty vampires. His second book, Dark Waters, was written some years later after he moved to Cornwall where he was heavily influenced by H.P. Lovecraft and his love of the sea. His stories are set in and around his home village where he finally feels he belongs.

KNOTWORK HILL
C.W. BLACKWELL

I reach Bill and Judi's cabin just before nightfall. The sun is setting behind the remnants of an evening storm and there's a heavy wind in the sugar maples, tree duff tumbling over the narrow drive. Judi's sitting on the front porch with a lit cigarette, blood stains on her white leather boots.

It's been an hour since I left Knoxville.

An hour since Judi told me Bill was dead.

"I slipped in it, Keeler," Judi says. She isn't looking at me when she says it, just keeps her eyes focused on the tip of her smoke. "Looks like I'm guilty as hell, but I swear I found him this way. I turned to throw up and I slipped in the blood."

I believe her. If there's anyone who doesn't deserve to be within a hundred miles of whatever happened here, it's Judi. She's the good one, the one that always keeps us grounded no matter how hard a job gets.

I tell her so.

She's crying now. "What do we do, Keeler?"

"Show me," I say. "You need to show me."

Judi mashes the cigarette into the porch boards and nods in agreement, but the nod just keeps going without her saying anything else, the wind pecking at her blonde curls.

I sit beside her, and she leans into me.

She's not like Bill and me.

She doesn't deserve any of it.

• • •

Bill Connelly was an ex-cop, SWAT. Before the academy he served overseas in the military. Not Iraq or Afghanistan, but places just beyond the edges of CNN's infographics. The places you don't learn about in fourth period geography class. Kinshasa. N'djamena. Manbij. When we ran an interrogation on contract, he was the one that made it real. He'd pull a fingernail or two. A tooth. Once he showed up with a leaky car battery with jumper cables and sharp, fanged leads.

I saw him use a potato peeler once.

He made it fucking real.

Looking back on all the contract jobs we did together, nothing compares to how Bill has ended up. When Judi opens the front door it takes me a moment to even register what I'm seeing. My legs stall in the threshold. Bill is tied to a dining chair, feet bound and hands behind his back.

A black pond of blood thickening over the linoleum. His eyelids are sucked into the sockets and there's a crust of coagulate over the cheekbones. The scalp is severed and there are crude carvings on his skull like Celtic knots.

"Jesus, Bill," I say, as if the pity would do him any good. "What the hell did they do to you?" There's no avoiding the blood on the floor. It makes a sick wet sound as I plant my feet. Whoever did this knew how to drain him quick. A brutal slice up the femoral might have done it.

I crouch to study his face.

Those sunken lids.

"They've taken his goddamn eyes," I say.

I turn to the door. Judi's lighting another cigarette, hands shaking. I give her a nod and she gets the meaning, hands me the lit smoke and lights another for herself. I take a long drag and let the smoke through my nose.

There's something about the lips.

A blond thread at the center of Bill's bloody mouth.

"You see this, Judi?" I say.

"See what?" She's still watching from the doorway. "It's a goddamn hatchet job, Keeler."

I look again, closer this time. I cup his bloodstained cheeks and squeeze gently, parting his lips. From the void of his mouth I pull a hairy braid of wheat. The stalk keeps coming, green leaves slick with blood and mucous. When it's ten inches past his teeth, there's a snag. I'm careful not to snap the stem. With the cigarette smoldering at the center of my lips, I gently guide the wheatstalk the rest of the way. At the base of the stalk, wrapped in roots, is a small woven bag. I go to the kitchenette and lay the stalk over the Formica counter. There's a steak knife in the drawer and I use it to slice open the bag.

I drop the knife and cover my mouth.

"What is it, Keeler?" Judi says. "What'd you find?"

I don't say a word, not yet at least.

Inside the bag are Bill's emerald green eyes.

• • •

The eyes aren't the only items in the root bag. There's also a pair of molars, along with a thin wad of gray hair. But mostly I'm interested in the folded cardstock. It's a small piece, coated with wax. When I unfold the paper there's writing on the inside. More Celtic imagery, but this time there are words encircling the symbols. It says: CMB KNOTWORK HILL.

We sit on the porch with a bottle of bourbon planted between us and the cardstock folded in my palm. There's a hollow chime overhead as a pair of tiger moths skitter against the porchlight. Night animals scampering in the outer darkness.

Judi takes a hard pull from the bottle. She plucks the cardstock from between my fingers and looks it over. "Knotwork Hill," she says, like she knows the place. "If I wasn't thoroughly creeped out already, I'm there now."

"I've never heard of it," I say.

"You wouldn't," she says. "Not something a city boy

would know anything about. I doubt Bill ever heard of it either. If it didn't have tits or a line on a quick buck, Bill wasn't interested."

I acquiesce with a flip of my hands.

She wasn't wrong.

"This place, where is it?" I ask.

"Halfway between here and Coker Creek. Just a few minutes down the way, really. Up an old fire road." She laughs quietly, shakes her head. "I just can't believe it's come up."

"There's got to be more to it."

"There could be. It's a place local kids hang out sometimes. Kind of a rite of passage. They go up late at night and see how long they can last before, well."

"Before what?"

"It's a dumb story, Keeler."

"Whoever did this to Bill didn't think so."

Judi holds her breath and lets it out slow. "Something called a bronach, some kind of Irish witch. The settlers built a small convent on Knotwork Hill and one of the nuns was double-dealing with the devil, so it goes. The teenagers like to freak themselves out over it. You know, as if she still haunts the place."

"Ever been there yourself?"

"Once. It's a real place, even if the witch thing is bullshit. It's just ruins now, of course. Christ, you're not thinking of going are you?"

"CMB," I say, avoiding the question. "We did a job with a guy named Brierley. Chet Brierley. He was off his rocker. Cut someone up pretty good for no reason at all but the fun of it."

"Bill mentioned him. Just a few weeks back."

"Did they do a job together?" It wasn't completely out of character for Bill to pick up extra work without me, but I was usually the first to know.

"I think so, although he hasn't been forthcoming lately. We've been, well, distant. Whatever happened between Bill and this guy, it seemed to upset him."

We search each other's eyes, and in the searching there is understanding. I stand up, thumb the cylinder of the Colt .357 I keep in my shoulder holster. "I'll follow you to the fire road," I say. "If whoever did this to Bill wants me to follow his little clues, I'm willing to oblige. If it's Brierley, I'll even enjoy hunting him down."

Judi sets the bottle down and comes to me, pats my chest gently. "Whatever you do, don't get yourself killed."

. . .

I call my guy in Knoxville on the way and have him do a quick workup on Brierley.

Chester Michael Brierley.

CMB.

Turns out he did three years in Morgan County for attempted murder, other stints in county jails all over the state for assault. He was a suspect in a double homicide two years back where the victims were found badly mutilated, but they never hooked him for it. There were rumors that he came from a wealthy mining family in West Virginia, the kind whose bank accounts are flush as the number of family tragedies.

Money can cure a plethora of ills.

Insanity isn't one of them.

It isn't long before Judi pulls off the highway, idling the car on the dirt fire road. I pull next to her and get out, walk to the driver window. She watches me in the dim glow of the dashlights.

"Check your phone," she says.

I look. "One bar, eighty percent charged."

"Doesn't matter what the charge is if you got no service."

"I got some cat videos I could watch."

"I'm serious, Keeler. Kill the son of a bitch if you have to, but be careful. I don't want to find you the same way I found Bill."

"I promise."

I watch Judi back the car onto the highway. She heads north, back toward the cabin. Tail lights winking into a distant curve.

She's got a hell of a mess on her hands.

I don't envy her that.

• • •

I drive slowly up the forest road. Insects streak and flare in the headlights and there's a fine dust spooling over the fenders. The dead crunch of gravel like the grinding of bones. I flick my phone and watch the reception subtract to null, then regain a single bar. I hammer out a quick text to Judi, flicking my eyes at the road and back to the screen. The progress bar stalls and the message hangs in limbo. I lift the phone to the roof of the car for better reception and suddenly the windshield fills with a piercing light.

A car horn blares.

Tires skidding.

I pitch the wheel to the shoulder.

The windshield blows out in a cataclysm of glass. A fir branch punches through and pierces the passenger seat headrest. Smoke jets from the stalled engine. The car settles and I pat myself down, feel my face for blood.

I try the key: nothing.

Just the starter hammering a dead flywheel.

The driver door doesn't open easily, so I give it a hard shove with my shoulder, and then another until it parts with a metallic groan. I step to the road. The air is cool, moonlight spilling over the roadway. A silver Toyota is spun the other direction, the back end sunk in a shallow ditch. Headlights crooked at the sky. I pull the pistol and keep it flush along my leg, walk slowly across the road.

There's movement inside the car. A woman sobbing and the panicked voice of a young man. I move closer, peer into the driver's window.

When he sees me, the driver's face fills with terror. Eyes like moons. He throttles the engine, tires spraying gravel into the tree shadows. Screaming. The car is high-centered and it isn't going anywhere. I holster the pistol and rap my knuckles on the fender, spin my finger in the air as one might roll down an old car window.

There's a moment of confusion in the car. A deliberation between the occupants. Neither realizes the dome light is on and they are illuminated as if by stagelight. Finally the driver window comes down and the young man asks who I am and if I'm friendly.

I tell him my name, but he doesn't return the courtesy.

"Are you hurt?" I say.

"I think my girlfriend broke her arm," says the young man.

I get a glimpse of the girl, her face pinched in agony.

"If you're okay, why don't you get out and we can push this thing back on the road?"

The car door opens, the driver steps out. He's young, maybe eighteen. Meager stubble around his cheeks and chin. "We're freaking out," he says. "We saw somethin' up thataways and it scared the shit out of us. Sorry if I ran you off the road. I think I was havin' myself a panic attack. I'm tellin' you, man. It was ugly."

I glance at my car, still smoking against the fir tree.

No use punishing him for it.

"Tell me what you saw."

The kid looks up the road to the jet black hills and shudders. "It got dark so fast. It's the solstice, you know? Supposed to be the longest day of the year but it sure don't feel like it. It was so dark up there."

"What did you see?" It comes out as an impatient

growl.

"There's a body maybe two miles up. Some guy was torn up pretty bad. I think someone just got murdered up there."

"You sure it wasn't a prank?"

"I wondered at first, but then." The kid puts his hands to his face and starts to cry. "I touched it. Then I smelled my hands and I knew. Oh god he was all tore up. They say there's some kinda witch up there but I never believed it. Till now, maybe."

"There's bears around here, last I heard. What makes you think he was murdered?"

"No bear coulda set him up that way."

"Set him up?"

"Up on the boulder," he says, choking out the words. His eyes glow wet in the moonlight. "Folded over with his face to the sky, insides on the outsides. Maybe he was scalped, too. There's chalk on the stone with markings like you see all over the trees up there. Ain't a bear in the woods could do somethin' such as that."

It sounds too familiar.

"Listen up," I say, "Any of you got reception?"

"Don't you think we'd have called the sheriff by now?" says the kid.

"Not a good idea," I say. It's a lie, but the last thing I want is some hillbilly deputy getting between me and the man that killed my partner.

"Why not?"

"You'd be the center of the investigation. The first

one to find the body."

"Jenivette found the body," says the kid.

"They'd find a way to pin it on one of you."

"Maybe they would."

"Best get the car back on the road," I say. "Once you get on the highway you message my friend and let her know I'm on foot. You and Jenivette can forget all about this."

"I shouldn'ta told you her name."

"As long as the sheriff ain't involved, it don't matter."

The kid nods slowly. "You won't say nothin' 'bout us bein' here?"

"Like I said, message my friend and we're even."

• • •

It takes both of us lifting the back end of the Toyota to get the front axle to stick. Once the car gets traction, Jenivette scoots over the console and the kid dives feet first into the driver seat without so much as a sideways glance. Gravel sprays like buckshot as they disappear down the road in a cloud of tan dust.

From the trunk of my car I find the Maglight and a bottle of water. I flick the light on, give it a slow pan over the treeline. Fir branches pendulous in the night breeze. I turn and light the road as far as it will reach. If the kid was right, there's a good chance Brierley could still be up there. Maybe even watching from the cover of the trees.

I start out on foot. The road curves in a hairpin around a grove of buckeyes and I pass over a dry wash where springmelt has drawn ragged furrows through the silty ground. My footsteps are all I can hear, as if I am travelling in vacuo through the darkness. The deadened air moving as I move. The moonlight is now bright enough to click off the Maglight, so I hold it in my left hand as a readied weapon.

My gun hand is free to draw and fire at will.

It's now midnight. The silence has given over to coyotes and whippoorwills. The forest opens to a vast wheatfield, the aching dry rustle like the sound of torn paper.

There is another sound.

Something out of place.

A ponderous croon.

A woman's voice.

I skin the Colt and thumb the hammer, searching for the origin of the sound. I turn a circle as I walk, revolver at the end of my arm. Finger on the trigger.

The voice again, this time with a curious lilt before a long and terrifying wail. I stop, scan the surroundings. I feel like I'm being watched.

A sudden rustle to my left.

There's movement in the wheatfield.

A bowed spine weaving through the awn and spike.

I thumb the Maglight, paint the field with the light. More movement. I look closer. It looks like some half-dead sea creature cresting and falling against the surface, snaking through a tide of wheat.

I watch it turn.

Wheat rattling.

It winds closer to the fieldline, the figure just visible behind the swaying stalks. A dark form in the grasses. Eyes like tiny kernels of fire. Watching me. I part the wheatstalks with the gun barrel, plant my knee in the dirt.

When I shine the light, there is nothing there.

All is still and silent.

Like it was never there to begin with.

• • •

Beyond the wheatfield, the road ends at a misty crossroads. To the east lie the ruins of an old stone building. Cavelike windows surrounded by ragged masonry. Some walls are orphaned and rise unshouldered like monoliths in the vaporous dark.

I wander among the ruins, gun and light clasped together. From the branches hang wreaths woven into crude shapes, twisting soundlessly among scrags of white lichen. There are Celtic knots carved into the fir trees and within these markings the moss does not grow.

It isn't long before I find the body.

It's just as the kid described. A torn figure sprawled on a large stone, his face locked in a grisly, silent howl. Viscera unspooled like curtain rope. When I look him over with the light I see that his eyes are missing and there are knotwork symbols carved into his cleaved skull.

Just like Bill.

But there is something else, a different kind of familiarity. Something about the blond eyebrows and narrow bridge of the nose. I thumb my phone to the saved photo of Brierley.

It's him. There's no doubt about it.

I spin around, search the shadows. If Brierley's dead, then all bets are off. I'm now dealing with someone else entirely.

Or something else.

The sound from the wheatfield returns.

A sick groan.

A dark form moving between the pillared firs.

"Come out," I say to the trees, watching the movement. "Whatever sick game you're playing, it ends now." There is no reply, only the creaking of branches and the whistle of the whippoorwill. I call out a second time.

A twig snaps somewhere in the dark.

The crunch of fir needles behind me.

I turn, blood draining from my face.

A creature stands over me, tall and crooked. Hairless skin sagging over the bones. Its sick-looking eyes are distended like a toad's throat and the nose is a fleshy pustule dripping with mucous. It shrieks, the mouth fanged and impossibly deep as if the jaw is unhinged.

I stumble back, fire off a round.

Then another.

The thing shrieks again and raises its arms, long fingers bent and clawed. I keep firing. The bullet wounds dot its chest, bloodless and puckered like corpse skin. It swipes and sends me backward into the dirt, the Maglight spinning from my hands.

I roll to my side and try to stand, but it pummels me again, this time hard enough to lift me into the air. The gun flies skyward and I crumple against a nearby fir tree. I brace myself against the trunk and spin into the darkness, staggering down a narrow trail. One hand on my aching ribs and the other batting branches from my face as I go.

No gun.

No light.

Just the moonlit trail winding through the firs.

I struggle to make sense of the thing that just attacked me, but I keep going, hoping the trail will loop back to the road. With any luck the kid was able to get a text to Judi. Maybe she came back for me. Maybe she's driving up the road now.

It's a big maybe.

There's a flicker just ahead. Yellow lights throbbing in the dark. The trees thin and I'm now standing in a torchlit clearing. A halfcircle of flames. In the center of the clearing is a large stone carved with Celtic knots, three ears of wheat draped over the top as if by some ceremonial rite.

It's a dead end.

I cough and my mouth fills with blood.

My ribs are badly broken.

I free a torch from the ground and head back the way I came, but I see the thing lumbering down the trail toward me. It's eyes shine when it sees me and it picks up speed. I square off with the monster, torch held firmly between it and me. I jab its face, but it bats the torch from my hand with a screech.

It lunges and I stumble back.

The sick smell of compost wells over me.

The clawed hand rakes my face, hard enough to whiten my vision. I give it a hard kick and it swipes again.

This time the whiteness fades to black.

My eyes flutter and still.

• • •

I wake in complete darkness. My hands are bound above me as if from a tree branch and there is a furious ache deep inside my skull. I hear the crackle of fire, the smell of smoke. I turn my head and blink my eyes.

Nothing. Only darkness.

There's a tacky wetness at my lashes.

My eyes are gone.

I struggle, but the restraints are too tight.

"Judi," I scream. It's the only name that could possibly come from my lips. The only name I want to hear.

"I'm here, Keeler."

Judi's voice. Judi's voice.

"Judi, thank god," my voice is just a pitiful croak. "Judi, it's not safe up here. That thing you told me about is real. It attacked me. I must have shot it half a dozen times."

There's a long pause before she speaks. The sound of

torches. Fir needles crunching underfoot. "I can't do that, Keeler," she says at last. Her voice is sad, apologetic. I feel her hand on my chest, fingers running gently down the length of me.

"Judi?" I don't want to believe it. "Tell me what's happening."

There's movement all around me.

A low murmur in a strange language.

The voices grow to a rambling chorus.

"You're part of something you don't understand," says Judi. She's touching my face, mouth close to mine. I can feel her breath. "Be brave for me, okay?"

I writhe against the restraints. Head full of razors.

"No, Judi. No. I don't want to die like this."

"It's too late, Keeler."

I hear the haunting wail of the bronach.

The smell of rotting leaves.

"Just let me go, Judi. Judi please."

"I can't do that, Keeler. The bronach needs three."

"Three?"

"Three benefactions."

"Whatever you've gotten yourself into, we can fix it."

"That's exactly what Bill said. You and him. It was always you and him. Two sides of the same coin. The muscle and the mind. Two cold and unrighteous hearts. I'm sorry, Keeler. It all ends for you now."

She joins the chorus. Chanting strange words.

I am suddenly enveloped by many hands. On my

throat, forehead. Fingers in my mouth. I try to bite down but my jaws are pried open. A wooden block between my teeth. All I can do is scream. I scream Judi's name over and over, even though it comes out as a lipless and incomprehensible howl. There is something in my throat now, a fibrous bindle that blocks my esophagus.

The root bag.

The wheatstalk.

They're shoving it down my throat.

I scream, but there is no scream.

The chanting grows.

A swell of croons and whispers.

The crackle of torchflame.

The smell of blood

and smoke

and wheat

and death.

C.W. BLACKWELL
ABOUT THE AUTHOR

C.W. Blackwell was born and raised in Santa Cruz, California where he still lives today. His passion is to blend poetic narratives with pulp dialogue to create strange and rhythmic genre fiction. He writes mostly crime fiction, dark fiction, and poetry. His recent work has appeared in Pulp Modern, Aphotic Realm, Econoclash Review, and Mystery Weekly Magazine. You can follow him on Twitter and Facebook.

https://twitter.com/CW_Blackwell

Lazarus' Respite
Michael Subjack

Walter Hopkins scurried out of school, doing his best to hide among the other children. He was eager to get home, and not just because he had a new Lego set to attend to (though he liked those a great deal). No, the name of the game for Walter was avoiding the ire of Jason Hansen, a bully with a special interest in Walter that dated all the way back to the beginning of the school year. This was hardly Walter's first time dealing with a bully, but as it was now May his ordeal with Jason had been the longest.

Poor Walter was a skinny kid with oversized glasses, a pale face covered in freckles, and a cataclysmic case of asthma. That deadly combination made him bully catnip, and despite the best efforts of his parents and teachers it never seemed to end. Once one bully was phased out another materialized. At one time Walter had been a happy and well-adjusted boy. While that was still mostly true, something else had started to grow inside of him, something that would give the grown-ups in his life pause.

Walter often imagined terrible things happening to Jason and the other bullies. The fantasies had gotten so vivid that he could often smell the blood and sweat coming off them as they begged for their lives. In these scenarios Walter was the one in charge, and the concept of mercy was a foreign one. Sometimes these fantasies were intense enough to cause nosebleeds, but that wasn't for anyone but Walter to know; just as the fantasies themselves belonged to him and him alone.

On this particular day Walter simply wanted to get home and finish his Lego set, and the tricky part was making it there without incident. The week had been bad enough as it was. During lunch, back on Monday, Jason had placed a chocolate pudding cup on Walter's seat right as he sat down. It stained the seat of his new corduroys, and Jason proceeded to nickname him Wally Poop Pants, a moniker that was still hounding him four days later. He had walked quickly away from school property, though the nickname was shouted at him by several students. While Walter normally headed west to get home he instead went north, opting for the woods that skirted his neighborhood. It would be a longer walk, and his mother had warned him against it because the woods contained disease-carrying ticks. Not to mention upturned rocks and roots that could lead to a sprained ankle, or worse.

While Walter loved his mother, and did his best to respect her wishes, she wasn't the one who had to deal with Jason Hansen. When he arrived at one of several entrances into the woods he cast a furtive glance around, making sure nobody saw him. The coast was clear, save for an old man watering his lawn.

Walter stepped inside and prayed for freedom, but fate had been consistently cruel to Walter. This day would be no exception.

As he made his way along the path Walter found the singing birds and smell of fresh pine not just pleasant, but downright therapeutic. Even if it was his against his mother's wishes Walter thought that, just maybe, this could become his regular route. Further down the path he saw a deer nibbling serenely on a patch of grass. He briefly imagined the deer as a much more vicious creature gnawing not on grass, but on the face of Jason Hansen. As he got closer the deer took off running, and Walter supposed he couldn't blame it. The only things that made a point to surround him anymore did so in the interest of being mean, and as far as he could tell deer didn't possess such hateful qualities.

The same couldn't be said for the two louts he heard talking up ahead. He contemplated turning around, but aside from having already come too far he might also run into Jason. Walter took a deep breath and forged ahead. As he got closer he got a better look at the pair, and he recognized them as two eighth-graders named Anthony and Spencer. Walter had mostly managed to avoid them, but he knew they had gotten into their share of fights and enjoyed picking on smaller children. This was not good, and it didn't smell good either. The formerly clean aroma had been replaced with an odor that faintly reminded Walter of a dead skunk. It seemed like even the forest was telling him to get out of there. He put his head down and walked past them as quickly as he could.

He wasn't quick enough.

"Hey, kid!"

It was Spencer, as far as Walter could tell. He pretended not to hear them and quickened his pace, but it was followed by the rhythmic thudding of heavy footsteps behind him. He felt a hand, roughly the size and weight of a Thanksgiving turkey, fall on his shoulder. He slowly turned around to face his would-be tormentors. Some might say such a maneuver was bold, but Walter knew they wouldn't punch him right away. Such acts of violence required a build up, and this dance had only just begun.

"Where you going, little guy?" Anthony asked, his glossy, gray eyes twinkling with gleeful malice.

"Home," Walter replied, doing his best to keep his tone neutral. Showing fear or aggression had a tendency to yield unpleasant results.

"You're not going home," Spencer informed him. "Not until you see what we've got to show you."

"What is it?" Walter asked, feigning interest.

The two older boys exchanged shark-like grins and guided Walter over to a spot that was just off the path. At first he didn't understand what the big deal was. He saw a tattered blue tent, a pile of threadbare clothing, and an almost full bottle of liquor. Is that the best these guys had? He thought that maybe the bullies at his school were finally starting to lose their touch, but then Spencer pointed a grimy finger the size of a summer sausage at a heap of clothing just beyond the tent. It took Walter a few seconds to realize that this particular pile of clothing was actually a man sleeping, and it took a few more seconds to realize that the man wasn't actually sleeping.

He was dead.

"You ever seen a dead body, kid?"

Spencer again. And as a matter fact, Walter had. His paternal grandfather two years ago. His mother had been worried the sight would traumatize him, but Walter was okay with it. The corpse had looked more like a wax figure than his grandfather, but this was hardly the same thing.

"Just a fucking bum," Anthony said with indifference before hocking a thick loogie just inches away from the body.

"We should tell somebody," Walter said quietly.

"Tell who?" Anthony asked. "The liquor store? Nobody cares."

A slight breeze picked up, sending rust-colored leaves blowing past them. The man's tattered overcoat briefly flapped before falling still again. The smell of body odor and urine invaded Walter's nostrils, causing him to wrinkle his nose and hold his breath.

"He fucking stinks!" Spencer exclaimed, clasping his hand to his face.

"Still want to tell somebody?" Anthony asked Walter, his voice muffled from the sweatshirt he had pulled over the lower half of his face.

Walter didn't respond. What he wanted was to be far away from here, if they'd let him. He took a cautious step backward and was relieved to see that the boys still had their eyes trained on the body. He did a "one Mississippi, two Mississippi" count before taking another step back. And he might have gotten away, but his foot landed directly on one of the dead leaves the breeze had blown past him. Ordinarily the crunch would have been almost imperceptible, but on this day it sounded akin to an angry elephant crashing through a glass house. The pumpkin-like heads of Spencer and Anthony snapped back and saw Walter trying to make his getaway.

"You're not leaving already, are you?" Spencer asked as each of them grabbed one of Walter's arms.

"I think he's going to tell somebody what we saw!" Anthony said.

"Better make sure he's dead first," Spencer continued as they began dragging Walter toward the body. He attempted to plant his feet, but the two boys dragged him with the ease of an alligator pulling a wounded gazelle into the water to feed on. Walter could feel his asthma starting to go into overtime.

Oh, please, he silently begged. I don't want to die!

Spencer and Anthony stopped about a foot away from the body. Walter could still feel his chest starting to hitch, and he knew he'd need his inhaler soon.

"What do you think, little guy?" Anthony asked, getting close to Walter's face. His breath smelled like garlic and stale Fritos. "Is he dead?"

Walter bobbed his head madly, hoping they'd let him go. He silently swore that he'd never set foot in these woods again.

"I think he's going to cry!" Spencer said, laughing.

"Is that right?" Anthony asked, blowing more of his rancid breath in Walter's face. "Are you going to cry, you little fucking bawl baby?"

Walter clenched his jaw, combating not just with his asthma now, but also with panic and fury. The sensation of all three was so overwhelming he thought he might faint, but Spencer and Anthony held him steady.

"Well, if you're mad at us now," Anthony said in a mockingly apologetic tone. "You're really going to hate this!"

They launched Walter toward the dead body. He lost his balance and fell on top of it, which in and of itself would have been bad enough.

What made it infinitely worse is that he felt it move.

Spencer and Anthony brayed with laughter as Walter scurried away. Unable to breathe he pulled out his in-haler with shaking hands, and shakily sprayed it into his mouth. His vision, which had become blurred and blown out, slowly returned to normal as he regained control of his breathing. He saw Spencer and Anthony looking at him with wide eyes, and the fact that they almost added a second dead body to the pile was not lost on them.

"You okay, kid?" Spencer asked in a low voice.

"Forget it, let's just go," Anthony said as he elbowed him in the arm.

"He moved!" Walter gasped.

Spencer and Anthony stopped dead in their tracks.

"Shut up," Spencer said. He was attempting to sound tough, but there was a slight tremor in his voice.

"I'm serious!" Walter continued. "I felt him move! He's alive!"

Spencer and Anthony looked at each other. Their fear was undeniable now.

"Seriously, we need to go," Anthony said as he started to back away.

"No," Spencer said, shaking his head. "We have to see if he's alive. Because if this little shit tells somebody we were out here, the bum can back him up. And don't forget why we came out here in the first place!"

Spencer proceeded to pinch his thumb and forefinger together and place them in front of his lips. Walter had no idea what the gesture meant, but that was the least of his problems.

"He doesn't even know what that is!" Anthony cried out, sounding exasperated.

"But the bum will!" Spencer countered.

"So we ditch what's left of the shit and leave!"

To Walter's great pleasure, Anthony's formerly gruff voice was becoming high-pitched and querulous. It almost sounded like he was going to cry.

"Fuck that," Spencer said, holding his ground. "I already got picked up by the cops last month! They find out we had weed, I'm going to fucking juvie!"

Walter still had no clue what they were talking about, but he found their panic cathartic.

"I'm going to make sure he's dead," Spencer continued. "Then we dump the shit and get out of here. And you…"

He pointed a trembling finger at Walter.

"You say anything to anyone, you're fucking dead, you got me?"

Walter nodded, though it was clear Spencer and Anthony had lost control of the situation. Regardless, he stayed still and kept a tight grip on his inhaler.

"What if he's not dead, Spencer?" Anthony whined. "What happens then?"

He was definitely close to tears now, but Spencer's mind was made up. He took several cautious steps toward the man's body and leaned forward, looking for any sign of movement. When there wasn't he knelt down, reaching a shaking hand toward the body.

"What are you doing?" Anthony hissed.

"Checking his pulse!" Spencer whispered back.

"Don't fucking touch it!" Anthony said, raising his voice, but it was too late. Spencer was slowly placing his hand on the man's dirt-streaked neck. Just as he was about to make contact, the body turned over with a thick rustle of clothing and the popping of worn-out joints. The man's face, almost completely obscured by dirt, looked up at Spencer with startling blue eyes before giving him a wide smile that displayed an incomplete set of rotting teeth.

"Hi there!"

The greeting was casual, bordering on friendly, and before Spencer could respond the man plunged a box cutter into his neck with a quickness and ease that was almost supernatural. Spencer fell back, his face comical with shock as the man withdrew the blade. Blood began to pulse from Spencer's neck in impressive arcs that splattered, violating the surrounding foliage.

Anthony opened his mouth to scream, but the man was already on his feet and striding toward him. In one swift motion he pocketed the box cutter and pulled out a length of cord. Anthony tried to run, but the man already had the cord around his neck. He tightened it and Anthony gasped, falling to his knees as his face turned red, then an ugly shade of purple. His eyes bulged as the man continued to tighten the cord, and Walter watched in wonderment and horror as Anthony's bulging eyes filled with blood. The scene, gruesome as it was, bore a surprisingly close resemblance to Walter's fantasies. He felt a strange sense of gratitude as Anthony let out one final, choked gasp before dying. The man let his body slump to the ground with a heavy thud before returning the length of cord to his pocket.

He turned to Walter and grinned.

"What do you say, boy?"

Walter didn't know what to say. The man sensed his trepidation and laughed.

"You don't need to be scared. I heard everything those two whistling assholes said, and I certainly know what they did. In case you haven't figured it out yet, I don't like bullies."

He spat on the ground, and Walter noticed with some distaste that the phlegm was green and speckled with bits of black and brown.

"My experience with bullies," the man continued. "Is that they stay bullies, even when they grow up. I just did the world a favor!"

He punctuated this simple proclamation with a look of dignified defiance, as if he was daring Walter to disagree with him. The thing was, Walter didn't disagree. Even if he did he certainly wouldn't let on, not after he saw what this guy was capable of.

"Give me a hand?" the man asked as he grabbed Spencer's feet.

Walter hesitated before taking another drag from his inhaler.

"Don't worry, boy. They won't never find them. And if they do, they certainly ain't going to blame you."

That was good enough for Walter.

Although the man did most of the work, Walter did his best. Since he was perceived as weak, even by the relatives and teachers that were nice to him, nobody ever asked him to help with anything. The task at hand was grim, but Walter wasn't going to let such a rare opportunity go to waste. The bodies were dumped in an old sewer pipe that the man claimed hadn't been used in thirty years.

"The redirected the sewers elsewhere," he told Walter matter-of-factly. "But that don't mean we still can't fill it with shit!"

He followed this with a loud, hoarse laugh, and for a brief instant Walter joined him. When they returned to the man's campsite Walter watched as he opened a bottle of booze and used it to wash away Spencer's blood.

"Need to take it easy with this shit anyway," the man explained as the blood and alcohol were swallowed by the freshly dampened soil. When it was done the man added the bottle to a tattered garbage bag filled with empties before returning to his earlier spot.

"Back to sleep," he said. "Be on your way now."

Walter, still slightly numb from the events of that afternoon, dutifully grabbed his bag and made his way back to the main trail.

"Hey, boy!"

Walter turned around to see the man propped up on his elbow.

"I got your back. Do what you need to do to forget about everything else that happened today, but always remember that."

And then, in a matter of seconds, he was prone and fully asleep.

• • •

"Wally Poop Pants!"

Walter was almost home, and was still thinking of an excuse to give to his mother. He was almost an hour late and knew she'd be freaking out by now, but at that moment he had another matter to attend to.

"Wally Poop Pants!" Jason repeated in a sing-song voice. He rode his bike past Walter and was now blocking his path. There was a time when Jason seemed impossibly tall and imposing, but now he just reminded Walter of an ant. A smelly, ugly ant.

"What are you up to, buddy?" Jason continued. "Your knees are looking a little dirty. Been busy in those woods?"

Walter didn't fully understand what that meant, but the mention of the woods brought on a sudden burst of inspiration.

"Hey, Jason," he said with a grin. "Wanna see a dead body?"

MICHAEL SUBJACK
ABOUT THE AUTHOR

Michael Subjack was born in a small town in Western New York. He enjoys good cigars and going on hikes with his dog Rosie.

He lives in Los Angeles but you can also find him on Twitter as @MSubjack. and on his Amazon Author Page
https://www.amazon.com/Michael-Subjack/e/B01GJ2QSGW

FOREST MAN
HOLLEY CORNETTO

"**T**ell me what you remember, Nate."

Jennifer sat across from me in a booth at the Tick Tock Diner. It was past midnight, and the place was mostly empty. A jukebox stood in the corner, covered in dust. The whole place looked like a relic of the past; maybe that is why I'd chosen it for our reunion.

I swallowed hard, considering my answer. How much did I remember? How much of what I thought I knew was real? "I remember the night at the bonfire, when we found out about Franklin. I had a crush on you. Did you know that? I was nervous."

She had so many piercings that her face resembled a pincushion. From the looks of it, her hair had once been blue, but was now faded to green from neglect. She was still beautiful, no doubt, but the years hadn't been kind. Maybe that's how it was with first crushes. Maybe, deep down, you always felt a spark.

"What else?" She shook a pill from the bottle in her hand, swallowing it without water.

"The song. I can't forget that song."

. . .

My family went to Lake Swart every summer when I was young. The water was pristine, the bluest blue I'd ever seen, and the shore was covered in white sand. There were fourteen cabins in all, and in any given summer, most of them were occupied. It was the same families every year, and we got to know each other well during those summers together.

It was tradition for our parents to throw a beach party the first night at the lake. They spent the night drinking beer, and we made s'mores. It was when everyone caught up with each other, and all that we'd missed since last summer. S'more Night was legendary.

The bonfire blazed, sending up smoke and debris that twirled through the evening sky. The whole beach was illuminated. From the boombox by the folding chairs a DJ promised to play 'all the hits from the seventies, eighties, and today.' The big red cooler, half buried in the sand, was so full of beer and soda that the lid wouldn't close.

Families started to trickle in. Brandon arrived first, wearing a Yankees hat and cargo pants. His pockets were already bulging, no doubt from whatever rocks he'd collected along the way. He was tall and lanky, with dark eyes and skin. Lee joined us next. He was older than the rest of the lake kids, making him our leader by default. He wore a red bandana and a Van Halen t-shirt. He had a lollipop tucked behind his ear like a cigarette, and a Walkman clipped on his belt buckle. Sarah and Jennifer arrived at the same time. Though sisters, they were opposites. Sarah was tall and loud. She liked makeup and manicures, and by the way she looked at him she liked Lee too. Jennifer was short and shy. When she laughed, she covered her mouth with her hand. I wondered if this would be the summer that I told her I loved her.

Marcus, the youngest of our summer regulars, arrived last, and a collective groan went out from the group.

"Oh great. The loser's back," Lee sighed.

"Aww, come on. He isn't so bad." I replied.

Brandon opened the box of graham crackers and passed them around. "Speaking of not coming back, did you guys hear about Franklin?"

I looked around the group. None of the others reacted. "What happened?" I asked.

"His family moved." Brandon answered, unwrapping a chocolate bar. "They won't be back this summer, or maybe ever." He passed the chocolate to me.

"That sucks." I broke off a block and passed it to Jennifer. I blushed when her hand brushed mine. I wondered if she had a boyfriend.

"That isn't what I heard," Marcus said, taking the seat to my left.

"Shut up, Dorkus. Nobody cares what you heard." Sarah snapped.

Lee leaned forward, feigning interest. "Well come on, weirdo, what'd you hear?"

I knew where this was going. Lee was looking for fuel, something he could use to tease Marcus for the rest of the summer, and that dope Marcus was dumb enough to give it to him.

Marcus cleared his throat, speaking in conspiratorial tones. "He vanished. They never found him."

"Bullshit." Lee tossed a marshmallow at him.

Brandon shifted uncomfortably. "Marcus, that is messed up dude. Why do you always have to go there with your creepy-ass shit? His family moved, that's all."

Marcus shook his head and brushed crumbs off his 'I Want to Believe' t-shirt. "He went missing here at the lake."

"No way." Jennifer speared a marshmallow and held it over the fire.

"Yes, way," Marcus continued. "It was in the paper. He lived in Greenbriar, one town over from me."

Lee scoffed. "This is the dumbest shit I've ever heard. If he went missing at the lake we would've known about it." He pulled a white Bic from his pocket and struck it, holding the flame beneath his skewered marshmallow. He was showing off, I knew. The marshmallow caught fire; he just laughed and blew out the flame.

Marcus frowned at the lighter. I knew what he was thinking: it was likely swiped from Lee's parents. Lee teased him mercilessly last summer for being a tattletale. Apparently the lesson stuck, because Marcus ignored it and went back to telling his story. "My family and his were the last ones here, remember? You were all gone by then. The police came and everything. They even asked me questions about where he was, and when I'd seen him last."

"How would you know anything, dweeb?" Lee flicked a bit of hot marshmallow at Marcus.

"Because after you guys left, we hung out in the woods. We found this cave down by the boulder path that…was weird." His face screwed up into a perplexed look.

Jennifer inspected her toasted marshmallow. "A hidden cave? I want to see it." She took a bite from her s'more. Melted chocolate dripped down her chin, and I shivered.

"Me too!" I said, a little too quickly. "Why don't we meet up in the morning, by the path?"

"We'll all go," Lee announced, decision made. "And when we don't find anything, I'm going to toss you in the lake, freak." I hoped he meant Marcus, but he was looking at me when he said it.

• • •

"What about you?" I asked, trying to get a look at the label on her pill bottle.

"I don't remember what I don't remember. Sounds stupid, right? My parents put me into therapy after that summer. You probably didn't know that. They put me on so many goddamn pills that I can't tell the real from the nightmares anymore."

I nodded. "I had nightmares, too. I kept dreaming about Franklin's face, and Marcus…I still dream about them." I couldn't bring myself to mention Sarah.

She fidgeted with an unopened pack of Camels. "Was the cave real?"

. . .

The next morning we met at the Boulder Path. It was an unmarked trail that led away from the beach into the forest, and we'd nicknamed it that because it was littered with glacial erratics. We used them for climbing, or hide-and-seek before Lee declared it to be a baby game and forbid us from playing. Franklin and I defied him once, but when Lee found out he gave us wedgies that made my balls sore for days.

I had a backpack full of snacks, and the canteen I'd gotten for my birthday was strapped around my shoulder. Ever the Boy Scout, Brandon's pack had a compass and whistle hanging from it. Lee was last to arrive at the rendezvous point, and of course he didn't carry any supplies. He never did.

We entered the forest and followed the trail past the usual places. Eventually Marcus wandered off the path, heading deeper into the woods. "It's this way, over by that hill." He pointed through a patch of trees and boulders, but I couldn't see the hill from where I stood.

Sarah stopped, looking down at her clothes. "I'm not going any further."

Lee tugged her arm. "Come on, Sarah. If Frog-Face says it's over here, then that's where we're going."

She shook her head, jerking her arm away and refusing to move. "You go ahead, but I'm staying here. I'm not going to get my clothes all dirty in those weeds."

Lee glared at her. "Suit yourself. Anyone else want to chicken out? Now's your big chance. Anyone? Just Sarah? Good." Lee sneered at her. "Have fun by yourself, chickenshit."

We followed Marcus deeper into the forest, dead leaves crunching under our feet as we marched on. Vines snaked up large oaks, and the undergrowth was dense and tangled. We all grew silent, in anticipation of something we couldn't name. Brandon produced a thick piece of yellow chalk from one of his many pockets, and marked the largest oaks as we passed. "So we can find our back here again if we need to," he explained.

"Good idea," Jennifer said.

I felt my face burn. "Yeah, Brandon. Good idea."

The forest grew thicker around us. I'd never been this far off the path before. Briars snagged at the leg of my pants, and no birds or insects chirped. The only noise was the crunching of leaves as we trekked on. Uneasy, I decided to break the silence. "How did you find this place, anyway?"

Marcus shrugged. "Franklin found it. He showed it to me. We were here for a week after you guys left, so we had a lot of time to explore." He stopped short at the base of a hill. Lichen-covered boulders of various sizes surrounded the hill and climbed the side, and he pointed between the largest of the two.

I stayed behind him and Lee, keeping close to Jennifer. She'd been unusually quiet since Sarah's departure, and I could tell it was bothering her.

I looked up at the mouth of the cave. It was a little taller than head height, ringed with ferns that hung down like teeth. It looked ready to devour us.

Lee laughed. "I'll be damned! I thought you were screwing with us. Maybe I can swipe some of my old man's smokes and bring them down here."

Jennifer tugged at my arm, reaching for my hand. I intertwined my fingers with hers, trying to keep the shit-eating grin off my face. "Should we go inside?" I asked.

"Heck yeah!" Lee shoved Marcus out of his way and walked to the mouth of the cave. "Damn. Did anybody bring a flashlight?"

We all looked at Brandon, but he shook his head.

"We could come back later with lights." Jennifer suggested.

I looked down at her hand in mine. I wasn't about to pass up this chance. "Hey Lee, still got your lighter? It could help us get a look inside."

Lee grinned and reached in his pocket, flicking the flame to life. "Follow me."

Jennifer's grip on my hand tightened. "I don't think

we should."

I tugged her forward gently. "We might as well look since we're here. You know Lee will just make us come back if we don't."

"Okay." I could sense the uncertainty in her voice.

"Holy shit guys!" Lee had already gone in, holding the flame on his lighter a few seconds at a time before letting it die and sparking it back to life. Marcus and Brandon were standing behind him, looking over his shoulder at something just out of my line of sight.

"W-what is it?" Jennifer asked.

"I don't know. A tree?" Marcus guessed as the flame flickered out again.

"Shut up, dipshit. Trees don't grow in caves. They need to photo…photo..." Lee flicked the lighter again.

"Photosynthesize," Brandon interrupted.

"It looks more like a statue," Jennifer said, straining to get a look from behind the others.

I stepped forward with false bravado. "Jennifer's right. Look, it has a face…" In the exact center of the cave stood the stump of some long-dead, petrified tree. Carved into it was a man's face.

"What's this?" Lee asked, and reached for a bit of string dangling from one of the branches.

Brandon had backed away and stood just outside the cave. "This is messed up, dude. That looks like a person. Those look like arms!"

Lee stood frozen, his hand on the arm of the statue. A few seconds passed before he laughed, a nervous laugh

I'd never heard from him before, and he lifted the string.

He must be afraid, I thought. I'd never seen Lee afraid.

Marcus looked at the strings and went pale. "It's Franklin's friendship bracelet."

"No…" Jennifer's voice was so low I was sure I'd been the only one to hear. She was trembling. I needed to get her out of here.

I looked at the others. "Why don't we come back when we have flashlights? So we can get a better look at it?"

Lee was staring at the statue, tree-stump, whatever it was. He turned on Marcus. "You put it here to try and scare us. Where did you find the carving, freak? Did you do it yourself? Been watching too much TV, and got bored? Decided to mess with us?" He shoved Marcus hard against the wall of the cave, his face inches away. "Well, I'm not buying it, creep." With each word he pressed a finger hard into Marcus's shoulder.

"Guys, come on. We should go find Sarah." I couldn't care less about Sarah, but I didn't know what else to say. There was no way I was going to get between Marcus and Lee.

• • •

"Yeah, it was real."

A waitress approached our table, notepad in hand. She was older, with a mustache shading her upper lip. "Know what you'd like?"

I ordered a cheeseburger and fries. Jennifer asked for a slice of pumpkin pie. When the waitress walked away, Jennifer leaned across the table. "What was that thing inside? Was it…him?"

I shook my head. There it was, the crazy part. The thing that had kept me from contacting her for the past twenty years. It was true that something had happened that summer, but we'd been kids, too young to understand. Our minds had created a story, a boogeyman, to blame instead.

She interrupted my thoughts. "You heard the song too, right?" She sang the words, barely louder than a whisper:

"Don't get lost along the way,

Forest Man is here to play…"

My stomach knotted. "I heard you sing it."

The waitress returned with two glasses of water. Jennifer refused to meet my eyes.

"You never told me what you remember."

Her gaze met mine. "Did I tell you I asked my parents about Franklin? I was so freaked out after we found his bracelet. I asked them what happened, why his family wasn't there."

I hadn't known. "What did they tell you?"

"Nothing. They wouldn't tell me anything. They said it wasn't my concern or some bullshit."

Xanax. The bottle said Xanax.

• • •

The next morning I went to the Boulder Path again. We hadn't agreed to meet or anything, I just felt drawn to it. I needed to return to the cave and see if I could find evidence that it had all been a joke. Maybe then Jennifer would think I was a hero or something.

When I got to the path she was already standing there, as if she'd been waiting for me. She grinned when she saw me. She was beautiful.

I held up my flashlight sheepishly. "I thought I'd go check it out."

She nodded. "Me too. I…I mean, it was weird, right? That tree thing? The bracelet? You don't think Marcus would do that to scare us, do you?"

I shook my head. "Lee maybe, but not Marcus."

She nodded.

We entered the woods, and left the path where Brandon's chalk marks began. I was grateful that he'd left them. I could tell an oak from a maple, and I knew that bigger meant older for trees, but that was where my knowledge ended. I was a child of the suburbs, not the forest.

We turned our flashlights on and entered the cave. I swept the beam to the center of the cave where the tree… thing…stood. It looked changed, somehow. I reached out to touch it, but Jennifer got there first.

Her flashlight clattered to the ground, breaking a silence that I hadn't noticed until that moment. When she pulled her hand away it was covered in something red, and sticky. She gasped, holding up a UFO-shaped key chain. "Marcus'?" she asked.

I nodded. "Do you think he left it here yesterday?"

She shook her head, looking down at her hands. "No. This…this wasn't here yesterday."

"Maybe he came back this morning?"

"I don't know, but something isn't right." She sniffed her hand and recoiled. "It smells like blood."

I shined my light along the cave's inner wall. It was covered with crimson words:

Take my hand and come with me

Tweedle, deedle, deedle, dee

I will follow where you go

Tweedle deedle, deedle doe

Don't get lost along the way

Forest Man is here to play…

The air in the cave was suddenly stifling. "That wasn't here yesterday, was it?" I stammered.

Jennifer shook her head.

"Someone must have come back here. Maybe Lee. Right? Lee came back and did all this…to get back at Marcus for trying to scare him. Right?"

She stared, unblinking, at the words on the wall. Her hands were shaking.

I led her out of the cave, and offered her my canteen. "Here, wash your hands off."

She moved mechanically. After her hands were clean I led her back to the path, out of the forest.

When we returned to the lake Sarah and Lee were on

the beach. Sarah's eyes were rimmed with tears. A fishing pole lay at Lee's feet. It looked like they were arguing, and that they'd been at it for a while.

Sarah frowned. "Jennifer! Where were you? I woke up this morning and you were gone."

Jennifer stared at her feet, silent.

"We went back to the cave. It was…different." I said.

Lee flinched, the movement barely noticeable. "What do you mean, different?"

"There was something written on the walls…it looked like blood."

"Blood was written on the walls?"

"No. Something was written on the walls in blood."

"What was?"

"I don't know…it looked like a story, or a rhyme. Something about a man in the forest."

"Forest Man?" Lee asked.

"Yeah. That sounds right." I answered.

Lee muttered under his breath.

Jennifer's voice was barely above a whisper. "What does it mean?"

He shook his head. "It's bullshit, that's what. It's Marcus being a freak. He should've let it go." He turned and stalked toward the cabins.

"Where are you going?" Sarah called after him.

"I'm going to pound that little jerk," he called back, vanishing down the road.

Sarah turned to Jennifer and me. "Is she okay?"

I shook my head. "I don't think she is."

When Lee got back to the beach, Brandon was following him.

"Well, what happened?" I asked.

"He wasn't there."

Jennifer tensed.

"What do you mean, wasn't there?"

Lee sighed. I expected him to yell at me, but he just ran a hand through his hair.

Brandon broke the silence. "He was supposed to meet me this morning. We were going to break into Franklin's room, to see if they left anything behind."

Sarah propped her chin on her knees. "Supposed to?"

Brandon nodded. "Yeah, but he never showed up. I went to his place. I figured he overslept, or there was a Twilight Zone marathon on or something. But his parents said he was gone when they got up this morning."

Lee kicked the sand.

"So now what?" Sarah asked.

"We go to his house and wait for him," Lee answered. "He can't hide forever."

• • •

Jennifer took a bite of pumpkin pie. Her coffee mug was empty, despite three refills. She looked older than 32, but her nervous demeanor made her seem younger. I don't know what I'd been thinking, looking her up after all these years. That wasn't entirely true; I thought if I saw her again something would click. Either we'd hit it off and I could finally tell her how I felt, or nothing would happen and I could walk away laughing at how ridiculous I'd been by holding on to those feelings for so many years.

"Would you be willing to go back?" It was a dumb move, asking her to go back there, but maybe I could help her make peace with the past. If I took her back, and she saw that there was nothing there, then maybe she could move on. Maybe she'd want me to help her.

She didn't look surprised by my question, but took her time before answering. "I think we should call Lee, too."

I dropped the fry I'd been holding. "Lee? I wouldn't even know how to get in touch with him."

She lifted her chin toward her phone. "I do."

"You have his number?" I tried to swallow the lump of jealousy that formed in my throat.

"Yeah. We dated for a while, if you could call it that. We were really just hooking up, I guess."

"Don't tell me." The truth was, I didn't want to hear it. I didn't want to picture them together. Goddamn Lee. He'd taken advantage of her fragile mental state.

"He was pretty messed up about what happened that summer, too. I know he'll want to come with us."

I frowned, chewing another french fry. I did not want Lee to come. I knew this much, but I couldn't think of a good reason to tell her no. "Fine. Call him. He can meet us there tomorrow, or not, but I'm not waiting for him."

What was the chance that he'd be able to drop everything and meet us by the cabins the next day, I thought.

The chances were pretty good, as it turned out.

• • •

Marcus' mom answered the door. "Have you kids had lunch? I can make you some pizza rolls and lemonade while you wait."

"Thanks, that would be great," Sarah replied.

Mrs. Matheson rummaged around the kitchen, and in a few moments placed a steaming plate of pizza rolls and pitcher of iced lemonade in front of us.

I kept watching Jennifer, hopeful she'd snap out of her trance. She stared forward, unaware of anything around her.

"Mrs. Matheson, could we ask you something?" Sarah rested her chin on her hand in a staged movement.

"What's on your mind, kids?"

"Marcus said that Franklin went missing last year from here, at the lake. He said you were all still here when it happened."

Mrs. Matheson looked at us and sighed. "It was a terrible thing, really."

"So it's true?" Sarah asked, eyes shining.

"Yes. Franklin disappeared, and the police did a search of the area. I'm afraid I can't tell you much more than that. We left soon after he went missing, because Marcus had gotten very sick. He was sleepwalking and mumbling. He was zoning out, almost like he was in a trance. Don't tell him I told you, but I want you all to watch out for him. Be kind. The doctors said it was stress induced. I didn't want to come back this year, but he begged. He said it would do him good to see his lake friends."

I took the last roll from the plate, wiping my greasy hands on my jeans. "We'll look out for him, Mrs. Matheson. Don't worry."

Lee nodded. "Could we leave a note for him in his room?"

"Sure! He'd like that."

Sarah lifted the plate from the counter. "You guys go ahead, I'll help clean up."

His room was exactly as I remembered it. All of his things were still there, right down to the Ninja Turtles duffle bag lying in the corner.

"Look around." Lee ordered. "See if you find anything useful, or any clues to where he might have gone."

Brandon searched the bookshelf. Lee paced, muttering to himself. He stopped in front of the desk. I watched as he lifted a notebook and flipped through the pages before rolling it up and sticking it in his back pocket.

I took Jennifer's hand, a gesture that was becoming more natural each time. "Let's check over here."

I opened the closet door and pushed the clothes aside. Jennifer made a strangled sound in the back of her throat. I saw a flash of red, and immediately pushed the clothes back. I was too late. She'd already seen the writing.

Lee and Brandon rushed over. Behind the clothes in his closet, in crimson letters, was the rhyme: Don't get lost along the way, Forest Man is here to play.

Lee kicked the closet door. "He's somewhere. And when I find him, I'm going to pound him." He stormed out of the room, and we fell in line behind him.

We spent the rest of that afternoon on the beach. Lee and Brandon cast line after line into the lake, catching nothing. Sarah spread out on a beach towel with a Nancy Drew novel in hand. I stayed with Jennifer, trying to get her interested in building a sand castle. She mostly watched.

None of us mentioned Marcus. No one said much of anything.

By sunset Mrs. Matheson had walked down to the beach. "Have you kids seen Marcus? He never came home."

Lee flinched. Brandon placed a hand on his shoulder. "No ma'am. We haven't seen him."

She turned and left, her face a mask of concern.

Sarah looked up from her book. "What was that about?"

Brandon threw down his fishing pole. "You know what! Marcus is gone, just like Franklin, and it has something to do with that cave."

"Don't talk crazy." Lee's face was twisted with rage. "It means that Marcus is trying to scare us. That's all."

Brandon shook his head. "Marcus wouldn't do this. He might be weird, but he isn't mean. He'd be afraid to be out by himself for this long, especially after dark. What if something's there? What if there's someone in the woods?

We need to tell our parents."

Lee swung his fist hard, and we all heard the sickening thud as his fist impacted Brandon's face. "We aren't telling anyone! Do you understand? We don't talk about the cave, or the woods. Nothing. And if I find out that you did, I'll kill you!"

"Jesus, Lee! Chill out. He won't say anything." Sarah bent down to check on Brandon, who was cradling his cheek. "You don't have to act like a freaking barbarian."

"I don't need this right now." Lee scooped up his fishing rod and headed down the road toward the cabins.

• • •

Jennifer went outside to call Lee while I paid the check. I exited the diner and spotted her on the corner, lighting up a cigarette. The flames lit up her face, reminding me of that night at the bonfire.

"Well?" I asked.

"He'll be there. Said it was about time we decided to go back."

"What about Brandon? If we're inviting Lee, shouldn't we call Brandon, too?"

Jennifer shook her head. "No. Lee never forgave him for all that shit with the police. He thought Brandon was trying to blame him for what happened to Marcus."

"Jennifer, I'm sorry I didn't do a better job of keeping in touch. I just..."

She shrugged. "It didn't touch you and Brandon, not

like me and Lee. You didn't understand."

"I understood well enough. I just didn't know what to say to you."

She took a long draw from her cigarette. "You don't have to live with the guilt. I was given a choice, and I made a bad one. The weight of that decision, the guilt I feel...it's haunted me since that summer."

"What do you mean, you were given a choice? Brandon told the police, and they didn't find anything. What else could you have done?"

She tossed her cigarette on the ground and stamped it out. "I don't mean the police. I mean him. He gave me a choice, and I told him to take Sarah."

I stood, staring at her. I wondered if she'd had one too many Xanax, or one too many therapy sessions. I wondered what her parents had told her, what her therapists had told her, and what stories she had told herself to make sense of what happened. After years of torturing myself I'd finally decided that Forest Man was just a story, one we'd invented in our subconscious minds because the truth was too frightening to confront. There was someone in the woods when we were kids. A kidnapper, or a serial killer maybe, and they had taken our friends.

· · ·

By the next morning the police were at the lake. Marcus hadn't come home, not that any of us expected him to. Not even Lee, despite his talk.

My parents sat me down and explained that they expected me to cooperate with the police. I thought about Lee punching Brandon, and I thought about Jennifer. I excused myself as soon as I could, and went to her cabin.

Sarah met me at the door.

"Where is she?" I asked.

Sarah rolled her eyes. "I don't know. She's been acting weird since yesterday. This morning she just left. I think she took my book with her."

"Thanks," I called over my shoulder, heading toward the forest path. I had a hunch that I knew where she'd be.

I left the path at the usual spot, and saw her sitting just inside the cave, right in front of...him. I don't know when I had come to think of the tree stump as a him, but it felt right. She sang in a low voice. "Take my hand and come with me, tweedle, deedle, deedle, dee..."

"Jennifer?" I placed a hand on her shoulder. She jumped.

When she turned around I saw that she was still in her pajamas, and was weirdly barefoot. Her feet were covered in dried mud.

"He wants to play."

"Who?"

"The Forest Man. He's lonely, and he wants us to come play with him."

I crouched down beside her. "Who's the Forest Man, Jennifer?"

"I will follow where you go, tweedle deedle, deedle doe..."

I grabbed her by the shoulders and shook her. "Jennifer?"

"Marcus sent Franklin to play. Lee sent Marcus to play. Now, it's my turn."

"Come on, we're getting out of here." I put her arm around my shoulder and hoisted her up, dragging her from the cave. "We're going to go back and talk to the police, okay? We're going to tell them everything. Screw Lee."

"No." Her voice was husky and low. "No, you can't tell the police. Promise you won't."

"This is serious. Something is happening, and we need to tell the grownups."

There were tears in her eyes. "Please, please promise you won't."

It was her eyes that convinced me. Her face was dirty, with snot and drool dribbling down her chin. But her eyes shined with…fear? I wasn't sure. "Okay, I promise."

I turned for one last glimpse at the cave, and saw Sarah's Nancy Drew novel propped against the tree stump. I half-led, half-carried Jennifer back to the lake.

By the time we arrived her parents had noticed her missing and panicked, fearing the worst.

"Thank you for bringing her back, Nate. I'm sure she's just worried about Marcus. I mean, we all are."

I nodded. There was nothing else to say. I wanted to mention the song, or the book, or those crazy things she'd said to me about the Forest Man, but when I looked at her I couldn't. I had promised. It would have been a betrayal.

My parents called me back home, and I went inside

our cabin and waited. My dad tried to interest me in a game of chess, but I couldn't remember how each piece moved. Eventually, he'd gotten annoyed and stopped trying.

"Why do I have to stay here anyway? Why can't I be with my friends?"

Mom sighed. "Because the police are searching the woods. They can't have you kids walking through a crime scene."

"A crime scene? They think it was a crime?"

Dad gave her a warning look. "Something happened. We don't know what. It's too soon to jump to any conclusions, so just let the police do their job."

"What are they looking for?" I asked.

"Your friend Brandon was taking them into the woods. He thought he knew somewhere they should check."

My heart felt like it would pound right out of my chest. Of course Brandon would.

• • •

We pulled onto the winding road that led to the lake cabins. I glanced at Jennifer through the rearview mirror. "Are you sure you're up for this?"

She nodded.

She'd grown silent as we approached the lake. Almost in a trance, the way I remembered from that summer. "My family never came back here." It was a stupid thing to say, but I needed to break the silence. "What about you? Did your family ever come back? To look for Sarah?"

She shook her head. "No, but they kept the cabin. I think in case she ever came back." Her tone was cold and blank, like she wasn't there anymore.

I cursed silently, noticing a rusted Ford truck in the driveway. Part of me had held out hope he wouldn't come. "There's Lee."

She nodded.

Lee looked ragged, and old. His chin sharp as a razor, and his cheekbones hollow and gaunt. He looked twenty years older than he should have. His hair had gone prematurely gray. It was funny to think this was the person we'd been afraid of as kids, the one who'd bullied us into submission.

He walked right past me and enveloped Jennifer in a hug. He held her longer than necessary, and whispered something to her that I couldn't hear. She gave a tentative nod, and then he approached me. "Been a long time, Nate."

"Yeah. Yeah, it has."

"Do you two want to unpack first, or head straight down to the cave?"

I looked over my shoulder. Jennifer was catatonic. "We should probably unpack. I think she might need a few minutes, so you can fill me in on what you remember from that summer."

His eyes went dark for a moment, and he didn't reply.

"Surely you remember something?"

He smirked. "Is this the part where I tell you not to call me Shirley?"

I sighed, grabbing the bags from my trunk. Jennifer was already up the stairs, turning the key in the lock.

He grabbed my shoulder, tight. "Is she okay? What did you do to her?"

I jerked out of his grasp. "I didn't do shit. Before we left she started talking crazy. Something about making a bad choice, or the wrong choice, or something. And then, when we got here, she just spaced out. Like that summer."

Lee rubbed the stubble along his chin. "Did she say what kind of choice?"

I must have given him a strange look, because he waved me off. "Nevermind. She's probably just nervous about being back." He turned, and I noticed a rolled up notebook protruding from his back pocket.

"Hey…" I grabbed it and tugged. "This reminds me. That summer, you took a notebook from Marcus's room."

He jerked it from my grip and looked around nervously. "Not out here. Let's go inside."

I nodded and followed him up the stairs. I noticed he didn't bring any bags.

• • •

Jennifer, Brandon, Lee, Sarah, and I all sat on the couch while Mr. Matheson reamed us out about lying to the police. "You kids know better. Every bit of time and attention you take away from these officers puts Marcus in more danger. They spent hours out in those woods looking for a cave that doesn't exist. You should all be ashamed of yourselves!"

I saw Lee pinch the inside of Brandon's leg. Brandon squirmed, but didn't make a sound.

It'd been Brandon who decided to tell the police everything. He told them about Marcus leading us to the cave, and the weird stuff we'd found inside. He told them about the rhyme we'd found written in the closet. When the police searched the closet, they'd found nothing.

Brandon then offered to take them to the cave. They circled the path for hours. He couldn't find his chalk marks, and they couldn't find the cave. The police finally decided he was lying to them.

When we left the Matheson house we were told to go back to our cabins, and not to wander into the woods. My parents were already packing.

"Wait, we can't leave. Not while Marcus is missing."

My mom frowned. "We can't help by staying, and what if there's a kidnapper or someone out there? It's dangerous. The police have cleared us, so we're leaving tomorrow."

"Mom, I—"

"Don't argue with your mother, young man. We're leaving, and that's our final decision. I'm sorry that you can't stay and play with your friends, but the other families are leaving too. There's no point in staying."

"Jennifer's family?" I asked.

He nodded. "Leaving tomorrow."

"Can I at least say goodbye?"

"Tomorrow."

The next morning I got dressed and ran to Jennifer's cabin. I sat on the steps, waiting. I sat for what felt like hours, before I decided to go tap on her window.

She opened after a few taps.

"Are you leaving today, too?" I asked.

She shrugged. "We were going to, but we probably won't. My parents will want to stay and look for Sarah."

"What do you mean 'look for Sarah'?" I saw a shadow in the room behind her. I stood on my tiptoes and caught a flash of red bandana. Lee. Lee was in Jennifer's room.

"She's gone. She went to play with the Forest Man. She won't come back; they never do. Don't be sad, she won't be alone. She'll be with Franklin and Marcus."

"Jennifer, did you tell your parents? Why is Lee here?"

She nodded. "Yes. I told them all about the Forest Man. They don't believe me; they think I'm crazy, but I told them…I gave him her book. He needed it so he could find her and bring her to stay with him." She tugged at her hair. Her face held no expression, but her eyes…her eyes shone with that same fear I'd seen the day before.

"Why is Lee here?" I repeated.

"Lee believes me about the Forest Man. Lee saw him too, he's the only one that understands."

Lee stepped forward and wrapped an arm around her shoulders, pulling her away from the window. "Come on,

Jenny." He flashed a menacing smile. "Nate's leaving."

Fear got the best of me. I panicked, and ran from her window.

. . .

We placed our bags inside. A fine layer of dust covered everything in the room. No one had been here in years, that much was certain. I flipped a switch on the wall, but no light came on.

"Hey Jenny, do your parents still pay the electric for this place?" Lee asked.

"Jenny?" I echoed.

"We oughta look around for candles and such. Did you bring a flashlight?"

I unzipped my duffle and pulled out a pair of mag lights. We searched the kitchen, eventually producing enough matches and candles to keep the place lit after dark. After everything was arranged I sat down in the kitchen, nodding to the chair across from me. Lee sat.

"Is that the notebook?"

He grimaced and tossed it onto the table. "Yeah, it is."

"What's in it?"

He tilted his chin toward it. "See for yourself."

I reached across and opened the notebook, now creased and yellowed. The first page had a rough sketch of the tree stump. It looked much as I'd remembered, the bark shaped like a face. No wonder we'd been terrified; it was creepy. Underneath the sketch were the words Forest Man, written like a label. A name.

I flipped the page. Next the song lyrics were written in red ink. At least, I hoped it was ink. I could feel the color draining from my face. I felt a paralyzing fear, like I was twelve all over again. Why had I come back here? What the Hell was I trying to prove?

I flipped another page. There was a sketch of a boy. It was little more than a stick figure with a UFO drawn on the t-shirt. The stick figure was touching…holding…a piece of the tree stump. I slammed the book shut.

"What the Hell is this, Lee?"

"It is what it is." He flashed his usual non-committal smirk.

I felt everything go red. I wasn't a little boy anymore. My hands shook as I reached across the table to grab his collar. "You listen to me, you fucking asshole. I've had it with your bullshit! You tell me what happened, or I'll beat it out of you."

His eyes widened. I saw my face reflected in them, and I looked furious. He pulled himself free of my grip. "Okay, okay. Calm down."

"Talk. Now."

He gave a sigh, heavy with years of baggage. "Forest Man is its name."

I rolled my eyes. "Not this bullshit again."

"Shut up and listen."

I shook my head, but did as he demanded.

"Something happened to me and Jenny out there. I

don't know why us, and not you or Brandon. But…the thing, it came after us."

"A person? Someone hiding in the woods?"

"No, not like that. We both started having dreams after we were in the cave. Me after the first time, and her after she went with you. He'd come to us in dreams, holding out his hand, singing that damned song. 'Come play!' he said. Sometimes he was alone. Sometimes, he came with Franklin, but it was wrong. Franklin was all covered in blood. He looked torn…Eaten. I don't know."

I jumped when Jennifer pulled out a chair to sit down. I'd been so engrossed in Lee's story that I hadn't noticed her come into the room.

She sighed and looked up at me. "It was the same with me, but Marcus was there too. Franklin was all rotted and gross, like a zombie movie or something. When he tried to talk, maggots fell out of his mouth. I heard words in my head. 'Come play…' He, he asked if I wanted to play. I said…I said no. But, then he told me that if I wouldn't play with him he'd be lonely, and he'd take us all. So, he told me to pick. To pick someone to come and play."

She lay her head on the table and sobbed. Lee put his arms around her, murmuring softly.

"You picked Sarah, didn't you?" I already knew the answer.

She nodded.

I turned to Lee. "And you? You picked Marcus."

He nodded, not meeting my eyes.

I grabbed the flashlight off the table and started toward the door. This was crazy, some sort of shared delusion between the two of them. He'd been in her room that last day at the lake when she was out of it. He'd done something to her. But, what if he hadn't? What if it was real? There was only one way to find out.

"Where are you going?" Lee called from behind.

"I'm going to find that damned cave to prove that there is no Forest Man!"

He grabbed the spare light and followed me out.

Jennifer rose from the table. "I'm coming too." Her voice was clear, determined.

I found the overgrown path and started down. I was angry, and that anger fueled me. Jennifer kept pace, but I could hear Lee coughing and wheezing as he struggled to keep up. All those years of chain smoking were finally catching up with him. "Slow down."

Jennifer paused. "Do you guys remember the first time we saw it? Lee took the bracelet. He touched it. When Nate and I went back there was a keychain on it. I touched it. Do you see?"

Lee panted so loud he sounded like a dog. "See what?"

"We had to choose because we touched it!" She shouted. "Think about it. Take my hand and come with me? We took its hand!"

We arrived at a spot on the trail that seemed familiar. It didn't look familiar, but it felt right. I knew we were in the right place. I veered off in what I hoped was the direction of the cave.

I stopped short, and Lee almost barreled into me. I had spent so long convincing myself that it wasn't real, that it couldn't have possibly been real. I felt the blood leave my face as all of the memories came rushing back.

Lee broke my reverie. "I'll be damned; I half imagined it wouldn't be here. That it never was here."

I watched as he slid his hand into Jennifer's, interlocking their fingers. I felt my face flush with anger.

I flicked the flashlight on and shone the beam into the cave. As I inched closer it started to come into focus. The tree stump, just as I'd remembered, except it was surrounded by trinkets. Necklaces, bracelets, keychains, keys, car fobs, cell phones, even a hoodie were all draped around it like offerings at an altar.

"Sarah's book." I said, realization dawning on me. It was real. It had all been real.

"What?" Lee asked.

"Sarah was reading a book that summer. Nancy Drew, I think. When I found Jennifer here, she'd left the book. That's how she chose Sarah. She left the book." I turned to face him. "Which means you took something from Marcus, didn't you?"

He rubbed the back of his neck with his free hand.

"Answer me!"

"Yes, alright? Yes. I nicked a keychain from his pocket that night at the beach. I brought it down here. Look, I didn't think it was real. I thought I was dreaming. I thought he was messing with us, and I was mad, okay?

I figured if we came back down here and he saw his keychain it would freak him out."

"But then he went missing," I continued. "He went missing and you knew, but you didn't say anything. You let us all believe he was trying to scare us, and you knew the truth!" I stepped closer, closing the distance between us.

"I didn't know. I was a kid. It was messed up."

Fucking Lee. He was responsible for what happened to Marcus, and for what happened to Jennifer. And now he thought he'd just step back in and push me out again?

"What are you gonna do, man?"

I stalked into the cave, he trailed behind me, trying to grab me, to stop me. I looked over my shoulder, then grabbed the tree branch, which looked so much like a hand. "I'm going to play."

• • •

That night the Forest Man came to me in my dreams. Franklin, Marcus, and Sarah were all with him, but there were others, too. Children I didn't recognize. They sang to me, taunted me, and offered me things.

"Come play!" they sang, "Come play!"

I shook them off of me. "I can't play with you, I have to take care of Jennifer."

The Forest Man stared down at me, millipedes marching in and out of his eye sockets. "If you won't come and play with me, who will?"

I fingered a white Bic lighter in my pocket. A lighter that Lee had dropped inside the cave all those years ago, and I knew what my answer would be.

HOLLEY CORNETTO
ABOUT THE AUTHOR

Holley Cornetto was born and raised in Alabama, but now lives in New Jersey. To indulge her love of books and stories, she became a librarian. She is also a writer, because the only thing better than being surrounded by stories is to create them herself. She can be found lurking on Twitter @HLCornetto

https://twitter.com/HLCornetto

Return To The Woods
G. Allen Wilbanks

Elliot Durant marched forward, raising his feet high to avoid the worst of the uneven terrain. He ducked awkwardly to avoid a thick, low-hanging branch as he weaved between the trees and dense brush. Elliot did not want to be back here but, circumstances being what they were, he had been given no choice. He stumbled, but managed to keep his feet despite the stiff outcroppings of manzanita grabbing and pulling at the orange material of his prison-issue jumpsuit. The guards had agreed to un-shackle his legs for this trek, though his hands remained cuffed together and linked to the body chain around his waist, making his balance somewhat precarious.

"This where you killed them?" asked the guard standing behind him. The man wore a black and tan uni-form and casually held a shotgun in his right hand, the barrel pointed at the ground.

"I didn't kill my family," Elliot responded automatically, though he knew no one believed him. His claims of a monster living in the woods hadn't convinced anyone that he didn't murder his wife and two sons. It was too outlandish; too implausible. The story only made him sound insane.

Another man, an El Dorado County assistant district attorney named Dirk Cecil, stepped up and grasped Elliot's arm to help steady him when he tripped over another manzanita bush. "Watch your step," he said. The self-important little bureaucrat tried to smile at him, perhaps to appear more companionable, but he was panting for breath and the expression quickly slipped away. The ADA was grossly overweight, and clearly unused to physical exertion more strenuous than standing up from his office chair or signing legal papers. Wearing a white button-up shirt and dress slacks – poor attire for a forced slog through the forest – he did not appear to want to be in these woods any more than did Elliot.

"I didn't kill them," Elliot repeated.

Dirk shook his head. "Doesn't matter anymore, Mr. Durant. The jury will decide whether or not you go to prison. Right now, I just need you to keep your end of our deal. You show us where the bodies are, and I don't go after the death penalty."

"I'm not sure I remember exactly where they were. Even if I can find the place again, the creature may have moved the bodies after it let me go."

"Even if animals have gotten at the bodies, there should still be evidence of where they originally were.

That will be enough."

"No," Elliot insisted. "Not animals. It was some sort of monster…"

"Enough, Mr. Durant! I'm getting a little tired of your monster stories. Play that song for the jury if you think it will help, but I don't want to hear another word about it."

"I…I think we're getting close to where…where it happened."

Elliot, the ADA, and their four armed escorts emerged from out of the trees into a circular clearing. Sunlight shone through the opening in the forest canopy to reveal bare dirt and patches of grass growing in an open space almost thirty feet across. The hard-packed ground revealed no footprints or other signs of having been recently visited other than one glaring exception. In the center of the clearing, in a scraped-out shallow pit, were the ash and charred remains of an old campfire.

"That's where we were staying," Elliot pointed toward the cold fire pit. "Our tent was right here, next to the fire. I don't know where it went. It was still here after…" He swallowed thickly and glanced at Dirk. "After."

"And your family?" asked the guard holding the shotgun. He glared at Elliot with narrow-set, dark eyes sunk deep in his long face. His cheeks, red from the hike, and heavy frown lines etched along his nose and mouth made Elliot think of an evil ventriloquist's dummy. On his chest the guard wore a silver name badge with T. Wallace etched into it in black letters.

"The tent was ripped open from the top and when the creature crawled in, we ran outside to get away." Elliot paused and glanced again at the district attorney. The ADA sighed, but otherwise said nothing. "We ran out and went that way."

The group moved in the direction Elliot had indicated. When they reached the tree line at the opposite end of the clearing from where they had entered another guard cleared his throat to get their attention. He gestured toward a spindly oak tree, and they all turned to see a filthy, black-and-white sneaker laying on the ground.

"That looks like Michael's shoe," said Elliot. "We were barefoot when we ran into the trees. I think it must have fallen there when the tent got dragged away."

"Where did you go from here?" asked the district attorney.

"We ran, but didn't get very far before it caught us. It grabbed Laila first."

"Your wife?"

"Yes. It grabbed her before we got more than a few feet into the trees."

"So, we should find her around here somewhere?"

Elliot nodded, unable to speak for a moment. A tear crawled from his left eye and tracked down his cheek. He tried to wipe it away, but the chain around his waist stopped his hand before it could get close to his face. He sniffled and hunched his shoulder to his cheek instead, using his shirt to blot away the wetness.

"Yeah. Somewhere close by. The boys won't be far

away either. The thing was...too fast. We didn't have a chance."

"But you got away, didn't you?" asked the guard named Wallace. He had an ugly tone to his voice, and his lip curled up in a sneer. "How do you think you managed that?"

"It let me go."

"And why would it do that?" asked the ADA.

Elliot shrugged. "I don't know. It just did."

But Elliot was lying. He did know why it let him go.

A screech echoed through the trees; a high-pitched wail like the sound a hurt child might make. The deputies startled and glanced around the trees, trying to gauge how far away the source of the cry might be.

Elliot flinched. He knew the sound, and what it represented. He opened his mouth to warn the others, but Wallace was already shouting orders.

"Trent, you and Mitchell go check that out. The rest of us will stay with the prisoner."

The guards, Trent and Mitchell, nodded. The two men disappeared into the trees, moving as quickly as possible while still minimizing the noise of their own passage. Elliot saw them draw their service pistols before he lost sight of them in the dense growth. Several minutes passed as Elliot and the remainder of his escort waited for their return.

The cry repeated, but this time it was followed by shouting and the sharp report of gunshots. The shouts turned to screams, and in turn were cut short a moment later. The group strained to hear any further activity, but there was nothing left to hear. Silence ruled the forest again.

Elliot did not move. He was frozen in place; not from panic, but rather from resignation. The new silence that surrounded them was eerie. No birds sang, and the normally incessant hum of insects had completely stilled. Only a faint rustle of leaves in the trees as the wind blew past disturbed the utter calm.

"Trent!" called out Wallace, breaking the moment. "Mitch! What's happening?"

A faint galloping noise sounded in the distance, growing louder by the second. Something large was running directly toward them, moving fast and steadily through the obstructing trees and brush. Wallace brought the shotgun up to a ready position, and the other two guards drew their pistols from the holsters at their sides. The ADA, unarmed, sidled closer to Elliot. Whether it was to protect him, or put him in the path of whatever was approaching, Elliot did not know.

A green and yellow blur flashed through the group of men. Wallace's shotgun fired as the guard was struck by their unidentified assailant; the blast ear-splittingly loud at such close quarters. The shotgun pellets flew harmlessly off into the trees as Wallace disappeared. There was no more than a splash of blood on the ground to announce that the man had ever been with them.

Elliot turned to face the attorney standing behind him. "Monster," he said.

Dirk's eyes were wide with panic and shock. He didn't seem so eager to discount Elliot's story now.

The creature flashed past them a second time, sending one of the two remaining guards staggering drunkenly while clutching at his throat, trying to stop the blood that geysered from his opened carotid artery. His partner dropped a second later with his belly fileted wide, his guts spilling onto the ground at his feet.

Dirk Cecil abandoned Elliot, bolting back toward the clearing. His gait was more of an awkward waddle than a run, his too-wide belly threatening to overbalance his too-short legs. The image might have been humorous, if their situation had not become so dire.

"Don't run," called Elliot. "It won't…"

The creature appeared from behind a tree directly behind the ADA. It leaped onto the attorney's back, riding him to the ground like a big cat taking down easy prey. With a high wail of celebration the beast dropped its head and buried its teeth into the attorney's shoulder. The man screamed, and the creature bit him again. Dirk's cries of pain ended only when the monster grasped the sides of his head with two of its clawed limbs, then twisted his neck hard to the side. The fragile vertebrae broke with a loud, wet pop. The attorney made one last small cough, then went still.

The monster lowered its head and sniffed the corpse beneath it, giving the bloody shoulder a few licks with a long, reptilian tongue. A rumble emanated from deep inside the creature's throat; a low, satisfied purr. Elliot stood numbly and watched. He did not even consider fleeing. What would be the point?

At last the creature straightened. Its head turned slowly until four, bilious-yellow eyes settled ominously on Elliot. The thing crawled off the lifeless corpse that had been Dirk and padded closer to him, shifting sinuously across the ground on six thickly-muscled legs. Elliot waited passively for whatever fate might await him. He hoped it would be a quick death.

Rising onto its hind four legs the creature placed a taloned claw against Elliot's chest. The ends of two vicious, pointed nails poked through his clothing, breaking the skin and drawing a small amount of blood that immediately soaked into his jumpsuit. The monster sniffed at Elliot's face as it examined him, its yellow eyes blinking in a nauseatingly random sequence.

"Please," Elliot whispered. "Please, just kill me."

"No," the monster replied, its voice also at a whisper.

Elliot sobbed, tears flowing freely down his face. His chest hitched painfully. "But why?" he begged. "Why are you letting me go again?"

"You know why," the creature said in that same low hiss. "If I kill you, then all are dead. No more come to me. I send you away. You go away, then you come back with more."

"I won't," he insisted. "I won't bring anyone else. Kill me!"

"No," the monster repeated.

It pushed Elliot, causing him to stumble backwards

and trip. With his hands cuffed and linked to his waist, he was unable to break his fall. The back of his head struck the hard ground, leaving him stunned and dizzy. The creature slithered up beside him, lowering its face to hover over his own.

"This was good hunt, better than first hunt. Now, you go away. You go away and come back with more."

G. ALLEN WILBANKS
ABOUT THE AUTHOR

G. Allen Wilbanks is a retired police officer living in Northern California. For twenty-five years he wrote collision and crime reports during the day to pay the bills, and short fiction during his off-time to stay sane. He is a member of the Horror Writers Association (HWA) and has published over 100 short stories in Daily Science Fiction, Deep Magic, and many other magazines and online venues. His stories have also featured in several internationally, best-selling anthologies. He has published two short story collections of his own, and the novel, When Darkness Comes.

For more information you can visit his website at www.gallenwilbanks.com, or check out his weekly blog at www.DeepDarkThoughts.com. G. Allen Wilbanks can also be found on Facebook www.facebook.com/gallenwilbanks/ and Twitter https://twitter.com/gallenwilbanks

The Lady in the Woods
Michael D. Nadeau

Curiosity

Riding in the back of a run-down pick-up truck was not on his itinerary. Sean checked his watch one more time, brushing his black hair out of his hazel eyes. He didn't really need to worry about how long this was going to take, since his dinner plans weren't until tonight with Siobhan, yet he couldn't help it. He slid the small window of the truck cab open, and tilted his head to yell at the driver. "How much further?" he asked the old man behind the wheel, the wind whipping his hair into his face again; he just wanted to get this hike over with at this point.

"Oh, about another fifteen minutes there laddy," the man said, cackling over something he found funny. "Are ye sure ye want to go in there?" he questioned in his thick, Irish accent.

"It's just a forest," Sean retorted, then turned away to watch the countryside go by. He was visiting Ireland to see where his family had come from, and one of the places he wanted to see was Cloosh Forest. It was massive, with some parts of it untouched by man for centuries, and his curiosity had driven him to see it for himself. This was the only place not on the tour guide's suggestions, but it had always had a certain allure for him. Something about the old ways, and the deep magic of the forest, just drew him here.

"Just a forest? Aye, and Tir na nOg is just a place," the old man countered as Sean closed the glass window.

Sean may love the old stories, but he didn't really believe in them; not really. He loved the thought of the woven tale, picturing his family sitting around the hearth and telling little ones stories. They would recount the Children of Lir, the story of Deirdre, and Fionn mac Cumhaill, among others. Not that they ever existed, he thought, but I would've loved to grow up with those tales. He had found an old diary in his mothers' belongings when she passed away last summer, and learned that their family was from Ireland. There were all sorts of story books as well, and he had gone through them for hours. That's when he and his sister had vowed to come back to where their mother was born and see the sights. Part of letting go, Siobhan had called it.

The truck's brakes squealed as it came to a stop at the edge of the ancient wood, its exhaust backfiring in protest. He had been riding in the back of this truck for over an hour down Station Road, and he was finally here. The sun was already burning off the dew as it came up over the tree line, and the morning fog retreated from its burning rays. Sean climbed out, stretching the kinks out of his legs and grabbing his pack. He walked around to the driver's side door and smiled at the old man. "Thank you for the ride, Mr. McBride," he said, giving the man a folded, twenty dollar bill. "Are you sure you don't mind waiting?"

"Bah, I've no need of your money boy. Just promise me you won't go too far in there. Jus' walk a bit, look around, and then come out. I'll be awaiting here for ya." The old man looked at the woods with a mix of awe and fear, wiped his brow, then rolled up the window.

Paths

Sean shouldered his pack and left the truck behind, stepping into the forest. There was no actual "path" out here in the middle of nowhere, but that's the way he wanted it. He had his father's compass, and had watched a YouTube video on the plane ride about how to use it. He was certain that he would be able to find his way back if he got turned around. He took a reading, then put it away as he started walking. His sister had warned him of the old stories, and of things that lurked in the dark parts of the world. She had always believed in that stuff; but not him. He gave up believing in anything when his mother died.

"Stupid doctors," he said to himself as he walked over a moss-covered rock. The doctors had told her that they could save her; that her cancer could be put into remission because they caught it soon enough. She died anyway, leaving Sean and his sister to fend for themselves. They weren't little children, he was almost twenty years old and she was a year older, but it was still hard. He walked on; looking at the massive trees and rocks, just soaking it all in, then his phone went off.

He had set an alarm so that he didn't lose track of time, something he was prone to do, and he chuckled to himself as he hit the button to shut it off. He checked the time and swore, seeing that he had been in here for over two hours, the exact limit he had set; he hadn't planned on walking for that long. Originally he had wanted to find a good place to sit, then he would open his mother's folklore books and read a story to her, like a tribute. No time for that now, he thought, as he turned around to get his bearings. Nothing looked familiar. He took out his compass and set the dial, yet he saw the needle spinning slowly as he stood stock still. Crap.

Sean looked up and thought he saw where he had come from, or some rocks that looked familiar at least, and he started walking that way as he tried to put his useless compass in his bag. His attention was on too many things though, and he snared his foot in a tangled root and fell, his bone snapping like the dry twigs all around him. He cried out in pain and shock, landing awkwardly on the forest floor. His bone was sticking out like a white flag of surrender, and Sean watched his blood mingle with the fallen leaves as his scream echoed through the forest.

The pain was unlike anything he had ever experienced. He finally sat with his back to a tree and looked down at his ankle, cursing the ruined mess that would never get him out of this forest. He screamed for help, knowing in the back of his mind that he was far from anyone that could hear him. Fear drove him to try anyway, that icy grip on his spine that said he was going to die here, alone and afraid. He took a water bottle out of his pack and drank, then poured the rest over his wound, prompting another scream. He had to clean it or infection could set in, that much he knew, but as far as how he was going to get on his feet again, that was beyond him.

After two hours he tried to get up, but his ankle quickly showed him the error of his ways. As he stood it made him scream again, and he slid back down the tree trunk onto the bloody leaves. The old man, Mr. McBride, had to have left by now, so that meant no one was waiting for him except Siobhan. She knew he was going hiking in the Cloosh forest, but not where. They'll find my body at least, he thought as he started to get light-headed.

Then he heard the singing.

The Lady

The sound was light and melodic, drifting through the leaves like a breeze. Sean looked around in a daze, but couldn't see where the singing could be coming from, as it sounded like it was everywhere at once. As it went on the song took on more depth, gaining in pitch and tone as it drew near. His first thought was that he had drifted to sleep, but the pain in his foot every time he moved cancelled that idea immediately. The tune was catchy as well, repeating a chorus that he couldn't quite catch, but that he could hum to. Over and over the lyrics drifted across the forest, finally getting louder. The voice seemed to focus suddenly, drawing into a single focal point as a lady came around one of the trees.

She was beautiful to behold. Long, white hair was flowing about her shoulders as if a strong breeze followed her, yet no leaves blew. She was dressed in a long, white gown, the tattered edges also swirling in this imaginary wind, and her piercing, green eyes seemed to look all around without moving. She wore neither jewelry nor shoes, and as Sean watched her walk across the twigs and leaves he could hear no sound of her passing. Her song ended right when she came up to him, the echoes of it reverberating off of the trees and rocks for another second or two.

"Who are you?" he asked in a tiny voice as she bent down to look at his ankle.

She seemed to flinch at his voice, recoiling just a bit before smiling at him. "My name is old, and probably not known to you or any you know in this age," she said, "Yet it would violate the pact if I am asked in sincerity and did not tell. My name is Cairenn, and I am here to help you...

for a price."

Sean knew that name. He had seen it somewhere recently. Then he had it; his mother's books. "Cairenn Chasdub?" he asked incredulously. "The mother of Niall?" It was impossible that this was the wife of the long-dead Saxon king, which was only an Irish legend.

"That was a long time ago, indeed," she said, staring off into the canopy. "But that is for another day. For now, in this moment, you have a choice."

"What choice?" he asked carefully.

"I can save your life, but it comes with a cost. If I heal you, you have to come with me and serve me forever in Tir na nOg," Cairenn said, the gravity of her words like a palpable thing weighing down the very air.

"Forever?" Sean asked, thinking of his poor sister who would be left all alone in a strange country. "Serve you?" Yet, if he refused, he may never see her anyway, dying here alone in the woods. This can't be real, he thought, I'm dreaming.

"Yes, but don't fret. Time moves differently there, and you won't even notice the flow as it passes you by," she said with a cryptic tone. "You will be one of my Will-o-the Wisps."

Consequences

Sean closed his eyes and nodded, knowing that he could always find a way around this later. He saw her reach out and touch his ankle, a white glow surrounding it and tingling up his leg. The veins in his leg started glowing white, and the light travelled up his legs to his body. Within seconds he was whole once more, and feeling better than he had in a long time; both physically and mentally.

Sean stood and put weight on his ankle, seeing that even his clothes were mended. Cairenn was already walking away, beckoning him with a hand over her head as she started to fade from view. He looked down at his compass and saw that it was no longer spinning, instead pointing north as it should. North, towards Siobhan. He dropped his pack, turned and ran north. He dodged branches and leaped over rocks, a new-found vigor propelling him faster than he should be able to run through the forest.

"You must not!" Cairenn called from far away, her voice like a distant wailing. "The ash will come!"

Sean ignored her and ran on, catching the fading sun through the canopy above. If he could get to the road he would be able to walk home, home to his sister. The stories are real...it's all real, he thought as he plunged on through the forest, making such time that he could start to see the road. He burst out of the trees then, stumbling on the grass and onto the pavement in the fading light of the day. How long was I in there? he asked himself as he rolled over catching his breath.

"Gods boy, where ya been!?" McBride asked, helping him up.

"You're still here?" Sean asked, looking around and

seeing the truck. He waited for me, he thought, I really am going to make it.

"No!" Cairenn's voice echoed through the forest like the wail of an injured animal.

"What in God's green earth was that?" McBride asked as they walked to the truck.

Sean smiled, thinking that he had gotten away, but then he felt something pricking down his spine. It was a tingling feeling, like something leaving him. He felt funny — light-headed again, but more pronounced. "We have to hurry," he said, as he quickened his pace to the truck. He fell into the side of the vehicle, holding the bed of the truck and stiffening in shock. His fingers were turning black, and starting to flake. "No...no, please..." he begged, his body frozen.

"What've you done boy...what did ye promise?" McBride asked, seeing the boy's fingers, and now his arms start to fall to black ash. "You went too far, didn't ye? I told ye...Oh laddy, I'm sorry."

Sean watched in horror as his arms, then his legs flaked away into ash, his consciousness drifting up like it was lost from his body. He could see the pile of ash, and the frightened look upon the old man's face, as he looked down at what used to be himself. He felt it then, a pull. He turned and looked at the forest, the deep woods pulling his soul back in. He had broken a vow to the Old Ones, and now he was paying for it. He heard Cairenn's voice then, as if from far away, carried on the wind.

"Now, Sean, you will forever be part of the old ways; but I do thank you for the books you left behind. I do so love the old stories."

Michael D. Nadeau
About the Author

Born in the usual way, author Michael D. Nadeau found fantasy at the age of eight with Dungeons & Dragons. He loved being different people as well as casting magic. By High school he discovered his love for reading thanks to a teacher. She fed his thirst for books by bringing her own books from home and lending them to him, even buying one towards the end of her class. He has now read hundreds of fantasy books, living in each of their worlds along with the characters. After awhile he started created his own worlds for his games with friends. Cities, gods, ancient and terrible beings and histories...then he would burn them all down.

He is the author of the Lythinall series: The Darkness Returns book 1, The Darkness Within book 2 (June 2020), The Darkness Falls (coming soon), and Tales from Lythinall — an anthology (coming soon). He also has several stories in Kyanite Press's Journal of speculative fiction and Eerie River Publishing anthologies, as well as writing for Gestalt Media's monthly contest regularly.

You can follow Michael here:
My website: https://karsisthebard.wordpress.com/
My Twitter: https://twitter.com/Salen_Valari
My Facebook page: https://www.facebook.com/LythinallSeries/

A Matter Of Recycling
Tim Mendees

Stuart dropped to his knees as the rain poured through the branches. His load had been heavy, and exhaustion racked his body. The storm that ripped through the woods outside of High Bend was gathering in ferocity, and patches of decaying, autumnal leaves spun and whipped against his rain-lashed face. Thunder crashed overhead as he raised his hands to the sky in supplication. Tears streamed down his face as he lamented, "No more! You have had your fill!"

The groaning branches seemed to cackle at his defiance. He knew it wouldn't be as easy as that, and he could only watch as the process started to take hold of his unclean cargo. At that moment all he could think of was an escape, some kind of release from the terrible compact he had unconsciously made with the woods. No solution was forthcoming.

* * *

As a child Stuart Fowler had spent many a happy day amongst the ancient trees and dense foliage. His grandmother had warned him of the things that lurked in the dark places of the woods, but he had paid no heed to her fanciful tales of the furtive things that stalked the undergrowth. It was just another of his granny's various quirks. She was known as something of an odd duck amongst the small village. Forever chattering about curses and unhallowed ground, a fact that did little to endear him to the other children.

Left with his eccentric grandparent at an early age, Stuart was always a shy and introspective youth. He had few friends growing up, since the local children were terrified of his witch grandmother. Instead of conventional friendship Stuart had chosen the woods as his companion, and he felt at ease amongst the creatures that called the trees their home. He was out there every day, rain or shine, living in his own little world.

When one spends as much time as he did amongst the changing seasons, and the life or death struggles of nature, you become accustomed to all manner of unnerving sights and smells. The lifeless bodies of birds and small, furry animals were common, and Stuart quickly built up immunity towards these squeamish moments which bordered on morbid fascination.

One afternoon, when he was ten, Stuart had decided that the time had come for him to venture deeper into the trees. He had always stayed near the house, as the dire warnings of his granny against the darker regions of the woods had scared him into obedience. Yet, for whatever reason, defiance drove him onwards that day. He put all of his fears to one side and strode confidently into the densest part of the wood.

Bracken tore at his legs as he pushed further onwards. The trees here seemed older, more sinister and twisted, than the ones closer to the village. Rural Cornwall was a place of dark myth and superstition, and he told himself this fact over and over to quiet the nagging voice in his head that told him to run. A strange groan stopped him in his tracks. Branches twanged, and the leaves rustled. Stuart stopped dead in his tracks, his eyes wide and ears pricked. He crouched down and parted the patch of overgrown weeds in front of him.

Before him lay a clearing. It wasn't large, but it seemed to be a rough circle of ground where nothing seemed to grow. The branches of the encircling trees seemed to knit together, creating a fence around the patch that reminded Stuart of a police cordon. Though it was only mid-afternoon it was already a dark and gloomy place, as though the canopy above worked to repel all light.

With a tremendous scuffle a large badger burst through the undergrowth and into the clearing. The injured mustela wheezed and groaned as it scraped its limp hind legs behind him. His black and white flanks were streaked crimson, and it had clearly been engaged in a fierce territorial dispute. Stuart watched in grim fascination as it dragged itself into the clearing and collapsed. After a moment of labored breathing it expired.

He stood, still gazing at the broken creature. He had never seen a badger before, except on the TV. Cautiously he picked his way towards the carcass. Suddenly the corpse started to ripple and undulate, and Stuart watched in horror as the badger was consumed from the inside-out within seconds. A swarm of ferocious insects from under the soil had burrowed into the animal, making swift work of the muscle and organs. The skin was next to be devoured, followed by the bones. They blackened and cracked, then melted away like stop-motion footage of decomposition. It was a horrible sight. Horrible, yet fascinating.

After this display Stuart found a new fascination. He would gather roadkill, or other carcasses, and deposit them in the clearing. The strange insects would, without fail, devour his offerings. It felt good, like he was contributing to the nurturing of the woods. Instead of letting the dead rot away in the elements he would recycle them to feed the woods. He had never heard of, or seen, creatures like the ones that dwelt under the soil. They looked more like prawns, or small lobsters, than the usual beetles and centipedes. He scoured books on entomology, but couldn't find even a close match.

He spoke to his teachers about the unusual creatures, but of course they didn't believe him. Nobody ever did, and he knew he would need solid proof. Armed with a dead mouse and a jam jar he set off to get his proof, but unfortunately the creatures had one Hell of a bite. All he walked away with that day was a wound, which soon turned septic and earned him the unflattering nickname of 'Green Finger Fowler.'

Stuart's visit to the clearing became an almost daily thing as he became more and more withdrawn from the rest of the village. He kept the insects fed using mice that his granny's traps had caught, but the supply of fresh cadavers soon ran dry. This is when the dreams began.

The dreams were always the same. Stuart would find himself in the woods feeling safe and appreciated. The branches would part for him, like magic. For the first time since his parents bailed, he felt wanted and loved. The seasons would shift and flicker past in seconds, and soon his feeling of well-being turned into one of crippling hunger. A sonorous, insectoid voice would plead for food. It would promise him everlasting friendship, and every night Stuart would wake in a cold sweat with painful cramps in his guts.

The forest was hungry, that much was certain. But what was Stuart to do? He scoured the village and its surrounding environs for tasty treats, but it was to no avail. The dreams got worse and worse, the pain in his stomach became less bearable with every passing day. He didn't know what to do. Then, one night, it happened anyway.

He had gone to sleep feeling light-headed from hunger, despite having eaten both dinner and supper. That night, however, he didn't dream. The next thing he knew was that he was shivering from the cold. Clad only in his Batman pajamas, he was kneeling in the woods. The only light came from a sickly-looking moon, and he gazed down at his hands.

The pale light shining on the sticky substance on his hands made them look black. Before him, in the clearing, lay a canine cadaver that looked suspiciously like Jim. Jim was his neighbor Mr. Carter's beloved spaniel, and next to the rapidly-devoured animal lay a two-pound hammer. It didn't take a genius to figure out what must have happened. Soon the body was gone, and so was the feeling of hunger. Horrified by what he must have done, Stuart picked himself up and ran home. He stopped at a small pond to clean his hands first, then he slipped back inside, unnoticed, and quickly fell back to sleep.

The following morning it was as though it had all been a dream. If it wasn't for the posters announcing Mr. Carter's missing dog Jim, which were attached to lamp-posts and flapping in the morning breeze, then he could have imagined it didn't happen at all. Sadly, it did. His guilt was offset, however, by a great feeling of warmth. Of inner contentment. Of love. His dreams returned to joyful ones, and his stomach returned to normal.

The respite wouldn't last.

Soon, the forest was hungry again. This time he knew what he needed to do. He started small. A rabbit here, a gerbil there, but it quickly escalated. The neighborhood soon became a fluttering mass of missing posters for be-loved cats and dogs. Stuart tried to space his feeding's out, but the woods were insatiable. They demanded more. Not long after Stuart's fifteenth birthday they got what they wanted.

* * *

The first one was an accident, as it often is. In the preceding year, against all predictions to the contrary, Stuart had found a friend. Darren was new to the area, and as a result was also shy and awkward. His parents' concern for his safety bordered on the neurotic, and he was soon bullied for being a 'mama's boy.' Stuart lived across the street, and the two boys quickly bonded over their love of comic books and WWF wrestling.

They were in the woods one day when tragedy struck. They were wrestling together out of the sight of the village, and Darren had Stuart in a tight headlock that was quickly wearing him down. Then, from out of nowhere, Stuart had an unnatural surge of strength. He lifted his friend aloft and dumped him over his shoulder. Stuart's vision blurred and swam as his friend went up in the air, and as he turned his gut clenched in horror. Darren was rocketing head-first into a pile of stones, like a dart to a board.

Stewart watched as his friend's cranium was split wide open. He gagged and retched as the viscous concoction of blood and brain fluid poured onto the ground, and it was so much worse than what happened with animals. The metallic stench of blood was overpowering. Stuart shook and rocked on his heels hugging his knees. Darren was dead, killed instantly when his skull met the unforgiving stone.

A strange stillness fell over the woods. Not for one second did Stuart contemplate going for help. An inner voice told him what to do, so he grabbed Darren by the ankles and dragged him deeper into the woods. Once at the clearing he rolled his friend into the center, and looked on icily as the insects got to work. It took them just fifteen minutes to completely eradicate Darren's corpse. All that was left was some clothes, and some personal items that hadn't been soiled by bodily fluids. Anything that had been was consumed, even cloth.

Stuart gathered up the remnants and sunk them deep into the mud at the pond. Once his hands were clean he snuck home, quickly changing into clean clothes. It was, by now, right about the time that Darren's parents usually got home. Stuart sauntered across the street and casually asked if Darren could come out to play. His parents instantly panicked when they couldn't find their child, and they went into a frenzy. Stuart showed Darren's father where they usually hung out, and at no point was he implicated in his friend's disappearance. It was as though some kind of force was controlling his actions. Keeping him safe. Guiding him.

Soon a poster of Darren appeared amongst those of Tiddles and Rex, but Stuart never felt guilt over the event. After all, Darren's death was an accident. All he did was recycle the body. The woods were finally satiated, and were quiet for the rest of the summer. Though, as winter set in, the hunger pangs returned with a vengeance.

* * *

Now in his twentieth year, Stuart had the blood of many on his hands. Every time it was the same. He would vow that this one was the last, that the woods would have to find another feeder. He would try to resist the call of the woods, but somehow it would get its way. The first few, all local people, were dispatched during blackouts or attacks of somnambulism. It was the only way to relieve the crippling pain from his abdomen.

The local victims, along with all the vanishing pets, soon raised panic to a fever pitch. Some amongst the village talked of the Beast of Bodmin, while others talked about cults and rituals. A few even blamed the rabbit warren of tin mines that riddled the area, and this theory quickly gained traction when hikers and farm livestock began vanishing. It was as though the ground had just opened up and swallowed them.

In a way, it had.

As time progressed and Stuart got a car, he took his hunt for suitable nourishment for the forest to nearby Betyls Cove. The docks were awash with junkies and prostitutes, both of which were easy to lure back to his home and dispatch. His gran had long since passed, leaving him with the house by the woods.

Unbeknownst to Stuart, a task force had been set up

in Betyls Cove CID to deal with the plague of disappearances. Top-brass was convinced they had a serial killer on their hands, and the wheels of fate were quickly turning against Stuart.

While he was at work one fateful day, DI Baker led an operation to search the woods near High Bend. There had been many such searches, but the small, muddy pond had never been dredged thoroughly. Baker had narrowed the start of the horrors to the vanishing of young Darren, and decided to start at the beginning. They uncovered a veritable treasure trove of evidence. They soon found keys, wallets, mobile phones and handbags that were all linked to the missing people. The items were taken to the station and examined.

Stuart's undoing was a red plastic handbag. A woman, matching the description of a missing prostitute, was caught on a CCTV carrying said handbag as she got into his car. This, and his proximity to the pond and woods, made him a person of utmost interest.

Stuart returned home to a surprise. There was a body in his bath. He had no recollection of how it got there, but this had recently become the norm. The woods had stopped cajoling him to kill, and had just started taking control whenever it was hungry. The village was swarming with police, and he knew that at some point they would ask to take a look inside his house.

The only chance he had was to get rid of the evidence. The weather was fierce, and night had dropped like a hammer. He dressed in dark clothes and hoisted the emaciated body of the poor, unfortunate person over his shoulder. He ran full-pelt through the trees, quickly dropping the body in the clearing. Once the insects had done their grisly work he gathered up anything that the bugs didn't want and headed to the pond.

DI Baker hammered on Stuart's door to no reply. He had gotten a swift warrant for Stuart's arrest, and had instructed the police with him to smash the door in. Stepping inside, Baker was taken aback by the interior. All the furniture and fittings had been crafted from fallen branches and chunks of lumber. The carpentry showed no finesse, and it had just been cobbled together with a few wonky nails. Stuart had gone as far as gluing sticks and leaves to the walls and ceiling, effectively bringing the woods home with him.

* * *

The two young officers guarding the pond stared in disbelief as the sodden, bloody, muddy form of Stuart Fowler, who had emerged through the trees carrying a pair of knee-high boots and a length of hair-extensions.

"Stop right there!" One of them bellowed as the other shone his flashlight into Stuart's bewildered eyes. With inhuman force he launched the boots at the officer holding the light. They hit him square in the chest, and knocked him off balance. As he toppled backward into the pond his colleague gave chase.

Stuart knew these woods better than he knew his own

hands. They were part of him. His home. His friend and parental substitute. They were all he needed, his whole world. He sprinted through the undergrowth, weaving between branches and hopping over roots. The rain continued to pelt down, and thunder rattled his teeth. Lightning flashed and the branches whipped wildly.

He raced onwards towards the clearing, but the policeman kept pace. Despite Stuart's knowledge his pursuer was in much more athletic condition. As the constable neared his quarry Stuart slipped on some mud, falling forwards just as he reached the clearing.

Stuart screamed as the insects burst through his clothing and into his flesh. The policeman skidded to a stop, his hand over his mouth in horror. Blood burst from Stuart's mouth as the parasites consumed his innards. The policeman scrambled back towards the village in a haze of panic and horror, screaming himself hoarse. He collapsed outside the church, banging on the stout, oak doors as he begged for salvation.

The case of the High Bend disappearances was quietly closed, and the public was assured that the nightmare was over. Though they couldn't elaborate as to what had really happened, certain whispers reached the anxious public. The constable who saw Stuart's return to nature never recovered his sanity, and currently resides in a mental hospital where he constantly gibbers about the strange insects in the woods and the hungry earth.

Those of a certain age remembered the words of the strange, old woman who lived in the house next to the woods. They recalled her saying that the woods were cursed, and that dark, furtive things lurked within them. The woods were once again shunned by the local, God-fearing folk, and every care was taken to keep their children out of the trees.

Deep down they knew that all it would take for the destructive cycle to begin anew was for another lost child to make the woods their home.

Rouse Them Not
Tim Mendees

> *"Wassaile the trees, that they may beare*
> *You many a Plum and many a Peare:*
> *For more or lesse fruits they will bring,*
> *As you do give them Wassailing."*
> *—Traditional Wassailing Song*

It was January the seventeenth, and snow covered the ground at the Angove orchard in High Bend. It was a particularly bitter Twelfth Night eve that year, though spirits were riding high. The annual wassailing was in full swing, and the cider was flowing freely. The sympathetic magic of hundreds of revelers flowed around the frigid apple trees, carried on the raised voices and the jangling bells of the local morris men. Before the ceremony was through each tree would be blessed, and would have spiced toast secured in its bows. All except two, that is. Some said they were planted on the graves of two vicious killers. Some said they housed the trapped spirits of witches, others said they were gods. But, whatever the blight, all were convinced that those trees were evil.

The Twins stood over a narrow, dirt track that led to the rear entrance of the graveyard like guards of the dead. Their bloated and warped limbs reached over the path and touched, entwining like fingers on two gigantic hands. They loomed over the path, ready to snatch away unwary mourners. The trees rarely bore fruit, and what fruit they did produce was rancid. On more than one occasion a foolish child had plucked a ripe looking apple and taken a bite, only to suffer from savage stomach cramps.

Daniel and Jonah Green looked upon the ceremony as nothing more, nor less, than a thinly veiled excuse for a drinking session. The two brothers had taken root on a hay-bale and had been steadily getting more and more hammered as the evening progressed. As was usual, on these occasions, their conversation had ridden the gamut from pretty wenches to masculine prowess, then to foolish dares in no time at all.

"How about we wake up the Twins?" Daniel slurred.

"What the Hell for?" Jonah grinned with bemusement. "They are just trees. Or do you believe that god crap?" He gulped strong cider and sniggered.

"No," Daniel said, rather too defensively. "I just think it would be a laugh."

"It would irritate the Hell out of the druids." Jonah mused.

"Exactly." Daniel smiled. "Just look at that daft lot." He pointed to where the revelers were singing a song to an old pear tree. "They seriously think all this malarkey will give them a better harvest next year. Ruddy saps, the lot of them."

"Heh, yeah." Jonah chuckled and downed more fermented apple juice.

"So, are you in?" Daniel asked, a boozy grin plastered across his young face.

Jonah thought for a second. A nagging doubt was trying to take hold of his brain, but it was swiftly drowned in alcohol. "Yeah, why not?"

"Ok, we can finish a couple of more drinks first. You know, to keep out the cold." Both men erupted into raucous laughter.

As the two men imbibed Mr. Edwards, the head druid and village squire, had led the procession away to the far corner of the orchard. They were far enough away not to put a halt to the mischievous plan. Neither man believed the folk tales of evil trees, but just enough doubt lingered to make wassailing the Twins a good test of their mettle.

* * *

Once another flagon of cider was downed the two young brothers started to wend unsteadily along the path to the small graveyard. They were rosy-cheeked and full of bravado on account of all the booze, but even that warm glow was suddenly chilled by the sight of the sinister apple trees.

The moon hung low between the twisted branches, casting ghostly shadows on the path. Daniel halted and put his hand on Jonah's chest. The elder brother stopped, looking at his sibling with bemusement.

"You are not getting chicken, are you?" Jonah smirked.

"No," Daniel grumbled. "Look." He pointed to the low, stone wall behind the trees. There was a bent figure sitting there, arms aloft in supplication.

"It's old Mrs. Fowles." Jonah chuckled. "What the Devil is the crazy old bat doing?"

"I dunno." Daniel shrugged. "Listen," The old woman was crooning a gentle song. "I think she's singing it some weird lullaby."

Both men burst into fits of laughter, which alerted Mrs. Fowles to their presence. She stood and fixed them with the kind of stare that could turn a man to salt at fifteen paces.

"Quiet, you pair of buffoons!" She scowled, her voice like nails on a chalkboard. Mrs. Fowles had long, straggly hair that, along with her aquiline nose and bent posture, gave her the look of a malevolent old crone. She was, in fact, a kindly octogenarian who made the best cream buns in the village. "You will wake them." She gestured at the Twins with a bent finger.

Jonah sniggered in derision. "Oh, come off it. They are just trees." He chuckled.

"You know nothing." Mrs. Fowles hissed. "These trees contain the imprisoned souls of exiled gods. Those idiots have made enough noise to raise the dead as it is, so I implore you to keep your blasted voice down."

"Hah!" Daniel snorted, deliberately loud. "Gods? What utter cobblers!"

"Idiot!" Mrs. Fowles snarled. "I warn ye to rouse them not!" She hitched up her skirt and started to hurry away from the brothers, and the Twins. Her face had turned as white as the snow underfoot, and fear danced in her rheumy eyes. "You will pay the price for rousing Nug and Yeb, mark my words! We will all pay the price!" With her final warning hanging in the air she scurried away, towards the church.

"Silly old fool." Daniel laughed.

"Yeah," Jonah agreed. "But..." His pregnant But left hanging he grabbed his brother's arm. "Maybe we should leave it alone. The old bat might have a seizure if we go on."

"What?" Daniel blurted. "Now who is getting chicken?"

Jonah huffed. "I am no chicken!" He held out his hand. "Gimmie the toast, and I can show you."

Daniel did as requested and watched his brother stalk over to the largest of the Twins. He scrabbled around and finally found a foothold. The nearest hollow that he could deposit the spiced toast into was several feet from the floor, but Jonah was strong and agile so it took no time at all for him to reach it. He stuffed the toast, which was soaked in mulled cider, inside, then gave Daniel the thumbs-up.

"Go on then!" He goaded. "Your turn!"

Daniel strutted over to the adjacent tree and grabbed

an overhanging branch. As he strained to pull himself aloft a voice came to him on the wind.

'Tasty'

"What did you say?" Daniel shouted across to his brother.

"I did not say anything," Jonah replied.

Daniel reached the v-shape in the branches, reaching into his pocket for the spiced toast. Jonah had climbed down and joined his sibling at the foot of the second tree.

"You alright up there? Do you need me to come up and hold your hand?" He shouted up.

'Hungry'

"What was that?" Jonah asked his brother.

"I did not say a word," Daniel replied.

"Yeah, you did." Said Jonah.

"I really did not."

"Well, somebody said 'Hungry'." Jonah looked around. The wassailing party was over at the opposite side of the orchard, and Mrs. Fowles had vanished. It was just the two of them, and the Twins.

Daniel looked down at his brother with a pitying look. "Nice try," He sneered, "but you are not going to scare me that easily." He grabbed a fistful of toast and stuffed it forcefully into the gaping hollow of the tree.

The tree began to shake and writhe. Jonah turned white, while his brother bellowed in agony and surprise. Daniel's free arm pressed against the trunk of his attacker, his dangling legs kicking against the gnarled body of one of the Twins. Jonah rushed forward and grabbed his brother by the boots, tugging hard.

Daniel screamed as he hit the ground. His arm was gone from just below the shoulder, and the crisp, white snow was dyed a pinkish-red. Jonah was trying to pick up his brother when a huge limb crashed down towards them, and upon impact Daniel's ribs were crushed with a sickening crack. Jonah jumped backward out of reach, and could only stand by impotently as his brother's bloody corpse was scooped up, disappearing into the hollow.

Jonah turned to run when the snow in front of his feet burst upwards. Thick, tentacle-like roots shot out of the gaping maw and looped around his left leg. The force of the tendril yanked him off his feet, and he landed with a painful blow to his coccyx that drove the air from his body. The root was dragging him towards the tree that killed his brother.

'Mine!'

The second tree took umbrage at its greedy sibling, and swatted its trunk with a large limb.

'He is mine!'

Jonah started to scramble backward as the root slackened its grip. He was nearly free when the ground erupted again. This time the roots were fatter, and came from the other tree. In moments he was being dragged under the soil towards his doom. The blood surged through the massive, twisted trunks. The shackles that bound them to this hallowed spot were straining, about to break.

'More!' Grunted the larger of the trees. 'Feeling stronger, must have more.'

'Yes. More!' The other replied.

The sound of merriment carried on the wind. They could smell freedom. The only thing that could free the Twins from their earthly prisons was the warm fluids of the Druidic bloodline that had imprisoned them in their current forms. For the Twins, as Mrs. Fowles had warned, hadn't always been trees. They had, indeed, once been gods.

* * *

By midnight the party had broken up, and the majority of High Bend was safely tucked into their beds. Their bellies were full, and their spirits high. The wind had risen, and the snow had once more began to flutter to the frozen ground. The only people left in the orchard were a handful of villagers that represented the founding families. They were huddled around the fire, imbibing deeply of the strong cider.

Squire Edwards had been accosted towards the end of the festivities by an excitable Mrs. Fowles, who had warned him of the antics of the Green brothers. He, like all of the founders, had Druidic blood. It was their ancestors who, as legend had it, imprisoned the diabolical gods within the ancient apple trees. Time had, however, twisted the truth into nothing more than a campfire tale designed to scare unruly children. Nobody believed in the Twins anymore, except for Mrs. Fowles.

"I will kill that pair of ruddy idiots!" Fergal Green

snarled. As the father of the two drunks, he was understandably annoyed that they had whipped poor Mrs. Fowles into such a lather. "They should know better than to upset old ladies." His mustache twitched with agitation as he poked the fire with a long stick of apple-wood.

The founders gathered every year after the wassailing to distribute rotten fruit from the last harvest around the roots of the Twins, as a kind of sympathetic magic. It was a tradition, like the wassailing itself, that they perpetuated despite not believing in it one iota. It was supposed to keep the Twins from getting restless by keeping them fed and appeased. They would finish the cider, dump the fruit and mutter the words, then they would go home and sleep off a beastly hangover.

The squire was pensive. As head Druid he had more faith than most. It wasn't so much that he believed in the old ways, rather it was that he wanted to believe in them.

"Come along, then," He addressed the group. "Let us get this over with. It is blasted perishing out here." He hoisted one of the sacks of rotting fruit over his shoulder. Each of the other men followed suit, except Mr. Green.

"Come on, Fergal." One of the others, Mr. Angove, nodded. "The quicker we get this done, the quicker we get indoors. I am freezing my spuds off out 'ere."

Fergal crossed his arms over his chest in defiance. He puckered his mouth, looking like a bulldog sucking a wasp. Squire Edwards rolled his eyes; they had to go through this nonsense every year.

"I am too pissed off to go along with this rubbish."

Green spat. "I am going to go and knock some ruddy sense into those two louts." He walked over to his diminutive wife, who was shivering next to the fire, and grabbed her by the hand. "Come along, Lilly."

Lilly Green tottered in the snow as she was frog-marched across the orchard towards the village. Edwards sighed in resignation, dragging the abandoned sack behind him as he led the procession towards the cemetery.

* * *

The snow danced in the pale light from the cloud-occluded moon. It had fallen sufficiently to eclipse any traces of blood around the trees, not that there was much left to hide. Their hungry roots had sucked up every last drop. The trees looked, to the casual, drunken observers, as though not a branch or root had been disturbed.

"Let us start with this one." Edwards pointed to the tree on the left-hand side of the path. Sinister, in both senses of the word, it loomed above them as they emptied the first two sacks around the roots.

The tree shuddered as the wind roared. The gust was savage, almost unnatural, and whipped, powdery snow into the faces of the druids. The men were startled by a colossal crack, and they stumbled away out of fear of a falling branch. In a second the wind dropped, and as they rubbed vision back into their temporarily-blinded eyes Mr. Angove let out a yell of alarm.

"What is it?" Edwards asked, somewhat nervously.

"Look!" Angove pointed, his voice tremulous and cracking. "The other Twin! It is gone!"

"What!?" One of the others, Mr. Gillman, barked derisively as he spat snow from his puffy lips. "'ow can it be gone?"

"I do not know you, big oaf!" Angove retorted. "Look, it is just bloody vanished!"

He was right. The four men gazed in bewilderment at the gaping maw in the ground where the tree had, moments before, stood. The hole steamed and melted the snow in an ever-widening radius. As one the men gagged, for the wind blew a disgusting gust of foul, fetid air into their faces.

Cautiously they approached the maw, with Edwards in the lead. He held one of the oil-lamps the men carried over the hole, and gazed down into a vast abyss. The void seemed to stretch on forever. It appeared to have no end, as though it burrowed into the heart of the planet.

The men muttered anxiously in hushed tones. Each one had sobered up in a second, and panic-fuelled adrenaline kicked the alcohol into submission. Angove voiced the notion that they should get the Hell out of there. Not even the ever contrary Mr. Gillan argued, so they turned as one to retreat.

The ground shook as it tore asunder. The other Twin rose on its roots like a demonic spider. Possessed of unexpected agility, alarming in something so large, it sprung into the air. Edwards shrieked in terror as the vast trunk slammed into the forest floor, instantly flattening the other men into a bloody pulp.

'More!' The tree boomed. 'Almost free!'

Edwards gibbered insanely and fell to his knees. The mind-blasting horror he had just witnessed had killed his fight or flight instinct. The tree righted itself, and its roots writhed in the gore hungrily. It trembled as the power from the blood coursed through it, loosening more of its ancient shackles. A moment later the shrieking form of Squire Edwards was dragged to his bloody demise by a hungry root.

* * *

Oblivious to what had transpired, the wives and children of the four men sat around the fire. They talked amongst themselves, blissfully unaware that their impending doom was currently scuttling across the orchard towards them. They didn't even have time to panic as the second Twin slammed upon them in a feeding frenzy. Ripping and tearing, it reduced the villagers to puddles of meat and blood in seconds.

The first Twin joined its brother.

'Not free.' It scowled, 'There must be more.'

The second Twin waved a root in the air as though it was searching for a scent.

'There.' It intoned after a moment. 'The blacksmith's heir.'

The Twins were regaining their godlike powers by the second, and their branches rippled with a powerful fluidity. They cloaked themselves in shadow and rode the wind towards the village.

Poor Lilly Green had been forced to listen to her husband rant and rave about what a good beating he was going to give his two wayward sons, and what made it worse was that she knew he was as good as his threats. Fergal was filled with a violent temper that could spill out over the slightest infraction.

As they passed through the gate to the forge, Fergal was so engrossed in cursing and kicking at the snow that he didn't see what made his wife freeze.

"Lilly!" He bellowed. "This is no time for buggering about!" He turned to glare at his wife, but the look on her face knocked the wind out of his blustering sails. She was slack-jawed and wide-eyed, as though she had seen the Devil himself. She silently raised a trembling finger, pointing towards the entrance to the forge.

Either side of the large double doors stood the Twins. Fergal cursed and grabbed a nearby ax.

"Very funny!" He screamed into the night. "I know it is you two idiots! I don not know where you got the wood from, but I am gonna chop your fake Twins down into fuel for the forge!"

As he stepped towards the trees Lilly grabbed his arm.

"Don't!" She pleaded. "It is them! It is the Twins!"

"Do not be so bloody stupid." Fergal raged. "It is a prank! But mark my words," He raised the ax above his head, "those foolish sons of mine are going to regret trying to make a monkey out of me."

As the ax swung through the air one of the trees swiped it out of his hands with a supple branch. Fergal cried in terror as a root shot out of the ground, binding him tightly around the arms. Lilly screamed as it reached a branch down, securing her husband's head and twisting it off like the lid of a sauce bottle. The tree lifted the headless cadaver and poured steaming, hot blood down its trunk. Lilly fainted and collapsed to the ground.

'Is it done?' Its brother asked.

The tree stretched and strained against its invisible bonds.

'No!' It bellowed angrily. 'There is one more, a woman.'

The tree jabbed a thin root into the milky neck of Mrs. Green.

'Is it her? Is it done?' The other asked.

The first tree snarled in fury. This wasn't the blood they needed. It scooped up the prostrate woman and hurled her through the double doors. The force of the throw sent her spinning across the yard and into the smoldering embers of the forge. It was she who was to be fuel, not the Twins.

They fumed and lashed their roots around in the air, desperately searching for that last source of Druidic blood; the final piece of the key that could free them from their prisons. Soon they would be free once again, free to rule and to destroy. They had endured centuries of static life, dreaming of the terrors they would unleash when they were finally freed. Now, freedom was so close they could taste it in every metallic spot of spilled blood.

Ding! Ding!

The sound of a bell snapped the Twins out of their fury, turning their attention towards the darkened street beyond. An elderly lady on a bicycle waved and called out, "Coo'ee!"

'Her!' One of the trees yelled.

The little old lady, Mrs. Fowles, peddled off as quickly as her legs could manage. She steered the bike down the hill, back towards the orchard. The Twins shimmered and became shadow once more, riding the wind in hot pursuit of the fleeing woman.

* * *

Mrs. Fowles parked her bicycle against the stone wall of the graveyard and leaned against the gate. She had positioned herself directly between the spots that the trees had, until earlier, been rooted upon. She pulled her heavy coat around her as the wind grew into a fierce gale. A thin smile crossed her cracked lips as the Twins materialized and settled back into their spots.

'Give us your blood!' One of the Twins demanded.

'Free us!' pleaded the other.

Mrs. Fowles pulled back her sleeves, revealing her wrists, and held them out in a cruciform for the Twins to feed upon. As a single root from each tree shot towards her throbbing arteries she started once again to sing her soft lullaby.

'You are wise not to struggle' Said one of the Twins as root violated flesh.

Mrs. Fowles gasped as the blood began to be drawn from her frail body. Her lullaby rose in pitch and urgency. It wasn't a mystery that poor Daniel and Jonah didn't understand what she was singing, it was in a long-dead tongue. The trees cackled and roared in triumph as the blood of the old Druid flowed. They laughed and laughed and then...Stopped.

It was now Mrs. Fowles' turn to laugh.

'What trickery is this?' Demanded one of the Twins. The blood was turning to ice in their roots. A heady, toxic mist started to dull their senses. Their movements became sluggish; wooden once more.

"I have got you now." Mrs. Fowles gloated. She hadn't been idle since she left the orchard. She had rushed home and consulted the books that had been passed down for generations. "In taking my life you have doomed yourselves to an eternity of imprisonment." Using herbs, and an elixir contained within an old family heirloom, she had brewed up a potent concoction.

"I drank the elixir of the Elders. Now you have tasted it too." Her breathing was getting shallow. She was doomed the minute she drank it, so all she had to do was stay alive long enough to take the Twins down with her. "Can you feel it? Petrifying your roots, drying your sap?"

'Nooooo!!' The Twins bellowed in unison. They spasmed once, twice, then went as still as stone.

Mrs. Fowles was nothing more than a papery husk by the time the Twins had been imprisoned once more; for good this time, as there was no more blood to set them free. The cold wind blew and scattered the savior of humanity's remains across the frozen orchard.

* * *

The mysterious disappearance of half of the village was never explained. Eventually the distant relatives of the missing founders moved into the properties, and the village returned to normality.

That year was the last time that the ancient tradition of wassailing was performed in High Bend. The old traditions died away, and were forgotten. The Twins were eventually cut down and incinerated, due to being infected with an unknown blight.

Despite the horrors of that fateful Twelfth Night, the ceremony reaped dividends. That year's harvest was lush and plentiful, and even the Twins bore fruit that year. There was around twenty-three apples, one for each of the missing. Nobody ate them, for they were horribly bloated and, when split, smelled like a rancid corpse.

TIM MENDEES
ABOUT THE AUTHOR

Tim Mendees is a horror writer born in Macclesfield in the North-West of England. He has recently been published in Twenty Twenty (Black Hare Press,) Death and Butterflies (suicide House Publishing,) Solitude (DBND Publishing,) and has had several short stories accepted for publication in forthcoming anthologies and magazines. His debut novella 'Miracle Growth' is coming soon from Black Hare Press. Tim is an active and recognisable figure in the UK Goth scene in his role as DJ, promoter and podcaster. He currently lives in Brighton & Hove with his pet crab, Gerald, and an army of stuffed cephalopods.

https://www.facebook.com/goatinthemachine
https://www.amazon.com/Tim-Mendees/e/B082VMY727/

Dig
Elizabeth Nettleton

It kept telling him to dig.

The voice whispered through the trees, soft and urgent, following him as he made his way into the woods. He reached a small clearing and the voice lay with him upon the soft ground, an unwelcome companion while he waited for the kill he so desperately needed.

Dig.

"Be quiet," he hissed, his lips grazing the dirt beneath him.

"What?" a small voice asked.

Dom looked over his shoulder. His son Peter gazed back at him, his brow furrowed over his large blue eyes.

"Nothing," Dom said. "I didn't say anything."

A doe made slow, careful steps in front of them, her brown fur dappled in the disappearing sunlight. Her nose twitched.

"Can she smell us, Dad?"

Dom placed a finger to his mouth and moved his other hand to his gun. Peter began to whimper.

"I don't want her to die, Dad."

"It's either her or us, Peter. We need to eat."

Peter buried his face in the dirt, and soon two lines of mud traced their way down his cheeks. The doe glanced in their direction and then ran, her long limbs tossing her into the brush surrounding them. Dom pounded his fist onto the ground.

"Don't you understand, Pete? I don't like hunting either, but we need the food. Sometimes we have to make sacrifices for the people we love."

"Aren't there other sacrifices we could make?"

Dig.

Dom twitched. "Stop saying that!" he snapped.

"Saying what?"

He stared at his son's tear-streaked face. "Not you. I was…I thought I heard something."

Peter pulled himself to his feet and peered into the trees. "I don't see anything. Does anything around here hunt people?"

An owl screeched behind them, and Dom jumped. His gun fell to its side and he picked it up with clumsy fingers. "I guess there might be some wild cats around. But otherwise no, not out here. I've been hunting in these woods since I was a kid, and it's only the other hunters you need to watch out for."

"Are there any other hunters out here tonight?"

Dig.

"No," Dom said firmly. He stood and wiped his hands against his pants. "We should move. That doe ain't coming back, and we need to bring something home for your mom."

There was a flash of brown and white ahead, and he guided Peter through the tangled branches to meet it. Thin twigs snapped under their heavy boots, and Dom wondered, not for the first time, whether he should have gone out alone.

"Did you go hunting with your dad?" Pete whispered as he stepped over a large rock.

"Yeah, right up until I was about your age."

Dig.

Dom swatted the air in front of him. "Stop it!"

"Stop what?"

Something moved above them, and Dom found himself staring into the flaming, red eyes of a vireo bird. It opened its wings and sang, then paused and sang again, repeating itself in case they wished to sing along.

Dig. Dig. Dig. Dig. Dig.

Peter grinned and jumped from one foot to the other. "Dig! Dig! Dig! Dig! Dig!"

"You hear it too?" Dom asked, staring at the bird.

"Hear what? Ooh, ooh, ooh!" Peter said. He pursed his lips and tried to whistle the bird's song. "Ooh, ooh, ooh!"

"I really wish you would stop doing that," Dom said through gritted teeth. Sweat pricked the back of his neck.

Peter's smile fell, and he stuffed his hands into his

pockets. "Sorry, Dad. I just really wanted to dig."

"What?" Dom demanded.

"I just really wanted to sing, like the bird. Are you okay, Dad?"

"I'm fine, Peter!" Dom snarled. He hurled his gun over his shoulder and marched deeper into the woods. Long, wooden fingers scratched his face, and Peter panted as he tried to catch up.

"Why did you stop hunting with Grandpa?"

Why did we stop hunting together? He paused, struggling to remember. The memories pulled away and returned in fragments, revealing themselves to him piece by piece.

"He left us," Dom said slowly. "We went hunting one day and didn't get anything. It was a bad hunt."

"Like today?"

Dig.

Dom's neck cracked as he turned to look at Peter. "Yeah, a bit like today, bud. And we went home, and Grandma got…I think Grandma got mad at Grandpa…"

No, that wasn't right. His mother was mad at him, not his dad. His fingernails were filthy, he remembered, caked with dirt and torn by stones. She scrubbed his fingertips until he wept, and scolded him for walking through the woods all alone. His eyes had flashed at her, indignant. She was a fool. He was a child of those woods; nothing could harm him out there.

Dig.

"We dug a trap!" Dom cried out. "That's what happened. We dug a trap and then Dad sent me home while he waited for some dumb animal to walk into it."

"Animals aren't dumb, Dad," Peter said reproachfully. Dom waved his hand at his son and grinned.

"We're going to dig a trap, son. Dig, dig, dig, dig, dig."

"But we don't have any tools!"

Dom leaned forward until their foreheads touched. "We'll do it the old-fashioned way: with our hands."

"I don't know, Dad," Peter said. He turned his face away from Dom. "I don't feel so good. Can't we just go home?"

"Not until we catch something, Pete. Now, get digging."

Dom threw himself to the ground and grabbed frantically at the earth. Roots and stones tore at his hands, and he fed the earth with droplets of blood. Pete watched his father warily, then knelt beside him.

Dig. Dig. Dig.

"I'm digging!" Dom said, sweat falling down his face. A pair of red eyes flew overhead, and he waved at them. "Hello!" he shouted cheerfully. "I'm digging!"

"We're both digging!" Pete said.

"That's right, son. We're both digging."

"Then we can go home?"

"Then we can go home!"

"Good, 'cause I don't feel so good. I don't feel… right."

Dom's hand brushed against something and he

yanked on it, releasing it from its earthen home.

"What's that, Dad?"

Dom admired the moon's reflection on its smooth, white surface. "It's just some deer's finger bone. Oh, what am I saying? Deer don't have fingers!" He fell upon the ground, laughing. Dirt crawled into his mouth, threatening to choke him, yet still he laughed. He pushed at the earth until he found an arm, then a ribcage and a skull.

"Hello, Daddy!" he said. He lay next to his father in the shallow hole and smiled. "This is where we stopped digging, son," he explained.

Pete stood above him, his expression hard. "This is where we stop digging, Dad."

"Oh no, we need to keep going. It's telling us to dig. Listen." He held a filthy finger to his lips and stared into the night sky. Silence answered him. "Huh, that's funny. I can't hear anything anymore."

"We're so hungry, Dad."

Peter's eyes flashed red, and Dom felt something cold inch down his spine. "I know Pete, that's why we dug this trap. Remember?"

There was a deep growl from within the woods.

"Pete?"

"I am a child of these woods, and we are hungry."

Dom's eyes widened. It had stopped telling him to dig.

ELIZABETH NETTLETON
ABOUT THE AUTHOR

Elizabeth Nettleton studied Law at the Queensland University of Technology, Australia, and now lives in Oxfordshire, England with her family. She enjoys writing dark fiction and horror, and her work has most recently been included in The Sirens Call eZine and the "Forgotten Ones" drabble anthology by Eerie River Publishing.

Website: https://elizabeth-nettleton.webnode.com/

Twitter: @ElizabethNett18

Pumpkinface
T.S. Hurt

"I heard his old man used to give it to him up the poop chute." Lucky proclaimed.

"That would explain a lot." Seth Tucker sucked air through clinched teeth and rubbed his own bum. He had gotten up from the log he was using for a seat to animate his joke for the rest of the buddies. The small patch cleared out in the woods for their camp was filled with callow laughter, and he almost missed the log when he fell back down onto it. This just made himself, Lucky Thomas, Brewster Donaldson, and Harry Pfiltzer laugh even harder.

None of them heard the doves in one of the trees close by stir, and over their raucous laughter they didn't notice as the birds flew off. Neither would they have noticed the sudden, eerie atmospheric change when something, or someone, approached the outer edge of their camp's circumference. It stayed just far enough away to remain hidden inside the disguise of the darkness, which was held at bay by the light from their campfire. Whatever had just rode in through the woods on the velvety curtain of night, unannounced and uninvited, brought with it a sudden rush of coolness in the air. One by one the chill made each of their voices soften, until they were all able to hear Lucky again who had been waving at them to quiet down.

"That's funny and all but, that's how the rumor goes anyway." Lucky went on. "I mean, Seth, you're right. It would explain how someone would get so goddamned pissed off enough to do what he's done."

"Must have been that, yeah." Harry Donaldson said with a mouthful of corn chips. "Found his old man with his own prick between his teeth. I can't say I blame the kid any."

All of them winced with a look of disgust at what Harry had just told them. It was the same look that they had all had when Lucky had said what he had a few minutes ago. "Didn't find Pumpkinface though." Lucky added.

"Shit." Seth interjected. "He's probably halfway to Hell already by now. What's it been, over twenty years since his last victim? I'm sure he's checked in at the old folk's home for washed up psychopaths by now."

They all started to laugh again, but Lucky cut them off before they could this time. "No, guys. It sounds crazy, but it might be true." He said. "That might be why no one ever found him." Lucky noticed the doubtful look he was getting from them all. "Maybe Pumpkinface did just get too old and washed up. Got over everything and moved on past it all." He went on. "Maybe he just got sick of living off the grid, and checked himself in to some looney bin somewhere. No I.D., no past, no food or protection."

Lucky looked at them all, their expressions seeming to change now, and he could tell he was gaining ground and making sense to them with what he kept telling them. "How long, exactly, do you think someone like that could actually make it on their own without help?"

"A psychopath?" Brewster, who had been picking at the dirt between his feet with his folding knife, spoke up. "A molested, Hell-bent motherfucker set on exacting revenge on just about anyone he chose who made the mistake of crossing paths with him?" Brewster stabbed at the dirt with the sharp end of the knife now to drive home the point of what he wanted to say to his friends. "I doubt he's anywhere sipping spring water to wash down his rainbow-colored mood pills while listening to Kid Rock on a portable CD player during recess, harkening back on all of the good ol' killing days."

"Well, genius," Seth interrupted, "where could he be then? There hasn't been a Pumpkinface killing in awhile now."

"How the Hell should I know?" Brewster was wiping the dirt from his knife on his blue jeans. "I'm just saying that it's ridiculous to think that Pumpkinface just quit it all. I know it's been a while since he's killed anyone around here. After all, he had his own signature style of killing and that set him apart from everyone else and, besides, everyone knew his identity. It wasn't like he was just some stranger who rode into town one night and set the whole damn place on fire, and it sure as Hell isn't like he just vanished without a trace either. If he turned up anywhere after the killings just stopped, I'm sure someone would have put two and two together and figured out that the guy that just showed up on their doorstep the other day might just be involved." Brewster closed his knife and shoved it into his pocket, as if to proclaim a victorious debate between himself and his friends.

"If you all want to know where Pumpkinface is just ask me." Harry looked at each one of his friends with an unmistakably severe look. "I know where he went." He was satisfied by the wide-eyed stares he was receiving from each of his friends, along with their clearly obvious attention. A long and antagonizing pause occurred before he went on again. "He sleeps with Brewster's mom every night."

"Fuck you!" Brewster yelled at Harry as the others broke out in laughter. Brewster could feel himself about to laugh too, and even let a smile show on his face before standing up and declaring that he had to go and take a piss.

Brewster stood up on complaining legs, leaving his circle of friends with their shadows dancing on the ground in front of them. The coldness had snuck up on him while at the campfire and, now that he was away from it, he could feel the lie that the night told him. There was no warmth under its blanket, just darkness and cold. Brewster zipped his cargo jacket closed and shoved his hands in the front pockets of his jeans as he kept walking. His legs were cooperating now that he had begun using them again. It would be a cold winter, he surmised. It was only October now, but he could feel the relentlessness of the chill in the air. It was a cold that was going to hang around for a little while, and he almost thought against unzipping his pants, knowing that the cold would get in where he would have wanted it to get in the least.

At least his hands had warmed up a little before he reached in to grab himself with one of them. A gust of frigid air blew across the back of his neck, and he used his free hand to lift the collar of his jacket up. When he did he felt his balls shrivel as the cold found its way in. Goddamn, he muttered to himself, and shook from both the cold sensation of the air and the satisfaction of finally urinating. He could still hear his friends, especially Harry who had put that awful picture of Pumpkinface and his mother curled up together in the same bed in his head, back at the campfire laughing. Brewster started to laugh to himself. What Harry had said was funny, he thought. He made a quiet snorting sound, but stopped short of an all-out chuckle when a twig snapped behind him.

Brewster's head whipped around quickly to search over his shoulder for the source that might have made the noise, but he could not find it. He finished his piss, and had left himself sticking through the zippered mouth of his jeans, when another rush of coolness hit that area. Only this time the night air had fingers, and it touched his pecker and then tugged at it with a sharp pull. There was hardly any time for Brewster to react, other than the sudden drop of his lower lip as his mouth opened wide in shock. His eyes fell on the glint of something shiny and metallic as it sliced downward, toward his belly but not quite stopping there. It was happening all too quickly for Brewster to comprehend exactly what was going on. He felt the cold fingers close tighter around his penis, then he was yanked up on his toes until he could feel the warm, nasty breath coming from the man's mouth.

Then the quick, decisive stroke fell upon Brewster, and how was he to know what to expect? How, other than to submit under the grim rush of it all, could his mind completely register a defensive response such a fighting, or even a scream? Brewster was paralyzed by fear. He was right where the person who, figuratively, had him by the balls wanted him, and he thought the man was not going to let go until Brewster felt the cold grip around his pecker loosen. That may have been the moment that Brewster could have fled, and maybe even gotten away, but he didn't. The moment passed as quickly as it had come.

A flood of something warm ran down where, only seconds ago, it had been cold. At first Brewster thought he might have pissed himself, but he had the wherewithal to realize that there wasn't anything left in the reserves. He felt around down there nonetheless, and when his hands came up in front of his face he saw that they were slick with something wet and sticky.

Blood.

Brewster's legs began to give out when the white-hot weight of what had just occurred ran over him, trampling his mind like a five-thousand-pound rhinoceros. Then the pain struck, right where his hands had just come back from.

Not that Brewster would be able to know what it felt like now, but his final thought, absurd as it seemed, was that he'd never get to put what had just made a dull thump on the ground inside his Junior year crush, Mandy Simpson. His only attempt, however insubstantial, at defiance toward the person who had just severed any possibility of using the now irrelevant body part was to stare into where he thought their eyes were. He felt them glaring back into his own, watching him suffer. A heartbeat later another cold, dark curtain fell over Brewster, and he was no more.

The rest of Brewster's friends were still beside the warm fire, inside the safe circle of camp. Harry was the first of them to wonder why Brewster had not come back yet. He might have even felt a tad bit sorry for what he had said about Brewster's mother fucking around with Pumpkinface, but he would not let guilt have its way with him. He had only been joking around with Brewster, and Harry did not like to think he had much of a conscience anyway. He and Brewster were buddies, had been since the first grade. Brewster had bailed him out of a few playground scuffles when Harry's jokes had gotten his ass in more trouble than he could have handled alone, and even Harry's indifference to his conscience would not keep him from glancing over his shoulder to look for his buddy. That was when he thought he had heard Brewster returning to camp.

Lucky and Seth weren't paying attention, and had been going on for awhile about the last football game their team had won against Polk County. Seth had shut down the final running play and clobbered the running back before he could get across the scrimmage line, but Lucky had ignored Seth's boasting and argued that, if it hadn't been for his own stellar pass completion percentage that game, the Lions would not have scored as much as they had to cement the crucial victory. Seth bit back by reminding Lucky of their freshman year when Lucky had not been so lucky, and had gotten sacked on the final play when he couldn't find an open receiver. That had ultimately lost them the regional title for the JV team that season, and Seth would not let him forget it.

"Choked." Seth mocked.

All their boasting and chiding each other stopped when they heard Harry scream, then they saw Brewster's head roll into camp from the shadows. It stopped just outside the campfire, resting against the outer, glowing logs. Seth looked down at the orb-like intruder, having momentarily failed to see what had made Harry yell out. Lucky was staring at it too, both leaning over to figure out what was happening. Then they saw it. Seth numbly thought that Brewster's head looked like everything in it had been scooped out with something. It had come to rest on its side, on Brewster's left ear, but since it was hollow the bright, yellow light from the fire outside mixed with the redness inside of Brewster's severed head. Through the holes where Brewster's eyes and nose should have been the mixed colors glowed orange, like it was emanating an evil aura. Seth was terrified, trying desperately to make himself turn away, but he could not.

He sat there motionless, unable to move until he felt someone's hand grabbing the hood on his jacket and yanking him up onto his feet. His legs must have fallen asleep, because he still had trouble moving even though he was standing with help now. Lucky's brash grip on Seth's hood finally got him moving. Lucky yelled out something, but some of Seth's senses were still scrambled and he couldn't make out what it was or who he was saying it to. He was able to look away from Brewster's head lying next to the campfire, which resembled a carved, amazingly detailed pumpkin, just in time to see Harry skirting the shadows as he wrestled with someone at the edge of the camp. During that brief moment of interruption Lucky had succeeded in causing some of Seth's mental wires to reconnect, and when he felt Lucky's other hand pull at the front of his jacket he knew he needed to go along with him.

Both of them took off running, and soon Harry, who had broken free from whoever he had been fighting against (now you know who played wide receiver for the Harris High Lions) caught up to them. Harry soon overtook both of his friends with a flurry of feet, and barely audible expletives. None of the boys stopped running until they had gotten back to Lucky's Cherokee, which was still parked at the trailhead. Lucky fumbled for his keys, hoping they were still in the front pocket of his pants. Seth and Harry were bent over with their hands on their knees, sucking in as much cold, crisp life as they could.

Thankfully Lucky found the keys quickly. "Get the fuck in!" He shouted at them as he opened his door, quickly unlocking the others.

Seth went around to the passenger side and threw open the door, but was halted when Harry hesitated to climb in. "What about Brewster?" Harry asked them, his eyes lingering along the dark, wooded trail they had just come from.

Seth realized that Harry was also mentally numb, and that some of his brain circuits must have gotten fried during their impossible ordeal. "Dude, he's not coming." Seth tried to delicately spell out the fact that something terrible had happened to their friend back at camp, but was not having much luck. Harry did not move, rather he looked at Seth for approval. It was almost like he wanted permission to let go of the door handle and run back into the woods after Brewster.

"Harry, get the fuck in, now!" Lucky screamed over his shoulder from his seat behind the steering wheel of the Cherokee. "And shut and lock the door!"

Lucky's terror must have woken something inside of Harry, because he urgently threw open his door and jumped into the back seat, slamming it shut with a bang.

"Lock it and hold on." Lucky told everyone, check-ing the rearview mirror as he pressed the clutch and threw the Jeep into first gear. He only caught a glimpse of the dark figure standing on the path of the trail head. It was grasping something pointy and shiny in one hand, and something round and smoking in the other. Then the Cherokee was kicking up a burst of dirt dust behind it, clouding Lucky's view. Lucky did not stop driving until they had made it off the mountain and back into town. He pulled into the Harris County Police Department parking lot, not caring that his headlights were still on high from the ride off the mountain. He had to slam hard on his brakes in order not to run up onto the sidewalk, and the Jeep jerked to a stop against the curb as his off-road tires squealed on the asphalt.

Sheriff Conley met the boys at the door. They were all clearly upset about something, trying to tell him several things all at once. He could hardly make out anything any of them were saying, but he recognized the boys from the high school and the football games he worked on Friday nights. They were all decent kids, who came from good families, but they were still teens. Who knows what they could have gotten themselves into?

He tried to calm them down by patting their shoulders, urging them one by one to slow down, but he was having no effect. Finally his deputy had come out to help, and he and Sheriff Conley nudged the boys in through the front door. Before the stiff hinge on it would allow it to shut the deputy shot back through the door, jogging over to the Jeep and shutting off the ignition. He grabbed the keys and hit the light switch so the vehicle wouldn't die, and he made sure the doors were shut.

It was that time of night when the lights of the cozy houses and apartments start getting shut off, but the inside lights of some buildings linger on. Maybe that was why there was still a glow bleeding down on the front stoop of the Harris County Police Department, but all too often there is more than one reason for things. This time there was another reason for the eerily colored glow, one which did not even match the color of the lights coming from inside the building. This light was angry and evil. That was it's color, and it had a face just as angry and evil as that, maybe more so. Behind that face there was nothing. If emptiness can really be a thing, if it was ever meant to be anything or be allowed to have a name, it would surely be called Pumpkinface.

T.S. Hurt
About the Author

T.S. Hurt has been telling lies since childhood. His favorite genre to read is horror/suspense, and this might either be the cause of why his path has led him into such dark places he explores in his writing or quite possibly, it is because he has never been able to escape the tethers of his childhood and truly enjoys the thrill of misleading his readers, urging them to come along on the journey with him.

Follow along with his twitter journey here:
https://twitter.com/TS17293197

Neumack Woods
N.M. Brown

The kids in my town play like other kids, we look like other kids and we sound like other kids. However, the children of our town are NOT like other kids. Other kids…other towns...don't have Neumack Woods.

It's heavily rumored that Neumack Woods is haunted ground. Legend states that if a child under the age of fourteen travels into the woods after 8pm, they'll very distinctly hear a baby crying. I don't know why it's 8pm, maybe because the sun's been long gone by then? I also don't know why the age has to be under fourteen, but I can take a guess. I'm assuming that it's because kids under that age still have most of their childlike innocence. They say that children are more sensitive to the supernatural than adults, so that's gotta have something to do with it.

My friend Ricky Doyle lives down the block and over aways from Neumack, and I'm staying at his house tonight. We've been talking about going out there for months, but just now had gotten the courage to set our plan into motion. We're going to sneak out at 8:15 and go check it out. Ricky and I are both eleven years old, since his birthday last week, so that checks out too. We shouldn't have any problem hearing the baby. It was all figured out, a perfect plan. We'd eat dinner, pretend to go to bed, sneak out, hear the baby and be back in bed before anyone even knew we were gone.

This was our chance to bring some credit to the story. No one we had known had ACTUALLY gone to the woods. It was always a friend of a friend, or a cousin's girlfriend's neighbor who supposedly went and experienced it. Not much went on in our town, and there wasn't much to do. I've always been mischievous, constantly seeking out adventures, and Ricky needs a friend so it works out for the both of us. His interest in all things creepy and spooky isn't as enthusiastic as mine is, and I think he mainly goes along with my plans because he's just happy to have someone to hang out with.

School dragged on forever, and finally it was time to meet Ricky for the buses. My mom wrote a note saying I could ride his bus home with him! Ricky's already at the bus loop by the time that I get there.

"Aidan, hey! Did you give your note to the front office to ride home with me?" I take a piece of paper out of my pocket and wave it around, like a flag of victory. "I got the bus pass right here!" I told him triumphantly. "What's your mom making for dinner?" I asked him. He told me we were having spaghetti, my favorite!

We ate quickly that night without a word, not that there was much chance for one. We were shoveling in huge bites super fast, like we had been starved for a week. Ricky's mother smiled at us, and she brought out a piece of cheesecake for each of us after we had finished.

"You boys want some dessert? Aidan, does your mom let you have cheesecake?" I was about to open my mouth to say no thanks, when I caught Ricky's eye across the table. He glanced towards the plates and nodded quickly at me. "Thank you Mrs. Doyle, I've eaten cheesecake with my mom lots of times. It's really good."

Before long we were saying our good nights, promising to brush our teeth. We stayed silent in his room after that, just waiting. I felt like I was going to jump out of my skin when it got closer to eight o'clock! Occasionally we'd get a glass of water from the kitchen, or use the bathroom, which were mostly excuses for us to see what his parents were doing in the living room. We were trying to track their progress towards heading to bed for the night, and finally we heard their bedroom door close.

Both of us had agreed to wait exactly fifteen minutes after that to leave the house. With our jacket hoods pulled low over our heads we dropped out of Ricky's window and entered into the back yard. It was chilly enough outside to where I'm thankful I brought my jacket, but not cold enough to be uncomfortable. Even if it had been really cold the excitement in my blood would have kept me super-duper warm, which was great.

"Aidan, do you have both flashlights?" Ricky asked.

I shook my head in response. "No man, I thought you had yours, I just have this one." I held it up and waved the beam around his face. He winced, putting his hands up. "Come on...It's bad enough I don't have a flashlight, now you want to blind me completely?"

I laughed at this, and told him we could try to share mine. I didn't want to risk sneaking back in and out of the house again just for one flashlight. I'd just gotten old enough for mom to let me sleep over at friends' houses that weren't in our neighborhood. We're just getting started with Neumack, and I couldn't mess that up. We entered the woods, then spent a good fifteen minutes walking around. We saw a huge, black lump off to the right in the middle of the trees. My breath caught in my throat for a second, and I shined the light towards it. It was an old, broken down, and probably abandoned white car. The windows were broken out of it, so it was easy to see into. We walked to it and peered inside, making sure to keep our distance in case someone was living in there. It happens, you know.

"How the heck did this car even get out here? There are trees everywhere. Maybe it's been here since they were babies." Ricky said. I instantly corrected him, not missing a chance to show off. "They're called, like, saplings or something. There's no such thing as a baby tree." I scoffed at him, but then I thought about everything else that he had said.

"Ya know, that is a good question. It doesn't make sense that the car's out here like this. Hey, when it's daytime we should come back and check it for broken glass. If not it can be ours! We can be the only eleven year old kids at school to have a car, or maybe we can make a base out of it!" I suggest excitedly. We continued to walk on, agreeing to check on the car again tomorrow.

The trail was very difficult. Both of us keep close together to share the beam of light, but that made us bump together a lot. I felt like a pair of Siamese twins in some kind of weird, three-legged race. We were bumbling and tripping over any, and every, thing in our paths. It was a blast! We were chuckling and stomping around so hard that I could barely hear any other noises, but something weird got my attention. I shushed Ricky by putting my hand up, pointing to my ear to signal him to stop and listen. There, under the noise of the wind through the trees, I could hear something. I tried to sharpen my ears and block out any other sounds. Yes, that was it! I couldn't believe it. I didn't know whether to feel scared, excited or worried.

"Ricky, do you hear it too? The baby! C-c-can you hear the baby?" Even in the moonlight I could tell that Ricky's face had turned a lighter color than normal. His eyes are wide, and he clenched his hands together. "Yeah umm...maybe we should go now?" He mumbled to me. I grabbed him by the arm a little more aggressively than I meant to, keeping him in place.

"Well, I'm going further. If you want to go back fine, but remember I have the flashlight. Sorry." I say, smoothing his army jacket out like that would somehow erase the act of me grabbing him. "I just want to get a little closer to make sure we aren't imagining it. Come on, please? We've come this far and can't head back just yet."

Against his wishes he reluctantly followed me on through the woods, both of us more scared than we are willing to admit. We seemed to be getting closer to the sound for a while, but then it just...stopped. Ricky looked satisfied, like he knew we could start heading home then. He was happy that we got our answer to the stories of Neumack Woods, but for me it wasn't enough. It didn't really answer anything, it just made more questions. I wanted, needed, to know where, if anywhere, it was coming from. The cry sounded very real, so I thought that maybe there actually was a baby out there. Maybe they were cold and hungry. Maybe they need help! My mom had a baby a few months ago. She's super annoying, screams and pukes all the time, but I would never want anything bad to happen to her.........to any baby, pukey or otherwise. Ricky wasn't having that though, and he all but dragged me the way we had come.

I followed Ricky back to his house, and we snuck back in through the window and tried to go to sleep. His parents were none the wiser. At first I couldn't stop thinking about the woods and that baby, but after a while the warmth and fluffiness of Ricky's bottom bunk's quilt cuddled me into a deep sleep. Eventually the lullaby of our snorts and snores drifted out of the cracked window into the night. The next morning at home I took advantage of my mom's tiredness, asking her after a long night awake with my sister if I could stay at Ricky's again next Friday.

"Unless you want us to both stay over here?" I wriggled my eyebrow at her. "What's one more kid in the house, right?" I say.

Mom turns to me, giving me an offended smile. "Don't you pull that crap on me, Aidan Stewart. I would have said yes, if you didn't try to reverse-psych me." She joked, kissing me on my forehead as she walked past. "I'm glad you two are such good friends." She added before leaving the room entirely.

The school week was long, and uneventful. It seemed to drag on and on. You know how things get when you're really looking forward to something! Things become a blur with the end goal in sight. I did all of my homework and went about the motions, mentally counting down the days, then the hours, then the minutes until Friday. The day had come! I came to school more prepared than last week. I had extra batteries, TWO flashlights just in case, even some nighttime snacks and Gatorade. It would be just like we're going night hiking! If that's even a thing, which I'm pretty sure it's not. I brought the game that Ricky had wanted to borrow too, and we met up and rode the bus to his house just like last week.

We went through the evening, having what they called 'Mr. Doyle's famous golden chicken breast' this time. The excitement had eaten away at my stomach over the day, and I didn't eat as fast as I ate the spaghetti. Mrs. Doyle had bought some mini cupcakes at the store, and gave us two each. We played some video games to keep ourselves occupied until his parents went in to their room. Before long we were out in the night air again. It was cold tonight, but in a different way. It was the kind of cold that my mom says will settle into your bones, whatever that means. My breath came out in puffs, and my teeth were trying their hardest not to chatter together with chills. I shook it off and pulled my jacket tighter around me, my hood over my head again like some kind of thief or ninja.

The vastness of the woods can be confusing, and it's easy to get turned around in there, but I felt less worried when we passed by the weird car. We both had our flashlights, and I breathed a little easier because I knew we were on the right path. I had no idea where we were going though. I was just walking, hoping to hear the crying. Now I know it sounds crazy to want to stay, but I had a plan. I had made sure my Dad's phone was charged the night before, and I took advantage of my parent's new baby exhaustion…again. I tiptoed into my parent's room like a ninja this morning to grab my dad's phone, turn it off and then put it in my backpack without anyone seeing. But it was all so that, when we went back in the woods, I could actually record the crying or any other creepy stuff.

This time we didn't stop at, or even mention, the car as we passed by it. Our once-treasure of a find gave way to a bigger mystery as soon as we got a little further down the trail. I got the phone out and turned on the flashlight feature, my excitement slowly turning into fear. I felt like I could totally puke right then, but I didn't. Ricky would have loved to use that excuse to leave the woods, so I tried to stay at least kinda calm. The thing that had caught our attention just after the car was a hatch, like the kind on those bunkers in war movies. We started to cautiously approach the metal hatch, which was positioned on the ground. We could see the moonlight glint off it from a couple of feet away, and I barely listened as Rickey begged me to walk away.

Then I heard it.

A noise startled us, something that sounded like a rock being thrown on concrete, and then the loudest scream I had ever heard in my life came from inside. The volume was so intense and distorted that it almost didn't even sound like a baby anymore! We scrambled back, and I dialed the police emergency number on my phone. I told them where we are and what our names and ages are, and when the dispatcher asked what the problem was I held the phone out towards the metal.

I yelled, practically screaming into the phone, "We're alone in Neumack woods, and there's a baby and this metal door thing! I think it needs help!"

Common sense told me that an unattended baby underneath a metal hatch would not have survived over the week from when we had last heard it, but it sounded so real! As we

were waiting for the cops a figure came running towards us through the woods. I haven't ever been good at fight or flight; 'freeze in place' is more of my thing.

After a moment we started to run, knowing it couldn't be the police that soon. The figure loomed closer to us, his walking speed nearly matching that of our running speed. When I looked back the second time Ricky's face disappeared from sight, and a cry cut through the woodlands. My heart dropped, and I realized this time that the screams don't belong to a baby.

I ran back to Ricky's house, alone, and his mother held me tight as I told her what happened. They called the police, and my parents too, not feeling like they had the option not to. My mom cried hysterically on the other end of the line, and I knew that she'd probably be mad later. Especially since she had to get Dad to wake up, then get the baby ready and then come and pick me up. By the time my parents arrived the police had just knocked on Ricky's front door, and the officer politely waited for my parents to enter the house before entering it himself. His face looked disturbed, like he'd seen something terrible.

"Please tell me it's not the baby!" I couldn't hold back my anxiety any longer. "Officer, did you find the baby? Is it gonna be okay?" He said a few hushed words to the adults, and my mother buried her face in my father's chest. I think she was holding back tears.

The officer cleared his throat, and he asked me to sit down. He assured me that no babies were hurt, or in danger, then he started to tell our parents what the police found out there in Neuman Woods, inside of that metal hatch door. It appeared to be locked from the inside, and they were the first adults to hear the baby cry besides the 911 operator. After some attempts they managed to pry it open, and then the officer paused. He told me to leave the room, but I heard him though...I heard it all.

What they found inside wasn't a baby. It was a very thin, weathered old man holding a tape recorder with the play button pressed. He was bare, except for a pair of dirty, brief-style underwear that appeared to be stained with old blood. His teeth were also reported to have been reddish in nature, and his gray beard was streaked with crimson.

The only sign they found of my friend was his blood-covered jacket, and his flashlight.

N.M. Brown
About the Author

N.M. Brown is an international best selling author from Florida. She's a happily married mother who sheds light on the dark corners of the mind that we like to keep hidden. Her other publications include stories in each of Sirens at Midnight, Calls From the Brighter Futures Suicide Hotline, Fantasia Divinity's Elemental Drabble Series, the Scary Snippets Collections, the Mother Ghost Grimm children's horror anthology, Dark Xmas, along with several others being released in the next year.

Thirteen
Craig Crawford

I watched them from the inside.

It's a lonely existence, bound to the earth for decades, rooted in a prison of my own doing by one who knew the ways of the world better than most. I couldn't do anything but watch as others passed by, my hunger a gurgle in the basement of my gut.

Incarcerated for my indiscretions, I can only stare out the windows, peering into the forests around me. It's madness. Powerless as the seasons come and go around me. Watching as the snow melts with the coming spring sun, only to shrink to the dark corners as the winds batter and sway the trees in the violence of the storms one after another. Even in the sun-bake of summer the heat is replaced by wind as the sentinel orb in the sky rains rays down on my prison.

Autumn is the one breath I get each year, when the weather softens, the tempests replaced by gentle winds crackling the leaves as they fall from the oaks and maples surrounding me. Though I am witness to the slow death of the Earth each year, and everything is ground back into the soil to herald the desolation of winter, I continue to endure.

It was my one hundred and twelfth autumn when my sightless eyes followed the trio hiking by. Two young men and a woman, dressed lightly in the fall sun, the woman sporting a pack and a stick. The taller man talked incessantly, constantly readjusting a sack off his shoulder, never still. I grew giddy at his boundless energy, but it was too much to hope.

The third, shorter and stouter, carried the inquisitor's eye, silently stopping before me, casting looks in all directions. "Wonder who built this way out here?" he echoed out, shutting the other man up.

"Some old hermit," said the second. "You know — some trapper dude or a crazy who can't stand to be around people. He probably came up here and built a shack, talking to squirrels and shooting rabbits and shit."

The young woman shoved him with an arm. "Randy, knock it off. This place looks like it's been abandoned for ages. No one lives up here."

"My dad told me this place has a spook about it, Sam," the third said. "There are legends of ancient druids and cults creeping around up here."

"And you think some cult built this place?" The second asked dubiously. "It wouldn't fit more than three or four at best. Sam's right, it looks like it's ready to fall down. Look at the roof: those wood shingles are curling and about to blow away or cave in. I bet the door is swelled shut in the frame."

The third took a step in my direction, and hope wriggled out from the depths of my decades-long despair. Bound in blood, there was only one path to freedom for me. The number was thirteen, and my memory stretched back over the other eleven, seeming eons ago, forcing me into something akin to rage and insanity.

He took another step toward the door.

"Harris, leave it alone," the woman said. "Randy's right, it'll probably collapse if you pull on the door."

He stopped.

I focused on the tree behind him, well aware my intense gaze had ruffled others in the past. Some people have a sense, or a gift, able to "know" when things aren't right. I was afraid the curious one would get the creeps, so I quieted my mind and metaphorically held my breath.

There had been an incident long ago where a child had seen me in the reflection of one of the windows before they'd broken out, and the last thing I wanted was to scare them off with an act of stupidity. I waited, forcing patience as he walked over and peered through one of the decayed, broken windows.

"Looks in pretty bad shape," the third one said, shielding his eyes and scanning the interior. "Wait."

He'd spotted the lumps on the floor, and excitement quivered within me.

"There's something inside," he said.

"Harris, you're not going in there. Just leave it alone."

"What is it?" the second said, coming up on his side.

"Don't know. Looks like old clothes, or maybe a sack or something. See?" and he pointed through the window, his hand and half his forearm inside.

I concentrated on the tree behind the woman: tall, probably three times my prison's height, half of its leaves yellow and orange and red, a few littering the ground around its trunk. I caught the dance of the branches as a faint breeze swayed them, shaking at its leaves.

"There is something," the second one said. "Let's go check it out."

"Leave it. There's something bad about this place."

It turns out the third didn't have the awareness, it was the woman.

"It'll be fine," and the third one tried the door.

True to his guess, the door was swollen by the countless seasons of rain and snow. It took the both of them, the second shoving from above while the third turned the knob and shoved his shoulder against it. They groaned and pushed until finally the protest of wood on wood gave and they both fell inward, slapping against the dirt floor.

The second one laughed as he helped his friend up. "That thing is rotted out. God only knows how long it's been since someone was inside."

"Are you alright?" The woman asked.

"I'm fine," the third said, brushing himself off. "We better be careful not to touch the walls, or the whole thing may come apart on us."

"True that," and the second headed further into the room.

"I'm staying out here."

"Sam, we're not going to camp here, just check it out. We'll be two minutes, promise."

Over the last century I've learned how to minimize my presence, how to sink into the background to keep from scaring off possible prey. It took me several decades to learn this, causing me no end of suffering and frustration in the beginning. In point of fact, it's only been in the last three decades I've managed to snare the bulk of my parole.

Curling up in the far corner, fading into the background as best I could, I watched out of my periphery vision as the two men entered. I was half focusing out the window — not directly at them. They scanned the room, both turning on flashlights in the gloom. There was a momentary pause in my direction. I looked away, sure they would bolt and run out the doorway like so many others.

The third held his eyes in my direction for several moments, but thankfully the second shuffled forward toward number Eleven. "Look at this, Harris. Is that a bone?"

He knelt down, and the third followed his course. He prodded the dried mass on the floor with the end of his light. Looks of confusion flickered on both of their faces: they had no clue what they were looking at, and how could they? I'd scored my last victory over four years ago, and having fed off of everything left over the only real remains were weathered and bug-devoured. Even most of the bone was masticated.

Except for the rounded piece of skull, which the second uncovered with the head of his light.

Had they taken more time to investigate the other room they might have uncovered the small hole in the floor. It was near the corner of the main room, and it led down into a smaller room. During my imprisonment I have learned many skills, including how to create lights to lure in those from a distance, and how to show myself at opportune moments.

Another, more rewarding talent lies in being able to move physical objects. As with my senses it took me until the turn of the century to learn how to move an object at all, but once I discovered I could do it I exercised those mental muscles until I could move all kinds of weights. The advantage lay in being able to move identifiable items like a flashlight from the deceased on the floor, rolling it across the boards to my hidey hole near the back.

In such a way I was able to remove all evidence from the previous eleven, so as not to spook numbers Twelve and Thirteen.

Except for the locket from number Four. Ancient, and gotten by accident, it had belonged to a young girl. Made from real gold, it caught the sunlight just right even buried in the grime and debris. It was the one thing which could make me chuckle: reminding me of an elaborate fishing lure, metaphorically used to tease the next one on my list.

"Whoa," came from the second as he spotted it.

Reaching into the dried remnants of clothing and dead beetles he pulled up the locket. Carefully taking it in his hand he brushed it off, showing it to his partner. Between their eyes flashed many ideas about what it might be, and whether it might have monetary value. "Hey Sam, come look at this!"

Like fishing, the moment always came when you feel the tug of a line and make the decision on when to try to hook your prey. Pull too soon and dinner could surely escape, neglect to pull fast enough and the hook might not catch.

I debated waiting. To get the third in their group was almost too good to pass up, but I was afraid I might not be able to concentrate with all of them inside. I would flay myself if I accidentally allowed them all to escape.

"That looks old," the third said. "Like really old. See the craftsmanship on it — that was handmade. Wait, see if it opens up. Sam, get in here and take a look at this!"

I cursed, but made up my mind. I slammed the door closed.

The two inside snapped their heads behind them, bewilderment flowing through their faces. "Sam, what are you doing?" The third called out.

A yell erupted from beyond the door, but I moved in, uncaring now if they perceived me. I needed to strike quickly and efficiently if I was to feed.

I chose the second — he was fidgety, and seemed

more likely to react quickly. I moved in as he stood up suddenly, looking about. I'm sure he felt my presence, but all at once he ignored the danger signs and headed to the door. He was easy to reach from behind.

His soul was a light I could see, pulsing from the center of his chest — I could feel the heat of it, the pure essence of the divine. He cried out as I sunk into it. Invisible hands, as I imagined them, grabbed and ripped at the connection to his body. I wrenched it, like a farmer trying to rend a root from the ground. I severed the connection between him and his soul and tore it loose.

The tall one shrieked and fell lifeless to the ground.

Exhilaration.

I fed on the essence as it bled back into the ether of the universe, but I got my nourishment and received the energy to reduce my quota by one. Closing my non-existent eyes, I reveled in the energy and sated a voracious hunger that had loomed for the last four years. It was akin to stuffing yourself at a banquet, squeezing in one last roll and downing one last goblet of wine: your belly bursting, but basking in the rapture of the feast.

So good.

I almost forgot the third, now my Thirteen.

A steady banging on the door, shadowed by an endless stream of cries and shouts echoed. Thirteen stood, eyes glazed over with shock and disbelief. He took a step toward his friend, but whether he saw me or not he felt me. I know it.

Realization set in against my ecstasy. I bristled with

energy — raw power. It was the same each time, like being an old man suddenly swollen with the vigor of youth again. I all but missed the moment: I had reached my Twelve. I was just one away from freedom.

I surged forward, real hunger settling in now. My quarry was in my domain, alone and afraid.

He yelled, backing away. The woman responded with a primal cry of her own, and had it been any other situation I might have grinned at their primeval communication, but the task at hand drove me forward. I felt his life-force the same as the other, and I was close to my own redemption. Power coursed through me, and I reached for his essence.

He scrambled away. His hands instinctively clutched at his chest as he first backed up, then twisted toward the window. He was powerless against my will.

Apprehension stole over me as I realized the broken state of my prison allowed other gaps; other exits. I dove upon Thirteen, summoning every ounce of wrath and rage as I swept over him. I used my abilities and tripped his feet into each other, toppling him to the floorboards with a crash. A howl, and a flailing of limbs, his only defense.

Except I was ethereal, and reached right past his swatting arms.

I reached toward his inner light, the brilliance almost blinding, but I wanted his core — needed it to free myself. My wraithen hands slipped past his own, and I encircled the core of his existence.

I touched coldness.

So cold it burned my hands — like shoving them into a fire, and I howled. I know they both heard it, because Thirteen shuddered and the woman screamed. I retreated to the far side, all of my new found vim gone, replaced by an ache stretching through my being. I roared and wailed at the pain, wondering what had done this to me.

Except I knew.

Through the glow of Thirteen's life force, I felt the pendant around his neck, hanging at his breastbone. A talisman of the hated metal ore, hanging from a necklace at his chest, protected their kind from me.

I'd felt its sear before, when the druid had cursed me a full century ago. It was life metal, capable of imprisoning me and hurting me, and my anticipated Thirteen wore it.

I doubt he knew the power at his breast, but either way I was powerless in the corner, my metaphysical hands throbbing. All I had strength for was watching as he got his feet under him and skittered across the floorboards to the window. His eyes never left the corner where I lay as he crawled out through the hole, fear on him like the stink of raw onion.

I howled again as his foot disappeared from sight.

So close.

I caught a last glimpse of the two as they tore back down the path, but hope was gone. I growled and snarled, shook the walls of my prison though I couldn't bring it down. My captor had been careful, and clever. I watched them go, bellowing after them though it made no difference now. They might return to retrieve their friend, but they would never step foot inside again.

I unleashed my rage, spent my energy lamenting the escape. So close to freedom, just to have lost it again after so long...

Darkness settled over me before my anger waned. Fatigued, had I still been human I would have slept, but such is my curse to never rest. I settled into the remains of Twelve and fed off of his faded essence. It was my only solace.

After a time I looked over Twelve's things and pulled him back into the center of the room, dragging him over the remnants of Eleven. I laid him out face-down, just like the others. His sack and his flashlight slowly tumbled toward my hidey-hole. I found the locket once more and placed it on the floor near his hand. I erased the drag marks from the dust on the floor with swirls and currents of stale air.

It would take a day or two, but I knew they would return with others. I could decay Twelve quickly, feeding on his remaining residue, but leaving enough to lure one of them inside.

Perhaps then I could snag Thirteen.

CRAIG CRAWFORD
ABOUT THE AUTHOR

Craig started writing in middle school, having gotten introduced to science fiction, fantasy andhorror by a new troupe of friends. A voracious reader, he started thinking about these people who actually wrote the stories he loved and thought he might be able to do it too.

In college Craig followed a track to expand his literary and writing smarts. He got his first publication free lancing for a gaming company called Palladium Books Inc., where he published two indices for source material for their RPG, Rifts. More interested in fiction, Craig turned his attention to novels. In 2008-2009, he earned a chance to workshop one of his fantasy novels with the Wolf Pirate Project. After the editor helped him flesh out another angle on the book, he earned a second spot with them the following year for another shorter fiction work.

Craig currently splits his time between writing short stories and novels. Mostly he writes fantasy, sci-fi, YA and of course, horror. You can check out his website to see what he's been up to.

Author website: craiglcrawfordbooks.com

Automatic Contamination
M.A. Smith

There was something wrong with that place, and we knew it from the very beginning.

The 'beginning' was a dust-fuzzed, summer's day when the last of the flocks of earth-movers and high viz clipboard carriers were wrapping up their work and wheeling away from the estate's perimeter. Everything within the boundaries of our test-tube town still smelled of new carpet and paint and fresh tarmac. The books in the brand-new library stood straight on unbent spines, and the graffiti that would one day cover the bricks of the village hall was no more than hissing dreams deep within the rowed cans of spray paint in the just-built hardware store.

I was old enough, then, to be pretty cynical about all of that. I was thirteen that summer, and the amputated woods and fields beyond the dual carriageway had begun to occupy my mind nearly constantly. The road itself cupped the estate's fringe like a defensive moat, and the low-level hum of the cars blurring along its length crept into my ears in my night-darkened room. I found myself falling into fitful dreams that I could not remember come morning, but that I knew had to do with that strange, half-land outside the town.

I still dream about those places. But now, God help me, I actually remember them.

Back then I knew that my parents wouldn't be happy with my 'running feral', as they referred to my participation in any activity that was not strategically planned and assessed for health and safety. Yet there was a point in the day where I could run free, right between the two hours or so between my shambling in from school and my mum and dad getting back from work. Later this would become the time for illicit alcohol and stunted, bumpy kisses, but at thirteen I still had one foot in childhood. All I wanted was to get out from under the shadow of all those crowd-ed up houses and pelt through a forbidden wilderness.

We'd been in our new house on the estate for may-be three or four months when I befriended Clem, who lived on my street, and Lucas, who lived a few streets down. We all went to the local school – as shiny, new and soulless as everything else – and were often together in those couple of parentless hours. Clem, and Lucas too, were left to their own devices after school. I don't even know where their folks were; I presumed they worked, but I never asked. The adult world was still a distant plan-et then, and one that we weren't concerned with. Or even interested in, to be honest.

On the dry and faded afternoon that I'm telling you about I'd just had time, crashing in from school, to change into jeans and a tee before the doorbell rang. I knew it was Lucas; Clem wasn't one for doorbells.

Sure enough, as Lucas and I stood in my parents' spotless kitchen, discussing which route we were going to take, an almighty thudding reverberated around the house. Before I'd even taken two steps to the front door I heard the snap of the letterbox being pushed up.

"Open the door, dickhead!"

I could see Clem's mouth smooshed up against the slot from the other side.

"Come on, Jamie!" More hammering.

"What the Hell is wrong with you?" I said, pulling open the door so fast that Clem, on the other side, lost her balance and began to topple backwards off the step. I caught her by the forearm, pulling her upright.

Clem grinned at me. "Fuck you, very much," She pushed past me into the hall, "dickhead."

I nudged the door closed with my elbow and followed Clem back into the kitchen.

"Ready, Clem?" Lucas said.

Clem merely patted the side of her backpack in reply.

"Which way are we going?" she asked.

"Jamie reckons we should cross the carriageway by the flats, next to the pub…"

"No way," Clem interrupted. "My mum's best mate lives in one of those flats; she'll get straight on the phone if she sees us."

"Where do you suggest, then, Clem?" I butt in.

She looked me, then Lucas, dead in the eye. "Underpass."

For the briefest of moments no one spoke.

"I don't know, Clem…" Lucas began.

Clem's lips began to curve upwards at the corners. "Scared?"

"Don't be an idiot," Lucas answered sharply. "What do you think, Jamie?"

I thought about it, but I really didn't want to go near that underpass. It was an aborted part of the estate; a botched start from back when the whole place was not much more than a raw scar in the earth, and I was still happy in my old, shabby little life. The underpass was a short, concrete tunnel that ran below the dual carriageway on the western edge of the town, and led…nowhere. When you came out the other end you were met with maybe a few metres of patchy tarmac and gravel, which then suppurated into rough grass and scrubby woodland.

It was creepy even before the stories had started circulating at school about the child-eating tramp that lived there, tucked tight against the dark walls of the pass. They said he was ready to reach out a clawed hand to grab any young flesh that happened, against its owner's every screaming instinct, to wander through.

Clem and Lucas were both looking at me, waiting.

"Okay, let's do it." I said. "That whole story about the tramp is crap, Lucas. Don't you think we'd have heard about it on the news, or had police crawling all over the estate if there really was a psycho in the underpass eating kids? This isn't fucking 'It.'"

Lucas thought for a moment, then nodded.

"Okay," he said.

I poured us all a glass of juice, and we chugged our drinks back in unison.

"I didn't actually believe it," Lucas said, as we headed out the door. "The place just gives me the creeps, that's all."

Clem laughed. "You did believe it."

"Shut up," he muttered.

It took us about half an hour to get to the underpass. It was on the furthest outskirts of the estate, beyond the parchment dry park and the pathetic 'nature' pond. The rise of a long, landscaped hill obscured both it, and the dual carriageway, from view, but as we neared it we could hear the low drone of the cars rise to an insectile whine.

"Are you sure you're alright with this?" Clem asked, and I couldn't tell if she was addressing me or Lucas. The snideness had gone from her voice, and I began to suspect that maybe she'd like to be talked out of what we were about to do.

"Course," I answered, for both of us. "Like I said, it's just a shitty story."

We trundled up the small hill. Reaching the top Clem plopped her backpack down on the ground and pulled out a bottle of orange liquid. She took a swig and passed it to me. I took a deep draught…and immediately sprayed it back out.

"Clem, is this spiked?"

The grin re-appeared. "Only a little bit. Can you handle it, Jamie?"

"What the Hell is wrong with you?" I asked her, for the second time in an hour. Yet I took another sip, more carefully this time. I drank again, then tried to pass the plastic bottle to Lucas.

"I don't want any," he said.

"Yes you do," Clem insisted.

"No, I really don't."

Clem grabbed the bottle from me and thrust it towards Lucas's face. He snatched the bottle from Clem. "Anything to make you shut up." He took the tiniest sip. "Happy now?"

We stood quietly for a moment, looking at the view. Behind us the estate undulated as far as the eye could see, uniform rows of clone houses dipping and rising in martially ordered blocks, the thin smoke from a couple of barbeques drifting above the roofs like a pair of long, grey balloon strings. We barely gave it a glance; what we wanted was ahead of us.

At the bottom of the hill alongside the dual carriageway ran a stunted, narrow path, largely overgrown with tall grass. It led nowhere, and terminated at the mouth of the underpass.

"Come on, losers," Clem said, and began striding down the slope, towards the path and the rush of cars.

"Honestly, it's fine," I said quietly to my friend as we followed after.

"Yeah, I know," he sighed.

Clem turned then, smiling back at us. It was a wide, beautiful smile that bloomed as bright and free as one of the meadow flowers that grew, unnoticed, by the side of the road. As quickly as the turn of the breeze it was gone, and she was just ordinary old Clem again, shouting back at us to get a move on.

There has not been a day that's gone by, since that afternoon, that I haven't thought of that smile.

At the bottom of the slope we walked in silence, single file, for a hundred yards or so, following the ratty little path. The cars passed by, separated from us only by a low barrier and a handful of inches.

We moved to stand side-by-side as we came to the open maw of the underpass. Concrete steps descended down into gloom, burrowing beneath road and earth. I realised that, despite their proximity, the noise of the cars had become a distant thing.

The one sodium light still working down there flickered, just out of sight. I knew that it was just the chancy play of light that made it look as though someone was down there, crawling along the floor.

"Are you sure about this?" Lucas said to me, and when I looked at him his blue eyes were wide, and the clouds above rolled, reflected across his gaze.

We were all quiet for a moment.

"I don't want to go back yet, Lucas." I ran a hand through my hair. "I feel like I'm suffocating in there. Do you understand that?"

A few beats of silence pulsed between us, a thick heartbeat in the heavy air.

"Fuck them," Lucas said quietly. "Ever since we came here, my folks have been acting like the Kardashians. Literally, the second we arrived. Automatic contamination."

"Fuck them," agreed Clem. "I wish we'd never moved to this shit hole. No offense."

"Alright then," I said, taking the first step down, "let's get out of here. For a couple of hours, at least."

And, together, we put our backs to the droid houses and pretend parkland and crossed over to…somewhere else.

*

Like I said, we knew there was something wrong with that place from the very beginning.

There was no bird noise, for a start. When we came out the other side of that underpass (limbs whole and bodies un-nibbled), that was the first thing that struck me. It wasn't that I'd been particularly listening to it before – the hard ratchet of the crows, the spiralling trill of the summer robins –but I became aware of it by its absence.

At the top of that step, on the other side of the underpass, a few hundred yards and a few hundred million miles away from the clean-slate sweep of the estate, there was no bird song. The skies, the swollen bellies of the trees, were empty of noise. There was nothing but the diesel hum of the cars behind us, and the noise of our breathing, wet and slow.

"Which way, Jamie?" Clem asked.

I looked around. We were in a ragged clearing; the patchy gravel of the path petered out maybe twenty yards ahead of us, just shy of the boundaries of a scrub forest. I could just make out the ghost of an old footpath, disappearing into the trees slightly to our left. Behind us the underpass dipped beneath the road, and the bright green of the man-made slope beyond hid the town from sight.

"There," I said, pointing to the faint track that ran into the tangled copse.

"You want another sip of party juice first?" Clem said, shifting her pack half off her shoulders.

"I'm good."

"Lucas?"

"Nah," he said, and began pushing through the dust-dry long grass towards the trees.

Clem cocked an eyebrow at me, but followed him.

I came last. I don't know, to this day, whether it was my imagination or not, but when we passed into the shadows of the ivy-strangled dog oak and stunted birch trees, the wasp-like whine from the road vanished. I don't mean it faded, or became muffled as we travelled further away; it completely disappeared, as if the cars had ceased to exist. Maybe they had. Maybe, if we'd looked round, we would have seen a soup-like fog behind us where the road had been, where the underpass had been. Maybe we would have seen it creep up the green slope beyond and, surmounting the summit, slide down into the folds of the estate, blotting and erasing.

Feeding.

But we didn't look round. We followed the dead, little path into the secret half-light of the forest instead, and it was magnificent.

Odd snarls of rusted, barbed wire sprouted in patches like fungus, in thickets and along the bases of trees. A cache of miniature bottles, medicinal looking and truly ancient, were piled in a cairn on a moss-varnished stump. Clem stopped to stare, horrified and thrilled, at a bird's skull nailed above a decomposing bird box high on the trunk of a tree whose leaves whispered in the small breeze. Everywhere was strangeness and wildness and dereliction.

And still we went deeper and deeper into the wood.

"Why is it so quiet in here?" Lucas whispered.

"Isn't it obvious?" said Clem, softly. "This place is haunted."

"Yeah, okay Clem," Lucas scoffed. "Like there was a kid-eating tramp in the underpass, right?"

"Don't you feel it, though?" Clem said, serious. "This place has gone bad."

We stopped then, at a curve in the dry-mud track. All around us the strangled and strangling trees nudged and batted at each other. We could see, a short distance beyond the bend, what looked like another clearing.

"I think we ought to go back," I said.

"Are you joking?" said Clem. "This whole thing was your idea…"

"It's getting late. Our folks'll be back from work soon. If my mum finds out I've been off the estate she'll blow a gasket, and I'll be grounded for a year."

Clem came closer to me, until her face was just a few inches from my own. She looked into my eyes for a moment, then a smile curved her lips.

"You can't take it, can you, Jamie? You and Lucas are both the same. You talk like big men, but when it comes down to it…"

"Hey!" Lucas cut in, putting a hand on Clem's shoulder.

Clem shook him off.

"You go back if you want, but I'm not. I want to see what that is."

I followed Clem's finger and saw what she had seen. In the corner of the clearing, obscured and overgrown, was a low, wood and corrugated metal shack.

"Fuck me," Lucas breathed, close to my ear. "What sort of person would live out here; in there?"

"It's abandoned," I whispered. "It has to be."

"Look," said Clem. "Next to the door."

We looked.

Next to the rough rectangle of the door was a crude mailbox, nailed to the wall at about waist height. A newspaper, un-rotted and bright against the corroded tin, poked from its open mouth.

"I bet you a tenner that's new," said Clem.

And with that she strode away from us, towards the shack in the clearing.

"Clementine!" I hissed.

The sunlight fell on her like God's own spotlight

as she stepped out of the dappling shadows of the wood. I remember hearing the papery sweep of the long grass against her bare legs as she moved away from us. I remember how a small swarm of flying insects followed her progress, and how straight and strong her back looked, the keys of her spine moving and visible through her light summer top.

I called her name again, but she didn't even look round. Lucas and I watched as she approached the waiting hovel, and reached out a hand towards the newspaper rolled tight in the mailbox.

"Shit," I said, through gritted teeth, starting to move towards her. I heard Lucas following behind me. Clem, wrenching the newspaper free, held it up and towards us in triumph.

She opened her mouth to call something back to us, and at that moment the crude door swung open.

I stopped in shock, so suddenly that Lucas slammed into my back and we both crumpled to the ground. Clem's arm, holding the newspaper, dropped. Seemingly in slow motion her head turned on the hinge of her neck.

Lucas and I couldn't see the figure who had opened the door – the gloom from within was too deep for that – but Clem could see. Whatever it was she saw drove the blood from her face, and stretched her mouth wide enough to allow passage for the scream that would come.

But it didn't come, because at that moment a withered arm shot out of the darkness, yanking her inside by the wrist.

I shot up from the ground and, jibbering, ran towards the hovel. I reached the door in the half second before it slammed shut, clutching at Clem's fingers which were desperately clinging to the frame. I noticed industrial type letters and numbers printed on the corrugated wall next to the door, and some part of my brain, amid the horror, began to calmly wonder as to their meaning.

"Jamie," I heard Clem's voice, begging, beyond the door. "Jamie, please, please…"

Behind me, Lucas was sobbing, high pitched and panicked.

I pulled as hard as I could, screaming into the dead air, but I only had a grip on three of Clem's fingers. Slick with sweat they slipped from my grasp and disappeared inside.

Just before the door slammed shut I saw a slice of something unspeakable. The elbow of a rough kitchen counter, mildewed and thick with filth. Knives. Meat hooks. Long bones, gnawed and cracked.

I almost passed out then. I would have, if Lucas hadn't hit me, hard, across the face. I realized he'd been shouting in my face, words I hadn't heard.

I don't remember running through the woods. I don't remember anything at all until we reached the underpass, and Lucas and I have never spoken of it since. We must have taken the dropped newspaper with us, as I do remember waving a car down with it. I remember how a few of the pages drifted away in the wind, tumbling over themselves in the false wind of the passing traffic.

The police never found Clem. They came to my parent's house every day for a week, told me that there was no shack in those woods. Told me that the woods were very small, that we could only have been walking in them for ten minutes or so in any direction before we'd have come to their edge. Wanted to know what had happened to Clem. That's what they kept asking me. She was missing, where had she gone, when had we last seen her, why had we made up a story about a cannibalistic tramp.

I wasn't allowed to see or speak to Lucas. The local adolescent mental health service was called in. My parents, grey-faced and close to tears, sat on either side of me on the sofa, day after day, as the parade passed me by. Only part of me was present to witness it, which was a relief.

The police never found a body, and so Clem was put down as a missing person. The police were sure that Lucas and I had been instrumental in her 'running away from home', but had nothing to charge us with and so eventually let us be. Clem's parents, equally believing Lucas and I bore some blame (which I guess we did) turned up at my house a couple of times and screamed at my parents, and we moved away not long after.

These events happened a very long time ago. You may remember the missing person appeal for Clem in the newspaper; it went nationwide, I think.

I'm writing this in my car. I've come back, you see, after all this time. The estate has grown old now, like me: it sags in places, it doesn't stand as straight as it used to.

It's whole, but stained and faded. It's become disillusioned; it's seen its acolytes peel away to newer towns and to fashionable city refurbs.

The engine's off now, and my breath steams in the cool interior.

I picture myself walking across town to the park; I imagine pulling my unwilling bones up that landscaped slope and walking, crablike and careful, down the other side. I wonder how the underpass will look. I picture the brittle dunes of skeletal leaves that will line its innards. I think of the path through the forest, and how I will follow it into the tomb-like dark of the trees.

I know that I'll walk for an hour or more, and will not come to the wood's outer boundary. Instead, I'll come across a clearing, where a shack lurks. Today's newspaper will poke from its mailbox.

I came here believing that, having seen it again, I can turn around and leave. I'd be satisfied that I am, and always have been, sane, but I know that I will not. Because that contaminated place has been waiting for me.

It's hungry again.

M.A. SMITH
ABOUT THE AUTHOR

MA Smith writes from Gloucestershire, UK, where she lives with her family. Her short fiction is published regularly in magazines that include Dark Moon Digest, Gallery of Curiosities, Andromeda Spaceways, Mythic and The British Fantasy Society's 'Horizons' anthology. Smith's novella, 'Severance,' is a sci-fi/dark fantasy re-working of the classic fairy-tale 'The Little Mermaid,' and was published in 2018 by Fantasia Divinity.

https://www.facebook.com/masmithwriting/
www.masmithwriting.com

Interference
Matthew A. St. Cyr

The sunlight was starting to sink, and had turned a deep gold by the time Samantha and Patrick reached the summit of Mount Wixatonic. Sam put her backpack on a large, smooth rock on the ground. She pulled out two water bottles and two granola bars, tossing one of each to Patrick. They sat together in silence, looking out at the vista that splayed out before them. From this vantage point you could see all of Harper below them, and as far as Worcester. The two sat, with their backs to the sun, watching seemingly microscopic life go about their daily routines beneath them.

"I've been doing a lot of thinking lately," Patrick said. "I don't want to spend the rest of my life as a tech in the emergency room."

Samantha swallowed the last of her granola bar, taking a large swig of water before answering. "Okay. Well, what did you have in mind?"

"Nursing school." He said softly, not turning to meet his gaze.

"Nursing school. . ." Samantha repeated thoughtfully. "You've been thinking about this for a while?"

"For about a year." He said quickly, quietly. "I've been trying to think of a way to bring it up."

"Well," Samantha took in a deep breath and held it for a moment, returning her gaze to the world below. "I think that's an absolutely absolutely amazing idea." She smirked when she saw his head suddenly whip around in surprise.

"Really?" He almost shouted.

"Of course! Why didn't you bring this up sooner?" She grabbed his hand, letting their fingers fold together.

Patrick shrugged, feeling a little self conscious. "Well, first we bought the house, then there were all the repairs that had to be done. I know you need a new car, and we just talked about trying to have a baby. Nursing school is expensive, and time consuming, so I guess I thought I was being selfish."

"Babe, listen. Yes, we want to have kids, but we're both only twenty-three. We've got plenty of time. As for money, we'll figure it out. Maybe I can take a loan out of my 401k to help, and you're not being selfish. Wanting to improve your career before we start a family is about as far away from selfish as you can get." She kissed his lips and touched her forehead to his, smiling.

"You're such a goober."

They sat in content silence for a while longer. The

sun had sunk low, casting the mountain's shadow for miles below them. To the southeast tiny specks of neon light sparked to life, some beginning to dance around each other like pastel fireflies.

"Oh, look!" Patrick said, pointing to the lights. "A carnival!"

"I read that there was one coming around. I think it's in Swinton." Samantha smiled. "Wanna go?"

"Most definitely!" Patrick stood, offering her a hand up. "Let's roll, Starsky!"

Samantha stretched as she stood and took one more look around. Her smile faded a bit as she looked towards the west.

"What's up?" he asked.

"I think we stayed up here too long, babe. It's going to get dark before we get to the bottom." She picked up her pack, slinging it around her shoulders and clipping it in the front.

"We'll be okay. We've hiked up here before, and I've got my map just in case." he smiled and winked at her. "No problem."

"Yeah, that's true." She playfully slapped his butt. "Let's do it, Hutch."

• • •

Starting their descent the couple laughed, joked and reminisced about old commercials from the 80's as they tried to remember as many jingles and out-of-production products as they could. That then turned into a game in which each of them would sing the theme song from an old sitcom, while the other tried to guess the show.

"Okay, try this one." Samantha said after wrongly guessing the theme song from Perfect Strangers. She took in a breath to start singing, but Patrick suddenly let out a yelp as he stumbled and fell, rolling several feet down the incline and landing up against a tree. Samantha froze in place for a heartbeat, shocked by the sudden outcry and motion. Coming quickly to her senses she hurried to Patrick, who wasn't moving.

"Baby, are you okay!?" she kneeled next to him. "Patrick?"

"My leg–" he took a sharp breath in.

"Okay baby, lie still." She took out her phone and flicked on the flashlight, scanning the light over his legs.

Both legs were covered in scratches and cuts, some fairly deep, and blood was running down to stain his socks a deep crimson. His left knee was deformed and swelling, and Samantha clenched her teeth and tried her best to ignore the churning in her stomach. She had never understood how Patrick could be so calm around blood and injuries. She usually fainted at the sight of a simple cut, let alone the carnage that was on full display now. She fought waves of dizziness as she got the first aid kit out of his backpack.

"Your legs are pretty cut up," she said. "And your knee is all messed up too. Like, really bad."

"It's dislocated." Patrick said wincing.

"I'm calling 911." Her voice wavered, trying to remain composed.

"No, I can–" His words were cut short by the sharp glance she gave him. "Okay." He said softly. "Okay."

Samantha dialed the phone and hit the send button. A ball of ice formed in her stomach as the words 'NO SERVICE' flashed across the screen.

"There's no signal." she said and then cleared her throat. "I can't call out."

"I can hobble down." Patrick said. "We'll find a big stick that I can use as a crutch, and I'll hobble down. It will be fine."

"How?" She countered. "It's almost completely dark out."

"We don't really have much of a choice here, babe. It's too dangerous to go alone in the dark. What happens if you fall? Then we're both down in seperate places, and we'd be pretty easy pickings for a hungry mountain lion wandering by."

Samantha hung her head. "Yeah, alright, point taken. Let's at least try to clean up the cuts on your legs so you're not dripping all over the mountain."

"Mmm." Patrick wrinkled his nose. "Patrick drippings."

"Gross." she said pulling out the antiseptic wipes and gauze, unable to stop herself from smiling.

"See?" He put his hand on her arm. "It's not that bad. Just like Nana always says: 'If you can laugh, all is not lost.'"

Samantha leaned forward and kissed him gently. "Let's get you patched up."

She worked as quickly as she could, wiping dirt, leaves and pine needles out of cuts and cleaning the wounds with the wipes. She then wrapped his legs from the knee down with gauze, while Patrick held the light for her. She found an Ace bandage and wrapped his knee as tight as she could.

"Well, I'm no nurse, but it'll have to do." She said, standing up.

"You did great, baby." he said. "Now see if you can find a real big stick that I can use to cosplay Gandalf while we climb down Mount Doom."

"You're such a nerd." she laughed and wrinkled her nose. "Stay here, I'll be right back."

"Hilarious." Patrick said, mocking a deadpan expression.

A few moments later she returned with a sizable branch that forked at the end. With a considerable amount of effort, plus some grunting and more than one expletive, Patrick was back on his feet. The branch was a little long, but since they were on a fairly sharp decline that worked to his advantage. He was able to stand on his own, but he would need Samantha's help to steady himself as they made their way down.

"We're going to have to leave one pack behind." She said. "I can't carry both and help you at the same time." Opening both packs she started to consolidate as much as she could. She managed to squeeze the food and water into her pack, but had to take their fleece jackets and tie them around each of her backpack straps.

"This will have to do." She said standing up. "Ready?"

"No, but let's try it anyway." Patrick winked. "What's the worst that could happen?"

"Worst case, for you anyway, I get rich off the crazy huge life insurance policy I just took out on you last week." She wiggled her eyebrows. "My plan is all coming together."

"You ain't right." Patrick furrowed his brow. "That's just wrong."

"Alright, Hopalong Cassidy, let's boogey." She said as she gently slapped his butt.

• • •

It took nearly an hour to travel about a quarter mile, with Patrick having to plan each and every step in advance. He was poking his make-shift crutch into the sloping ground ahead of him, testing for holes, rocks, sticks or slippery leaves. There were a few times that the stick caught just the edge of a large rock, or large patch of moss-covered log, and Patrick thought he was going to go down. He managed to adjust his balance and stay vertical, much to their surprise and relief.

It was full dark, with no moon, when they reached the first signpost for Dunn's Falls to signal that they were about halfway down the mountain. Both breathed a sigh of relief. The steepest part of the mountain was behind them, and in about one third of a mile the trail would be much wider and have far fewer obstacles in their path. These were the trails that were mostly used by recreational hikers, mountain bikers and even a few joggers looking to up their cardio game. Once they got onto them it would be far smoother sailing. Patrick leaned against the wooden sign post, stretching his back as best as he could. Leaning on the make-shift crutch was not doing any favors for his spine.

"Babe, I need to take a minute here." he said.

"Yeah, I could use a rest too." she agreed. "Are you thirsty?"

Patrick slid himself down the side of the signpost, careful to keep his bad knee straight on the way down. He took his phone out of his pocket, flicking on the flashlight and shining it on his legs. He could see that his left knee was swollen at least three times its normal size, even under all the bandaging.

He imagined Dr. Sessler in the ER, his frizzy grey hair jutting out every which way as he stroked his beard as he examined Patrick's knee. I suspect you have injured yourself, he would say. Doctor Obvious–that's what most of the staff called him when he wasn't around. He had a slightly annoying, yet somehow charming, idiosyncrasy of always overstating the obvious in any situation.

Patrick was pulled out of his thoughts by Samantha handing him a bottle of water. She also handed him a couple of pills from the first aid pack.

"Aspirin." she said.

"Thank you." He said taking the pills and holding onto one of her hands. He pulled her close and kissed her lips. "I love you."

"I love you too." She smiled.

They sat for a moment and looked at a small cluster of stars that shone through an opening in the canopy of leaves overhead. Patrick glanced down at his phone to check the time.

"We should get moving again." he said. "It's about a quarter of eleven."

With a small sigh she stood up and dusted her bottom off, then extended a hand to help him get to his feet. Once he was up, and had his crutch in position, he leaned against the sign for a moment as she put the water bottles back into the pack. Just as she was zipping the side compartment an unearthly sound echoed through the trees.

"Jesus! What the Hell was that?" Samantha jumped.

"Pretty sure that was a fisher cat." Patrick said, "It's okay babe. They rarely attack people, unless provoked."

"That was not a fisher cat, Patrick." She said. "I know what they sound like, and that was definitely not it."

"Well, there's only one other thing that I can think of that it could be then." he said.

"What?" her voice cracked and she hated herself for it.

"Sasquatch." Patrick said matter of factly. "Looking to make you his forest bride."

"You suck." She said wryly.

"I'm sure if it's not a fisher cat then it's some other small little critter that makes a lot of noise." Patrick started to take a step forward "As a matter of fact, I'm sure—"

A loud crack silenced Patrick for just a beat before he screamed, falling to the ground. His phone flew out of his hand and landed several yards downhill, casting long shadows among the trees. He writhed on the ground like a serpent, unable to speak, only uttering guttural growls of agony.

"Patrick! What? What happened!?" Samantha was at his side instantly.

She frantically shone her flashlight on him, trying to figure out what was happening. The light caught a glint of metal, and as she looked towards his legs ice filled her spine. The culprit came into focus: Patrick's right ankle was caught in a bear trap, the rusted, metal teeth pierced deep into his flesh.

"What…." Patrick's eyes fluttered as he fought the waves of pain, feeling himself blacking out.

"Stay with me baby, I need you to stay awake for me." Samantha tried to steady her voice. "Your ankle is in a bear trap. I'm going to try to open it, and I need you to pull your leg out when it's open, okay?"

Patrick nodded, still fighting the urge to pass out.

"Okay," she said. "On the count of three, yeah? One—two—three!"

She pushed down with all her might on the trap, trying to loosen the main spring, but it wouldn't budge. Patrick howled in pain and fell back, losing consciousness.

"Shit!" Samantha took in a deep breath and tried again.

At least with Patrick unconscious she didn't have to worry about causing him more pain. She again pushed down with all of her strength, but the jaws wouldn't so much as move and inch. Patrick's eyes fluttered, but he didn't wake up. She sat back and put her face in her hands, the blood rushing in her ears.

The only reasonable thing to do is go for help, she thought. Even if I got his foot out of the trap, his left knee is busted up and now so is his right ankle. There's no way he'll make it without being carried.

With her mind made up she untied both jackets from the backpack, rolling one up as a pillow and putting it under Patrick's head. The other she draped over him as a make-shift blanket. She dug the water and granola bars out of the pack and placed them next to him within easy reaching distance, then she went and retrieved his phone. She placed it next to the food.

Thunder rolled in the distance, and she looked skyward. She couldn't see any clouds from her vantage point, but the thunder was coming from the west.

"Damnit, that's all I need." she said. The thought of Patrick waking up alone and injured on the side of a mountain during a thunderstorm made her sick to her stomach, and she needed to move quickly.

She wrote a quick note on a white water rafting brochure that Patrick had picked up at a rest stop along the interstate a few months ago, telling him that she had gone for help and not to move. She put the note on top of his phone and kissed his cheek.

"I'll be back as soon as I can." She said. "I love you."

• • •

Samantha made her way through the darkness as fast as she could. The widened trails and the more gradual incline made it easier to move at a quicker pace, not to mention being free of the burden of the backpack. She used her phone's flashlight to light the way, occasionally stopping to check and see if there was any signal–her heart sinking each time in disappointment.

The thunder was getting closer, and louder. There was something in the sound that made her uneasy, but she couldn't quite put her finger on what it was. Somehow the thunder sounded wrong, and on more than occasion she was sure she heard the same unearthly sound they heard before Patrick stepped in the bear trap. It was closer than before. It sounded like an animalistic howl, if it were filtered through the sound of an old dial up modem. It seemed as though the sound, and whatever was making it, was following her.

At last she was within sight of the small, wooded parking lot. A single amber light buzzed lazily from its perch atop a small billboard, a map of the mountain on the sign. Moths and other assorted insects flew it tight, circular patterns around the light, casting flitting shadows over the lot. Their car sat directly next to the lit billboard.

Just as Samantha grabbed her phone it began to ring, surprising her to the point where she almost dropped it. It was Patrick. He must have woken up and somehow had signal. She quickly answered.

"Baby! Are you–" She was cut off by a loud whine and hiss. Pulling the phone from her ear, she looked down to find that the phone was in video chat mode. On the screen Patrick still lay unconscious on the ground. Oh dear God, she thought, there's someone up there with him. On screen the mysterious figure continued to move around Patrick, bringing the phone it close to his body and lingering on his legs. The video came to rest on the bear trap stuck on his ankle.

A crackle of static, then the video shifted. The bear trap was now inexplicably off of his foot. Whoever was operating the camera was now holding the trap in front of the camera, and they were moving back up towards Patrick's head.

Patrick's eyes fluttered open and immediately looked towards the camera, eyes wide in terror. Before he could utter a word, the trap was thrust down violently onto his face, the metal jaws sinking deep into his skull on either side. He shuddered and twitched for a moment, letting out a muffled scream, then fell silent.

Samantha watched, horrified, frozen in place. The screen went back to static, followed by a blinding flash. Her hand was immediately wracked in searing pain that quickly traveled up her arm, and an instant later she was unconscious.

. . .

When she opened her eyes again she found that she was lying next to the sign post that she left Patrick next to. The jackets and backpack were still there, but he was gone. His phone lay on the ground, still in video call mode. Blood covered the ground, the jackets and the signpost.

Spears of icey fear stabbed at her gut as she got to her feet. There were no drag marks, no other footprints, no animal tracks, nothing. It was as if he simply vanished.

"Patrick!" She screamed into the darkness. "Baby, where are you?"

She fell to her knees sobbing. Patrick was gone. Something was very, very wrong here. As she knelt, trying to catch her breath, a scream split the night air like a razor.

"Patrick." She held her breath and listened.

Again, a scream that seemed impossibly far away. It was Patrick, she knew it was. He needed her. She steeled herself and stood up, limbs shaking wildly. She had to find him. She began to move, feeling like she was walking through water. Her feet were clumsily catching on rocks and twigs as she moved as quickly as she could in the direction she heard Patrick.

Lightning flashed, illuminating the trees around her in brilliant light. The thunder that immediately followed crackled and hissed. Much louder now, she could hear what had been eluding her before—there was a sound of static in the thunder, much like the snowy static on a television. The lightning flashed again, and the thunder followed almost immediately. She looked up and the sky was still completely clear, the stars shining brightly. The sound of the static in the thunder lingered in the atmosphere, echoing off the trees and rocks around her.

A feeling of being watched crept it's way down her spine and she turned off her flashlight, suddenly feeling vulnerable and exposed. The static was still hissing and as the light from her phone died she was shocked to find that the trees in front of her were still illuminated with a flickering light. A fresh shot of icy fear shot straight into her heart and she slowly turned around to look behind her.

Sitting in a low tree branch, about eye level with her, was a small, flatscreen television. Snowy static filled the screen, casting dancing shadows around it. The thunderous static hissed from its speakers. Samantha blinked hard, trying to wrap her head around what she was seeing. Suddenly the entire world felt wrong. The air smelled of electrical discharge, and the hairs on her arms stood on end.

The television's volume increased to almost deafening levels and the snow began to fade, giving way to a picture. Patrick was sitting up against the trunk of a large tree, the bear trap still over his face. She could see his chest rise and fall sporadically, and wet, gurgling sounds emanated from beneath the trap.

A figure appeared to the right of the screen. At first it looked like nothing more than snowy static, but quickly took on a humanoid shape. It moved like a man, but it was completely made of static.

The static man moved quickly and silently in front of Patrick, obscuring her view of him except for his legs. There was a fast flurry of unnatural motion, and Patrick's legs began to writhe in agony. The figure moved to the side, she could see that the trap had been removed from Patrick's face. His eyes fluttered as the thing reached a luminous arm out and put it's hand to his face. His eyes suddenly opened wide.

Patrick let out an agonised scream. The creature joined in with its unearthly howl, both of which could be heard through the television and in the distance.

Samantha stood with her hands clasped tightly over her mouth, tears leaving small, clean trails on her dirty face and hands. The lightning flashed and the television switched off, leaving her standing in the darkness. Her legs shook as her rapid breath came out in rasps. The pit in her stomach shifted, and her jaws clenched. She fell to her knees and vomited so hard that she felt as though her back may break.

Out of the corner of her eye she saw another flicker. The static man was standing next to several large pine trees, silent and still. Though it had no face, or distinguishing features, she could tell that it was staring at her.

She pushed herself up on shaking arms, forcing herself to stand. The static remained motionless. Samantha began to back slowly away from the thing, and after about three steps it shot itself straight up into the air, creating a flash of lightning and a clap of thunder. Samantha stood and looked upwards for any sign of the being, but found only stars.

She stood frozen in a horrible state of indecision. Should she return to Patrick to help him? Was there even anything that she could do? Was he even alive? What was that thing? Would it be coming back?

She knew her best hope, and Patrick's, was to find help as fast as possible. Her legs felt as though they were made of rubber as she began to move down the path again, her mind swirling with a thousand thoughts and questions. All she knew for certain was that she needed to get help and get back to him as fast as possible.

It wasn't long before there was another flash of lightning and crash of static thunder. Again the static hiss remained. There was a bright flash, and snowy static appeared in the trunk of a nearby pine tree in a vertical fashion, as if a television was turned on its side. The white screen once again gave way to a picture. This time it was of a large, dead oak tree in a small clearing surrounded by thick woods.

She could see the static man hovering around a branch about halfway up. His arms were moving rapidly, but it was unclear what he was doing. Holding her breath she stepped closer to the screen embedded in the tree. The static man suddenly moved backwards, and a dark object fell. Samantha squinted and moved closer, trying to figure out what she was looking at until it became terribly clear.

It was Patrick hanging from a noose, the bear trap

still attached to his face. His body twitched a couple of times, and then fell still.

Samantha hadn't realised how close to screen she had gotten until it filled again with snowy static, and a loud hissing split the silent night air. The screen rippled, forming waves that moved like liquid across the surface, and a hand made of snowy static reached through the screen to grab her wrist.

The static hand burned her flesh as she struggled against it, and she could feel her flesh bubble and pop beneath. She tried to grab hold of the fingers to pry them off, but her other hand was shocked with a spark of electricity that left her fingers numb and paralysed.

"Please, no!" She cried.

The hand pulled her closer to the screen. She could feel intense heat and electricity as her face came centimeters away from the screen. Tiny tendrils of static reached from the screen, latching onto her face and burning like tiny matches. Two large tentacles shot out on either side of the screen, wrapping themselves around her body. Intense waves of pain wracked her as the smell of burning clothing and hair hit her nostrils. In one swift motion she was pulled into screen with a sickening sucking noise, then the world went black.

• • •

Samantha opened her eyes. Patrick's lifeless body hung five feet in front of her. His body was badly burned, and the bear trap had been reattached to his face. It was only a few seconds before she realised that she herself was in unbearable pain. Her hair had been burned off down to the scalp. Her clothes had been burned off, the nylon straps of her bra melted into her skin, but the cotton had burned away. Her arms had been stretched behind her and over a branch that hung at shoulder level. There was a noose made of vines hanging around her neck. She could feel liquid dripping down her legs, but she couldn't tell if it was blood, urine or melted flesh.

A flickering light illuminated the woods in front of her. The static man appeared and floated in between the trees, weaving in and out of them as if playing a game. It circled her several times, each pass coming a little closer until finally it stood at the bottom of the large, dead oak. Slowly it ascended through the air until it was directly in front of her. She could feel it smiling, though it had no face. She could smell electricity over the scent of Patrick's and her own burnt flesh.

"Please." She whispered.

Luminous tentacles of snowy static shot from its sides and wrapped around the branch she was standing on, immediately catching the wood on fire. She lowered her eyes to see the thin branch engulfed in flames, and what was left of her lower lip trembled as her gaze shifted from the static man to Patrick.

"I love you." she said, just before the branch gave way underneath her.

She fell quickly and barely felt the sharp snap in her neck. The last thing she saw before the darkness took her was the trunk of the dead oak she was hanging from, the bark glowing as static spread outwards into the rest of the forest.

MATTHEW A. ST. CYR
ABOUT THE AUTHOR

Matthew A. St. Cyr was born, raised and still resides in Massachusetts. From a young age he was fascinated by the unnatural and the unexplained and as a student in elementary school would often write book reports on books about UFO's, ghosts and Bigfoot, much to the disturbance of his teachers. Surprisingly, the Children's Public Library in Fitchburg, Massachusetts had a rather robust selection in what could be considered occult subjects back in the the nineteen-eighties.

As a youth, his interests in the mysterious and unexplained led to an obsession with magic and illusion, which became his primary focus for much of his young life, eventually finding work as a professional magician for a number of years after high school. This led to his discovery of bizarre magick, a lesser known genre of the craft which relies more on story telling than it does flashy boxes and sawing pretty girls in half.

He began to write small tales of terror to accompany his illusions and prestidigitations and while he still performs a wonder or two when the mood strikes him, he fell in love with the writing of the tales and it eventually became his main focus.

Today, Matthew spends his time dreaming up new stories from his home in Western Massachusetts, which he shares with his wife and three cats. On occasion, when the stars align just so, he will still perform the odd piece of magic for friends, family or even the occasional stranger, especially while spinning yarns around the fire in his backyard.

You can follow Matthew's ramblings at:

https://matthewastcyr.blogspot.com/

Facebook: https://www.facebook.com/MatthewAStCyr

Twitter: @MatthewAStCyr.

Getting Away from It All
Greg Hunter

When the first wound spoke to Jonathan, he was several miles off the designated trail — this was by design, although the cut had come by accident. It was a three-inch-long abrasion above his left ankle, which he'd caught sliding down the subtle incline that led him away from the trailhead on the first day of his long weekend. Provided he evaded the detection of the park's rangers, he would be set for three nights of camping without another soul around.

He was surprised by the voice from the start, but the surprise was in proportion to his agenda: an innocuous, if technically illegal, weekend of getting away from it all. At the end he would clear out his site by the same standards of the park's designated overnight areas, probably even with more diligence than those areas' campers. He would certainly cleanup without the kind of noise pollution that had led him to this, his single renegade activity.

Sing-alongs, shouting matches, bawling infants — they amounted to toll beyond the price of a park permit, one which he no longer wanted to pay.

He'd initially mistaken his ankle wound's first words as chatter from a party of like-minded purists, people who would hopefully make camp at an agreeable distance. This impression did not last long. When the wound spoke again, its nearness was audible, obvious, and very unlike conversation traveling through the trees.

North now, the voice said, *to the ground beneath the peak.* A hushed confidence.

As the speaker repeated itself, Jon scanned the oaks around him, seeing no one. He was waiting to catch sight of a bright Patagonia vest, or for a polyester tent bag to appear between the trees. He looked in the direction of the wound only after repetition, the fourth North, which forced into his reasoning the possibility of a speaker at his feet. Even then, at the earliest consideration of something extranormal, he'd still expected a face. Someone prone in the grass he'd somehow failed to notice. Even a frog, whose croaks could become audible as such, would amend themselves in his ear as soon as he'd identified the thing. But instead it was the wound, tremorring slightly as sound escaped it once again.

North now, to the ground beneath the peak.

Jonathan had hydrated carefully and only thirty minutes earlier had let loose a clear, colorless stream, but he twisted open his canteen and took several gulps, addressing the most likely source of his delirium. Next a handful of trail mix, in case it was an instance of creeping hunger. An egg white omelet the morning of these trips had always been sufficient, but he'd have to reevaluate his whole meal plan. He began to retrace his steps southwards, disappointed about his early return, but not willing to be a cautionary tale.

An itch traversed the ankle wound, and the voice grew in volume. Jonathan paused at this, but did not allow himself to stop for long. The sudden strain on his faculties might work like quicksand, intensifying its hold with any loss of composure. He stepped forward again, and once more reopened his canteen. When no voice sounded, Jon quickened his pace, until the wound spoke even more loudly than before. He raised his foot, as if to shake the sounds away, and fell sideways into the sage scrub. He grazed his palms, drawing blood.

North now, to the ground beneath the peak, the wound urged him, and as he raised his red palms to examine them the skin began to ripple and hiss.

Beneath the peak, the hands said, *beneath the peak,* their twinned voices thinner than his ankle's.

Jon put the hands at his sides, feeling both faint and unsure about heading farther south. If steps to the north might quiet the voices then he could resolve at least one problem.

It was mid-afternoon, if his sense of time had maintained itself. Beyond the tops of the oak trees the sun shone widely, but gently. He began to calculate the hours until nightfall. What this would determine, Jon didn't know — he was far off the park paths in any case. His hands hissed the peak, the peak, and he started to walk north again, erasing any southward progress. If he could quiet them then he could think, really think, and outline his best plan of action.

The ground beneath the peak would be three, maybe four miles away. He had not conceded that the voices would direct him, but this was a consideration in silencing them for a while. It did seem to keep them quiet. Once northbound the voices relented for a few minutes, while Jon stepped over bushes and between tree trunks. After a few minutes more he allowed himself to again consider the likelihood of delirium, of hunger or heatstroke — explanations incompatible with his gear and keen meal planning, but among the few plausible ones. He would not turn to face the south, but perhaps that was its own sign he had nothing to fear. He'd walk north of his own volition.

More water was wise in any case, and he reached toward his backpack's side pocket for the canteen, squeezing it against his ribs with one wrist and nudging it out of place. He gripped the canteen between both wrists next, keeping his grazed hands off of the metal. Beneath the peak, they said, and his ankle followed, more loudly: *North now, to the ground beneath the peak.*

Jon knelt among the scrub and vomited. Mostly water, with only the faintest sting. He considered certain things, such as if the wound scabbing over would end the talk or only muffle it. How long would that take, and would a scab trap something under his skin? If the only step was to let something out, to widen the wounds, then he could do it. He'd packed a multi-tool. But then the ankle broke his concentration, commanding him to move.

By the time the sky began to iterate, to reveal shades of gold and purple, Jon had walked far longer than he'd planned to that morning. His boots were new to the spring camping season, and his feet hadn't fully made a home in them. They felt weighted and swollen now. When he came upon a stream, he stopped and untied the laces, not worried about being scolded. He peeled off his socks next, examining the imminent blisters. He listened for a hum, or something like one, but he couldn't be sure they'd speak. Not until they burst, then he'd know.

Putting the socks back on was more difficult than taking them off, the fabric soaked with sweat and bundled up into itself. He stretched the breathable wool micro-knit as he eased them along his feet again, warping them beyond future use but cautious about troubling his blisters. When he was finished he felt soreness in his fingertips too, having used only the very ends of his hands. Then the ankle urged him north again, his grated palms echoing the ankle.

They — *he* — would reach the ground beneath the peak by mid-evening, Jonathan figured. Perhaps the day's fading light would still be there to illuminate whatever he — he — would find, for better or for worse. He uncapped his canteen and found it empty, remembering he'd drained it an hour earlier. Ahead of him the sage scrub grew thicker, no obvious footpath anywhere before his destination and few traces of people trying to get through.

He had not asked them why this place, or what to expect. For much of the walk, refusing the speakers any replies had helped preserve the possibility that his day had largely been imagined, a bulwark against certain frightening conclusions. You did not talk to things that weren't real — and if you weren't talking, they weren't real.

This stance had benefits even beyond Jon's awareness. He decided at last to ask something, to be better prepared for whatever they'd eventually see. It was best to be direct — what will we find? But after settling on a question, he could not ask it, could not speak.

There was no portent, no tightening or burning at the back of his throat. There was just the non-response of some station between mind and speech, something slack, diminished, or occupied. With this he panicked, really panicked, more than before. Jon's breathing hastened and he turned around, desperate to avoid the north, the peak, the stopping point. On pained feet he ran like a marionette, knees rising at odd angles, legs making rapid, irregular strides. His wounds growled, repeating their demands in raised voices. It was easier now to block them out, to listen to his lungs, the sound of labored breaths still able to escape Jon's mouth.

He cleared the scrub in single strides, the backs of his hands slapping aside canyon flowers and mariposa lilies. He managed this for several minutes, until the flora grew denser, stems and leaves nicking his forearms and hostile choirs trilling along the skin. He parted one bush to find a wide tree before him, his face colliding with the trunk before he could stop.

Jon knew it was a broken nose without knowing exactly what that meant. The blood dripping onto his quick-dry shirt looked black in the dim evening light, marking either the end or the beginning of something. He thought for a moment that he was about to sneeze — the sensation was very close to that, then the voice came through his nostrils. It was in his ears almost before it left his nose.

North, now. To the ground beneath the peak.

Jon reversed again and started walking.

The valley was still when he reached it. His wounds were silent, their bearer not in a condition to speak. The flowers and scrub thinned out before the bottom of the mound, and the peak cast a long, angular shadow across the grass. Nightfall had not fully taken hold. Jon could see them well enough: men and women covered in the day's scratches and cuts, blood spotting along their outerwear. Some of them raw, their bodies overtaken. The bearers all looked upward at the crag, dozens of them, not making camp but waiting. Jon stationed himself among them, sliding through small gaps between bodies until he stood in the innermost ring. Surrounded, although he couldn't say that he minded.

GREG HUNTER
ABOUT THE AUTHOR

Greg Hunter is a writer-editor based in Minneapolis. He is kind to animals and serious about breakfast. He is a regular contributor to TCJ.com, and his writing has also been featured at LARB, The Rumpus, The Official Catalog of the Library of Potential Literature, and elsewhere. Find him on Twitter @gregjhunter.

Fairies in the forest
Jason Holden

The drive had been a quiet one. Warren, Alex's son, had hardly spoken to him for the two-hour drive. The kid was fourteen now, and Alex knew he had more interest in his phone and social media pages than he did in spending time with his dad. Since the divorce Alex only got to see his son for two days every third weekend. It wasn't enough, so he'd decided on a trip to his own father's old cabin. He hadn't been there since his dad died a year ago, and the last few trips had not held pleasant memories. He had been losing his mind towards the end of his life, and improperly diagnosed dementia had left him unstable. He had been raving about magical creatures, fairies mostly.

However, the cabin held some good memories from his childhood. Playing in the forest that surrounded it, and sitting by the fire and hearing his dad tell stories of magical worlds, were fresh in his mind. His dad had always had a vivid imagination, so things like camping out and hunting for the fairies became obsessions towards the end of his life. Alex was sure Warren would lose interest in his devices once they arrived in that wonderful place, and then they could finally get some quality bonding time in. Pushing the button in the dash panel, Alex muted the sounds of the car's radio, putting an end to Freddy singing "Radio gaga". Then he leaned over, and with two fingers flicked the wire holding the earbud into his son's ear, sending it tumbling down.

"Hey, aren't you even a little curious where we're going?"

"Grandad's cabin in the woods." Warren made to put his earbud back in, and started playing a game on his Switch again.

"Aww, come on mate! I haven't seen you for three weeks, at least talk to me for the last fifteen minutes of the drive, yeah?"

Warren smiled, putting his Switch in his backpack as he looked out of the window at the pine trees whizzing by.

"Remember how Grandad would play the guitar and sing all those silly folk songs about goblins?"

They talked the rest of the journey. It was just what Alex had hoped for with this weekend, to reconnect with his son, and so far it was so good. On the approach to the cabin they took a narrow, winding road, which eventually straightened out and would lead them right up to the door. As soon as he hit the straightaway Alex put his foot down, releasing the full 240bhp from his VW Golf's engine. Having driven this road many times he knew every dip and every bend. Besides, he wanted to show off a bit to his son. Then, out of nowhere, he slammed hard on the brakes. Alex and Warren were flung forwards, and the car's back end let loose, throwing them into a fishtail. They came to a stop, just inches from a tree that had fallen across the road.

"Christ, that made me clench. Are you alright mate?" Alex opened his door and stepped out, walking to the fallen tree. Across the trunk someone had carved the word DANGER! in thick, jagged letters. Warren came up alongside his dad as Alex was rubbing his fingers into the grooves that made up the letters.

"Do you think Grandad did it?" he asked

"Yeah, I think so. You know he wasn't well towards the end, though by then you were with your mum at the other end of the country. For once I was glad you weren't close by, It's better that you remember him how he was before."

"I'm sorry Dad." Warren slipped an arm around his dad's waist, and Alex's heart jumped a bit. He couldn't think how long it had been since his son hugged him last. Since the divorce, maybe even further back?

"Grab the tow rope from the boot mate. Let's get this thing shifted."

Warren made his way round to the back of the car and opened up the trunk. Grunting, he lifted the spare tire out to get at the tow rope that his dad had stored underneath it. It slipped from his hands and fell, rolling towards the bushes. He watched it go, bouncing across the ruts of the road before wobbling and coming to rest against a bush at the far side of the road. Warren threw the rope to his dad and went to fetch the tire, but as he bent low the bush it rested against exploded into movement. A jackrabbit burst out, cannoning into Warren's chest and knocking him from his feet before disappearing back into the bushes. Hearing Warren's shout, Alex dropped what he was doing and rushed round to the back of the car.

"Alright there mate?" He asked, picking his son from the ground before collecting the tire. Warren rubbed at his chest where he'd been struck, "Yeah, yeah. It was a rabbit jumping on me." He followed his dad back to the car, "It's weird, I could swear that rabbit had horns or something."

Alex laughed, "Yeah? Maybe it was a unicorn rabbit?"

They made the rest of the trip to the cabin at a slow pace, just in case of anymore surprises left by the old man. Soon enough Alex parked the car, and they unloaded their gear and opened the cabin. Instantly they were hit by a stale smell, damp and unpleasant. Warren propped the door open with his bag, and went to open the windows around the cabin while Alex moved their gear for the weekend inside. Loaded up with suitcases and shopping bags Alex weaved his way past the furniture to the bedroom his father used to sleep in, now his he supposed. He dropped the bags on the bed with a muted thump, sending dust swirling into the air that made him sneeze. He watched the dust motes play in the air, dancing in the breeze from the open window. Something parted them through the middle, sending them flying in opposite directions, dancing more frantically before settling again.

It whizzed past his ear, grazing the lobe and buzzing loudly.

"Bloody countryside, full of damn bugs!" He exclaimed, flapping his hand through the air at the already long-gone source of the sound. Putting his hand to his ear he pulled it back, surprised to see blood on his fingertips. "Whatever that thing was, it was big for a bug." Shrugging, Alex moved off to gather the rest of their things from the car.

On his last trip in Alex was called into a room by his son. Inside Warren had found notebooks and old, leather-bound journals, all of which were full of writings about fairies. They were complete with drawings and collected "proof" of their existence. Two wings that looked a lot like they belonged on the back of a dragonfly were taped inside, one on either side of a drawing of a small green humanoid. The writing above it was neat and clear. It read "Tooth fairy", and the next page held a larger picture of the fairy's hand. The fingers were lined with hooks that the book stipulated were "for gripping the teeth of humans, to achieve smoother extraction".

Everything was labelled and explained in great detail, including the loud noise the four wings of the fairies made in flight. Warren ran his hand across the page, smoothing it carefully.

"Even if it's all made up, this book is amazing. Maybe we could get it published in the fantasy section or something?"

Alex closed the book, touching his ear where it had been cut as he shrugged. "Like I said, he wasn't well."

He moved to a small bird cage next at the other end of the table, picking it up and turning over in his hands. The lock that held the door closed was broken, and the door flapped open as he turned it.

"I tried to get him to leave this place for months, but he was stubborn and wouldn't move an inch. In the end he left himself, then checked into a home. Must have felled that tree on his way out I guess. I don't know why he left all his stuff here." Alex put the cage down, releasing a shower of dust into the air. "Come on, let's make a brew and unpack."

They spent the rest of the day cleaning out the cabin, unpacking and talking. Warren complained about all the work they were doing, but Alex could tell he was enjoying himself as he explored the old cabin. They even found the guitar that was the subject of many happy memories for Alex, and to his dad's amazement Warren started to play on it. It turned out he had been learning all summer from a girl at his school. He blushed when he said it, and Alex knew not to push the subject. He couldn't help feeling a little inward, fatherly moment of pride at the thought of his son's first girlfriend with the way Alex had talked about her.

With the cabin clean and fresh, Alex cooked bacon sandwiches for himself and Warren. They sat at the freshly polished table and ate in silence, until Warren asked,

"Can I please go look at that book of Grandad's again dad? I know it's hard for you to see, but it's really cool, and the pictures are good."

Alex rubbed a hand over the stubble on his check, feeling the rasp on his fingertips.

"I don't know mate. I just want to forget that part of his life. He was always so clever before the last few months. You know he went to the dentist and had all his teeth pulled? He told the dentist it was so he could just get it over with and move onto dentures, but he kept telling me how he did it so the fairies couldn't get them. It was so real to him."

Warren wouldn't let it go though, and before the evening was over he sat in one of the great chairs with the thick, leather-bound book on his lap flipping through the pages.

"Look here Dad," he said holding the book open and showing a picture to Alex,

"This looks like the rabbit I saw with horns. Says here it's a Jackalope, doesn't like people much, a bit mean. Sounds right, it did jump at me."

Alex looked and shook his head, "You're just imagining things mate. If these things in your grandad's book were real don't you think there'd be proof in the world? Real proof, not just the ramblings of an old man in an old book?"

Warren went quiet, flipping through the pages of the book some more. Alex could see he hurt his son's feelings with his short reply, so he tried to apologize.

"Look, I'm sorry..."

Warren cut him off, "No, you're right Dad, it's fake. It's a good job too though, look at this one."

Alex took the book and sat on the arm of Warren's chair, gazing down at a picture of a large creature. It was covered in moss, and had what looked like branches sticking out of its body seemingly at random. The blazing, yellow eyes seemed to stare right through Alex, and his stomach grew tight as he read through the text.

The Wendigo:

I have only encountered this Fae once in all my time studying the criptoids of this forest, for this I am grateful. Large and powerful, with an all-encompassing need to feed on raw flesh of living things. I saw it burst from the trees and chase down a deer as easily as though the poor creature was standing still, lifting it from the ground and ripping it clean in half before gorging on the flesh that once held so much life.

Alex coughed deeply, his throat tightening slightly, "Fucking Hell," he whispered.

Warren looked shocked, and couldn't help smiling up at his dad.

"Don't tell your mum I swore." Alex ruffled Warren's hair and handed the book back, "Pictures are good though, I'll give you that."

As the sun set the bird song they had heard drifting in through the open windows faded away. It was replaced by a chill in the air and the hum of insects, along with an odd, high-pitched shriek that broke through the other sounds on occasion. It made Alex's spine tingle. As he went around shutting the windows to keep out the chill evening air he joked that, whatever that bird was, it had probably kicked out of the dawn chorus for its bad vocals.

Once finished with the windows he got a fire burning in the old fireplace, then he made his way to the fridge for a beer. He paused at the cupboard with his hand on the glass. The day had been perfect, and Warren had hardly looked at his phone all day. The trip had been a success so far. Taking down an extra glass he filled it a quarter of the way with beer and topped it up with lemonade.

"Here you are son, made with real beer. To celebrate a successful day."

Warren looked amazed at the offering, "Really? Real beer?"

"Just one more thing not to tell your mum, but yeah."

Smiling, Alex sat down opposite his son and got comfortable in front of the fire, beer in hand. "Now, tell me all about this girl."

They talked until well after dark. Alex had another beer, but despite Warrens pleas he wouldn't let him have more. Alex made him stick to just lemonade, with the promise of 'maybe tomorrow' floating in the air to soften the blow. They were disturbed from their conversation by a loud bang on the window that shook the glass, making the both of them jump. They stood up and walked to the origin of the sound, peering out with their hands cupped to the glass. Alex shrugged, not seeing anything,

"Maybe a bird flew into it?"

"Yeah, there's not much else out here. Let's lock up and go to bed anyway. I've got some good plans for tomorrow."

The night was cold in the cabin, so Alex loaded up the fire and closed the damper to allow it to burn steadily for as long as possible. They huddled under extra blankets and lay down to sleep, but soon they were woken by another loud bang at a window. This time the bang was shortly followed by a crash, then the tinkle of broken glass hitting the floor.

Alex was groggy from the beers, and from being disturbed during R.E.M sleep, but when Warren screamed he was up in a flash. Parental instincts took over, flushing all the grogginess from his system. Bursting through the door to Warren's room he felt prepared for anything, but what he saw stopped him in his tracks. Alex stood, open mouthed at the sight of his son.

A small being was on Warren's face, its feet against his chin and hands wrapped around one of his teeth. It was pulling, and as it pulled at the tooth Warren screamed in pain. Alex shook the shock out of his system and dashed over. Grabbing the fairy round the waist he yanked it off his son's face.

The tooth came with it, blood arcing through the air. Both of Warren's hands came up to cover his mouth, and he sobbed in pain. The fairy in Alex's hand made the same high-pitched shriek they had heard before, bashing down onto Alex's hand with the tooth. The tiny thing stabbed the tooth into the flesh between Alex's thumb and finger on the hand holding it, so by reflex Alex released his grip. The fairy flew out of the broken window, toting its prize.

"He was right?"

Alex stumbled against the door, and as his legs gave way he sank to the floor. The sound of Warren's moans brought some strength back to him, and he crawled over to the bed.

"Are you alright?"

"It pulled out my tooth, of course I'm not fucking alright!"

He was crying more now, and under the circumstances Alex supposed he could forgive his son's bad language. He stood, slowly walking from the room and through to the kitchen to get some ibuprofen for Warren's pain. He didn't know what else to do, but didn't have much time to think about it when another of those nerve-jangling shrieks sounded behind him. He whirled around, grabbing the thing closest to him and swinging it through the air in an arc. The old guitar collided against the airborne fairy with a hollow thud, sending it smashing into the nearby wall.

He finally understood why his father had left in such a hurry: the fairies had come for him, just like they had come for Alex and his son now. The desire to leave overpowered everything else. He went to Warren's room, giving him the pills and starting to gather their things in a panic. All he said was, "He was right, my dad was right," in disbelief, over and over again as he shoved everything he could find into their bags.

Taking Warren by the arm he semi-dragged him towards the front door, and to the safety of the car that lay beyond it. Halfway across the sitting room Warren broke free of his dad's grasp.

"The book!" He cried, making a lunge for the chair where he had left it before bed. Warren scooped up the book where his grandfather had so painstakingly recorded the reality of these tiny beings, then he ran for the door his dad held open for him. Orange lights flashed as the car was unlocked, illuminating the surrounding clearing. Warren dived inside with Alex close behind, but as Alex reached for the door his face was gripped with pain. He was unable to do anything but spin around in the direction it was pulling him.

Tiny hooks were digging into his cheek, pulling him away from the car. More pain racked his body as other fairies swarmed over him, grabbing his body all over. His hands, his head, and his legs were all covered in the tiny creatures. One flew down in front of his vision, and it was indeed a tiny humanoid. Four wings on its back, like those of a dragonfly, and eyes like an insect. It hovered in front of his face and looked at him for what seemed like a long time, and when it opened his mouth he was powerless to stop it under the weight of all the others.

He felt a stab, which sent a wave of pain through his mouth and along his jawline as the hooks pierced one of his bottom molars. Then there was pressure from the small feet against his chin, and then blinding pain. Next was the taste of copper as the tooth was slowly and strongly pulled from his jaw. As the tooth came free Alex was released from their grasp. He bent forwards, spitting blood across the window of the car as the fairies flew at each other, fighting over the tooth and shrieking in a blur of airborne combat.

Alex made for the car, slamming the door behind him as he dived into the seat. Pressing the button on the dash the car revved to life, the tires spraying gravel and debris from the path underneath them as Alex set off up the path that would lead them to safety.

As he reached the tree line he found the road blocked again. In front of them stood a giant creature, no doubt attracted by the noise of the fairies' squabble. It towered over the car. The glowing eyes of the wendigo left trails behind them, like a will-o-the-wisp might, as its head rocked slightly from side to side. The eyes burned into Alex's own, freezing him in fear. With every step forward that it took the ground shook, the tremors rocking through the car.

"Dad, GO!" Warren unbuckled his seat belt and leaned forward, hitting his dad on the shoulder, "GO!" and then more quietly as his gaze locked onto the ever-advancing wendigo, "please."

The fear in his child's voice overwrote his own. He pushed the gas, hurtling right at the creature. One of the wendigo's legs was in their path, and they rammed it. The impact jolted them as it struck, and the collision sent them spinning, nearly into a tree. The fae gave chase after it recovered its balance, but as fast as it was it was no match for the speed of the car.

Once the wendigo was long gone from the rear-view mirror, and his adrenaline had subsided, Alex slowed the car. His fear soon gave way to nausea, and common sense. They needed to stay safe. It wouldn't do to escape those creatures just to wreck into a tree and kill them both, or wreck the car enough to leave them to the mercy of the horrors they had seen back by the cabin.

They drove through the dark in silence, not stopping once in the two hours back to the city. When Warren awoke in the morning his mum was already there to collect him, and his dad was gone. It was the only time Alex ever went back to the cabin, and even then he didn't go all the way up the trail. He stopped where the tree had been lain across the path, and he dragged it back into place.

Where the word DANGER had been carved he painted inside the grooves to make the letters a bright red so that they stood out more, then he drove away as fast as he could. His retreat was followed by a chorus of high-pitched shrieks that sang out from that part of the forest.

Jason Holden
About the Author

Jason is a human. He lives here and there in the UK, always with his wife, daughter and fur baby. His primary goal is to raise his daughter to adulthood without any major damage. When he can, he writes. He thinks he does it well, but you can be the judge of that. He has been published in a few anthologies here and there, has been praised and put down for his writing. You can find and follow him on Facebook. *Jason Holden-Author* Although he asks you only follow him on Facebook and not through the streets. That's just creepy.

The Von Brunner Woods
Evan M. Elgin

The greatest fear in humans is not that of the unknown, this is an old-time conviction. I like to think that within the 21st-century, in our technology-obsessed paradigm, that the greatest fear to humanity is a swift, sudden reminder that deep down in our primordial core, we are still no different than that of any other wild animal. It might be easy to dismiss that idea, but after coming face-to-face with that side a few years back I can at least try to help you understand.

It was a Thursday afternoon. I had been just getting over a nasty case of the stomach flu, which I had had since the following Friday. After ten days of being stuck inside, relegating my time between quick rushes to the bathroom and downing liters of chicken noodle soup, I had grown a little stir crazy. As my nausea had finally worn off, and I was returning to my old self, I decided to make use of the free time and take a little nature walk in one of my favorite conservation areas.

The Von Brunner Woods was a short drive south from my hometown in Charles Park, right along the Fox River, and about an hour west outside of Chicago. It was steeped in local history, being the area within the city where the first European family settled – the Dutch Von Brunner family.

This space of the protected forest was an isolated one that lingered just along the west side of the Fox River, but could only be accessed from the east. To get there you had to actually cross right through downtown, moving over the Main Street Bridge to the east side. Next you would take the first right down a side street, passing a few pristine, Victorian homes along the riverside before descending into deeper elms and willows. By then you'd reach the entrance to the park, which had a modestly-squared parking lot. A life-sized replica of an old Dutch windmill – a stocky structure with a wooden paneled body and four narrow wind blades – sat next to the pavement. Its presence overlooked the trailhead: a footbridge made up of iron and wood that brought you back over to the west side.

To my elation I pulled into a parking lot that was completely empty, and I backed my sleek, black SUV into an open spot closest to the bridged trailhead. I thought to myself that recovering from the flu midweek really did pay off. I was ready to take full advantage of the quietude, having that piece of public land all to myself as I left my car and crossed over the bridge.

I entered a forest that was rife in late-summer bloom. Wildflowers grew between oaks and elm trees; robins danced in the canopy above me, and even a gentle wind kept that late-August humidity at bay. I've always been a great admirer of the nature-based writings of John Muir, and even though my job and family life pretty much relegated me to a suburban existence the Von Brunner Woods, in all of its natural and rustic glory, always stirred something of deep reverence inside me. It was a place where I could collect my thoughts, and enjoy my time alone. I could walk by a few of the old stone and clay foundations of its original settlers, and meditate on their existence; I could sit on one of the many park benches that lined the trail and just take in the earthy smells of wildflowers and river algae off the wind.

Fifteen minutes into my deep focus I came around the bend of the trail, just in time to hear the chirping of the birds immediately take a back seat. Then, to my surprise, I heard what I thought were separate footsteps. The heaviness of the crunch told me that whoever was making the noise was a good sized animal, maybe that of a deer or even a cougar (they're extremely rare for northern Illinois, but entirely possible). The trail then straightened out ahead like a corridor of green foliage, clinging tightly to the narrow, dirt trail I walked upon. Among the solitude I watched as a black shape sauntered from the right side of the trail up ahead, and it stepped out onto the pathway in front of me.

My mind immediately went back to the empty parking lot, second guessing if there was a lone car there when I pulled in. Then I thought that maybe he was a DNR officer who hiked in from the west side, but when I looked at the man I saw that he was much more youthful than myself. He was somewhere in his early twenties, maybe even late-teens. He was a little unkempt in dirt-stained denim, a stretched-out undershirt, and a ratty, blue-knit sweater. His black hair was long and scraggly, matching his acne-pocked face, and he sported prickly stubble coupled with murky, white skin. The young man also walked odd, carrying a stride that was singular – carefully keeping each step in front of the other, like he strolled across an invisible tightrope.

I've always been a little socially awkward when encountering other hikers on the trail. It wasn't that I didn't want them around, but I take walks in nature to get away from people, and I guess it just unconsciously conflicted with the experience. Nevertheless, it was always good to be friendly with others. They had every right to enjoy this public park as much as I did.

"How's it going, man?" I said.

As we were about to cross paths along the trail I looked into his beady, dark eyes, which were kept firmly on his rubber sandals and mud-drenched, white socks. His awkward footwear matched my greeting.

Your early thirties are probably the second-most perplexing time of your life, next to being a pre-teen. It's an age when you reluctantly realize you have more in common with the "maturity" of the middle-aged than the reckless vibrancy of youth, but my dorky greeting went ignored as the young man's eyes jerked upward and glared at me – by then I was already focused on his mouth.

The young man had this smeared redness around his thin, chapped lips, like he had just finished gorging on a jam-heavy, peanut butter and jelly sandwich. Even with my initial shock I managed to ask him again what was up. The wind had grown heavy between my two greetings, so maybe he just didn't hear me the first time. But after my second hello he just continued to scowl at me, and walked right on by.

His manic look was that of primeval tension, immediately triggering a fight-or-flight response deep in my bones. I also couldn't turn away. I felt like I was looking at something different, but in human form.

I followed his body until the point I couldn't look over my shoulder anymore. I stopped and turned back to him, kindly asking if everything was alright. The young man just continued walking down the trail, using the sleeve of his sweater to finally wipe away the jam that smeared around his mouth. He then started to jog, turning into a full-on sprint and swiftly disappearing around the curved bend along the trail.

I stood back, puzzled. What was with this guy? Was he just painfully shy or something? Better yet, was he on drugs? How the Hell could he get here? I wasn't even fifteen minutes down the trail when I encountered him, and the only entrance was the parking lot. The trail itself was just one big loop. The western boarder of the park was that of Highway 31, which ran north-and-south along swampy land before hitting broadleaf forests a few miles in. And, most importantly, what the Hell was he doing walking out of the woods instead of being on the trail?

I continued my hike with caution, stopping every few seconds to look behind me and run questions through my head. The encounter I had with that young man was more than just one of tense discomfort – it was one of pure intimidation. There was this rabid, territorial posturing in the way he looked at me, one that made it seem like I was not wanted in that public park, that somehow he was holding back on physicality when I least expected it.

In reality I feared the young man might be guilty of something, but just what was it? My answer was quickly given to me when I almost tripped over it. Out of the corner of my eye I briefly caught the sight of something white, bloodied, and matted settled upon the dry dirt. I gasped and hopped a few steps over it, and once I regained my balance I turned around.

My stomach prickled with pins and needles when I realized the object I almost stepped on was that of the severed dog head – a west highland terrier, by the look of it. Its murky eyes stared blankly back up at me; its once shiny, white fur and pointed ears were covered in dirt and blood. The westie's severed neck was cut uncleanly, looking savagely gnawed off. The rest of its torso wasn't in sight. That's when I spotted streaks of splattered blood leading from the trail and into the foliage.

I turned my head to face the deep woods, and my

gaze followed the blood through the tapering elms. My eyes narrowed, and I stepped closer to the forest edge. The rest of the canine's corpse was about twenty-five yards in through the trees. Its limbs and body matched the state of its head but, unlike some carelessly discarded piece of flesh and bone, the corpse was placed in an upright position upon a bed of fallen leaves. Branches were propped up all around it to help it retain its sitting position, and three cairns of rocks were crudely placed around it.

A chilly numbness came over me, even though it was obviously hot. All I could think of was seeing that young man's face, his sleeve quickly wiping away at his mouth, and the excess "jam" covering it.

Wailing suddenly echoed through the forest and washed over my back, with the sound of crunching leaves running from the right to the left behind me. I turned, ready to face the culprit, but the scamper of footsteps faded back as the high-pitched screams ended on a coda of guttural glee.

Immediately I reached for my pocket to grab my smartphone. I was only met with an empty pocket, and the cruel reminder of my need to "unplug" when I was out in nature (a habit I ironically picked up on the internet as to not get distracted on my nature walks).

Pulling my hand from my pocket I decided to jog the rest of the loop. I was too far down the trail to retrace my steps, and I knew the bridge was just around one more bend in the pathway. As the trail rounded, then straightened out once more, the trees to my right broke apart and

I could see the bridge. I only ran faster at the sight, feeling the fatigue that still lingered with my flu.

When I reached the railing post I paused, panting. The sweat beaded down my face; I felt like I was ready to throw up once more. Straightening out my back I closed my eyes, and let my face and chest get shaded from the hot sun. That's when the crackle of leaves came from the forest once more.

I turned back down the trail I had just fled, my eyes frantically scanning the natural landscape until I saw him. Somehow he had cut back through the woods, flanked me from the left, and had gotten right up behind me. He stood about ten yards away in the trees, peeking out behind the thin trunk of an ash that barely kept him covered. We both stood there frozen, just watching each other. I was too afraid to move, so I tested him.

"What's your fucking deal, pal!?" I finally yelled.

I tried to sound boisterous and angry, hoping it would scare the kid off. But the young man merely twiddled his fingers in front of his mouth, reminding me of a menacing child, and proceeded to laugh with a girlish chuckle. It was enough to make me stop pretending to be tough and just run. I turned and sprinted for the bridge, letting my feet pound across the wooden boards. Each stride brought me further across the slow-moving river, and into the sight of the parking lot. I ran clear across the bridge, not stopping until my feet were slapping against cement.

I told myself that this had to be some kind of dumb, millennial joke. It was for some internet video channel, right? Turning around I expected some spikey haired, muscle-bound idiot to come jogging down the bridge toward me, holding a camera in one hand and laughing obnoxiously as he announced that it was all "Just a prank, bro!" I wished it ended like that, but in the tranquility of nature there was no one else but <u>him</u>.

The young man didn't chase after me, but he was still in sight. He stood, stolid, at the other end of the bridge as he watched me. There was a distance of about fifty yards between us. I couldn't see the veiny whites around his black eyes, but I could definitely see the scowl he still protruded out at me.

After nearly a minute of stillness he finally moved – running his sleeve across his mouth once more. His hand then lowered back down to his waist, flicking his fingers quickly. Suddenly he snarled incoherently, sprinting across the bridge after me.

I ran toward my truck without any more hesitation. I ran so fast that I ended up stumbling right up to the driver's side and slamming my hip into the door (a dent that vehicle still carries). My fingers frantically fiddled with the keys, dragging them from my front pocket. I didn't realize how shaken I was by the whole encounter until they fell from my trembling hands.

"Really?!" I yelled.

Of all the bad clichés, I had to get butterfingers in the worst time possible moment.

I snatched them up with intensity, squeezing them so tightly into my palm that I almost drew blood. I proceeded to slide them into the door, and was about to unlock it when I paused once more. A soft wind passed through the trees, and the calmness of nature washed over me. There were no pursuing footsteps from the young man, no pounding of the wood boards as he attempted to get to the other side.

Glancing over my shoulder once more, I saw him again.

He stood on all fours, kneeling upon the midway point on the bridge. Through the old, iron crossbars that ran under the railing his vacant eyes peeked through the spaces. More girlish laughter fell from his mouth, as if he was genuinely satisfied from tormenting me. Rolling out his pinkish-gray tongue he deeply licked the old metal, evoking a slithering sound from his mouth. My skin ran with goosebumps from hearing the itching sound of a slimy tongue lapping across the grainy bars.

Resting back on his hands and knees, and putting his backside against his heels, the young man barked at me. When I failed to respond to him he threw his head back, unleashing an ungodly wail until his voice cut out. His head pivoted forward, snorted in some air through his mouth, and he began to crawl on all fours. The young man wriggled faster than any seasoned infant.

I was already in the car by the time he neared the end of the bridge, and I peeled out just as he stood erect. My getaway didn't stop the young man, who charged after my car as he screamed and wildly flailed his arms about. I hit the gas pedal all the way down, my motor roaring. Looking through the rearview mirror my heart only palpitated more, though luckily his erratically moving body was growing smaller and smaller. Even then he still continued to chase after me, and I eventually lost sight of him as the road began to curve.

The shadows of willows washed over the interior of my car; my whole body shook, and I panted rapidly. I tried to decipher what exactly I just experienced, and by reflex I turned the radio dial that was tuned in on a local station.

Fate made it all known at that moment when a stern voice broke through the speakers:

Warning: This is a Public Emergency Announcement for the Fox River Valley. Authorities are in the process of locating a patient that was in transport to the Northern Illinois Hospital of Behavioral Health. The patient is a white male, in his early twenties with long, black hair, dark eyes, and unkempt clothing. If seen, please contact your local authorities and do not approach. He is considered extremely dangerous to himself and others. This message will repeat in fifteen minutes. Now back to your regular broadcasting.

It was in that very moment that I knew: humanity's greatest fear, within the 21st century and beyond, is not that of the unknown. Humanity's greatest fear is the ravenous animal that lingers within us all, and those, whom either by choice or illness, thought or empathy, are willing to embrace it. In the end we're no more civilized than any other apex predator – we're just better at hiding it.

You still might disagree with me on that assurance, but at least you now understand.

Evan M. Elgin
About the Author

Evan M. Elgin is a writer of both published and self-published fiction. His work has been previously featured in SERIAL magazine, while his debut novel Vive La Superior! is available on Amazon. He currently lives in a black void of "suburban weirdness" that makes up greater Chicago.

Instagram: https://www.instagram.com/evan_m_elgin
Twitter: https://twitter.com/evan_elgin
Facebook: https://www.facebook.com/evanmelgin
Amazon Author's Page: https://www.amazon.com/Evan-M-Elgin/e/B07Z47CFTF/ref=dp_byline_cont_book_1
Website: https://evanmelgin.wixsite.com/writer

Jodie's spot
Mark Towse

The ring of fog looks other-worldly from the top of this hill — impossibly symmetrical and well-formed, and my mind wanders with all the wondrous possibilities that could produce such a phenomenon. My parents say that I have an overactive imagination, but it's better than not having one at all.

If Jodie was here right now, she would be bouncing up and down with excitement. Her eager voice hangs in my head, "What is it, Steve?"

"I don't know, Sis," I whisper.

I have been walking for hours now — the blue skies have given way to matte dullness, and it's impossible to tell what time it is. Shrugging off the backpack, I unzip the front pocket and take a mouthful of the tepid water. The pause in movement allows the cool air to wrap around me, and goosebumps prickle my skin.

I like to lose myself in nature, become part of it, and

I refuse to bring a watch or phone out with me. Mum and Dad used to insist, but not anymore — not now that it's just me. It's a gamble, though. The car is a long way back, and I know I would never find my way in the dark. Jodie would want to investigate, though. For her sake I thread my arm through the strap of the pack, and march on.

"This is for you, Jodie!"

I was sixteen when my sister went missing, just over a year ago — and I still struggle to accept that she's gone. Sometimes, when I'm hiking, I think I see her climbing a tree or scrambling down a rockface, but I know it can't be so. She's here somewhere, though. It was always our favourite place, and I think she used to love being out here even more than I did. Since the day of her disappearance, I have been haunted by bad dreams. I guess Mum and Dad figure I'm old enough to deal with it. It sure doesn't feel that way. Besides, they have nothing to give.

They do not look at me the same way anymore.

Occasional, distant whistles from the birds fill the air and break the hushed soundtrack of my feet on the soft grass. The snap of a branch underfoot suddenly startles me, and I mock myself with a snigger. It is so quiet out here — exactly how I like it. That is how we both used to like it. Nobody knew she was coming out that day. She never told a soul — left a note for Mum and Dad that she had gone to her friend Melissa's house. She did not return that night, so they rang Melissa and uncovered the lie. It was me that checked her closet and found her hiking shoes and favourite backpack missing, the one I bought her last month for her fourteenth birthday.

The closer I get to the ring the more I expect the magic at some point to fade, and for the imperfections to show, but the mist is not getting thinner or any less alluring. It is only a few feet away now, but it is impossible to see through — so dense, and full of mystery.

I have never seen anything like it before.

Jodie would have gone into overdrive now, non-stop chattering about how awesome it was. Even now, as I draw up to its outside edge, it is no less impressive. Slowly, I raise my arm and plunge my hand into its smoky coldness — the illusion is quite spooky — my handless limb emerging from the grey vortex. Tentatively I step forward, into the vapour-like wall. My body gives out a shudder as the iciness hits, and I am immediately disoriented by the deafening silence and starkness that greets me. Regardless, I continue walking towards the centre. Visibility is poor, and I cannot see the arm in front of me nor my legs beneath me. It is making me lightheaded, and slightly nauseous. The absolute quiet has prompted a ringing in my ears that is getting consistently louder, and the cold has well and truly wrapped its coat around me.

The walls of vapour did not look this thick from the hill. I seem to have been walking for ages. I am getting worried, and momentarily consider turning back, but then the relief kicks in as I finally emerge from the greyness and can see my limbs once again. I did not realize how fast my heart was beating, but as I double over and suck in some of the less icy air, I feel it relentlessly pounding against the wall of my chest

I made it, though. I am here.

It is like a perfect circle inside and the grass here is so incredibly green and lush, as though the wall around it serves only to preserve its beauty. It is flawless — every blade appears to be the same length, and the colour is luxuriantly emerald throughout. How could there be a rational explanation for this? What bullshit would Dad come up with?

It is then I realize I can no longer see the top edge of the mist — as though the walls have extended towards the sky. Suddenly, I feel disoriented — which way was I facing? I grab the compass from my pocket only to find the arrow is stuck — immobile — as if there is no magnetic field here. Shit! The flawlessness of mist formation and grass beneath my feet gives no clues at all, and an urgent panic sets in — a sense of dread — I need to leave.

Which way?

Everywhere I look I see grey — a cocoon of blandness that no longer offers mystery — just an oppressive entrapment. And, spurred by the chill that runs through my bones, I turn and begin to walk back towards the grey wall. Just as I reach the edge a deep, guttural groan comes from behind that stops me dead in my tracks. Slowly I turn, and see the ground rising behind me like a drawbridge — the groan still emanating as it shakes the ground beneath my feet.

My legs will not work, and I am mesmerised by the opening in the ground that is appearing before me. The earthy trapdoor continues to lift with mechanical precision — a perfect square with approximately eighty-inch sides and a living, breathing lid about twenty inches in depth. It spits out more of the grey mist that attaches itself to the existing walls around me. They are closing in on me.

The noise is haunting — as though the earth is letting out a long, smoky exhale. A strange noise leaves my lips — a nonsensical garble of disbelief. And then, from the blackness within, I see something spit out from the hole and begin to float towards the floor. I dare not take my eyes away from the moving lid, but from the corner of my eye I see it land a few feet in front of me. Finally, the groan ends, and the earth stops moving. Briefly I move my eyes away towards the crumpled piece of paper on the grass.

As I bend down to retrieve it, I notice the unmistakable graphic on the front of the faded wrapper. I immediately recognise it as Jodie's favourite chocolate bar.

Fuck — no!

I run. I sprint into the icy cloud around me, each breath cold and cutting, but the mist does not give. I do not seem to be getting anywhere.

Another groan from behind me.

No — no way!

Urgently I turn, and the mouth of the earth still looms.

"Steve!" her voice drifts from the blackness.

No — this is not happening.

Please — no!

"Steve, help me, please."

What is this? It cannot be real. Is it my imagination — a projection of the guilt that I feel? It must be.

"Steve," her voice again — distant — desolate.

She never took a phone or watch with her that day. My parents blamed me for that, and of course I blame myself. I went looking for her every day after she disappeared. I thought she would be okay — I thought we would find her. She is strong — was — was so strong. Suddenly, I break down — the tears come, and I begin to bawl uncontrollably.

Her body was never found.

"Please, Steve."

But I cannot do it; I cannot go in there.

Wiping the damp from my eyes, I slowly start to back away. The word "sorry" leaves my lips croakily, barely audible. Something grabs the edge of the grass — it is not human, but resembles a hand of some sort — brown, twisted and knotted with small, spindly branches that act like fingers. Then a hand wraps around the opposite side. More mist expels, and another groan sends tremors towards me.

Holy shit!

As the spindly arms begin to pull the unknown creature from the ground, a pair of bright white eyes emerge from the darkness. I continue my retreat, but I am not putting any distance between us — it's as though the mist is a gaseous barrier holding me in position. With another loud groan, the face finally comes into view, and I let out a silent scream. The makeshift hair is a scattering of dry, tinder-like twigs that continues down the muddy cheeks and underneath the chin. Patchy moss decorates the rest of the earthy face and spreads across the branches that form the human-like shoulders.

Even with the foliage covering most of her face in a muddy, lichen-ridden complexion, I recognise it to be my sister. Or at least some of her. The moss that forms the mouth begins to part, "It's so peaceful down here Steve, but I'm lonely."

As she continues to pull herself from the pit the first rickety leg plants itself on the grass in front of me. "You'll like it down here; the smells and the gentle patter of rain — we can be part of nature together, for eternity."

I try to speak but cannot find any words.

The second leg emerges, and now the thing is completely out and thrusting itself to an upright position. It is close enough to touch — standing perhaps seven feet tall in front of me. I can smell the dampness from the moss that covers her, and with each tiny movement I hear the gentle cracking of the bough that forms her twisted spine.

"J-Jodie."

"It's your fault, Steve. No watch, no phone — that's what you always said. Don't tell anyone where you are going, otherwise it's not an adventure anymore."

"But I..."

The right arm reaches towards me and wraps itself around my left ankle.

"I'm sorry, Jodie!" I scream.

But the left one follows, stretching itself around my other leg.

"Come on, Brother," she says.

I crouch down and with both hands, grip the vine-like limbs and try and work myself free, but they are so damp and strong.

It's useless.

She begins to pull me towards her along the soft wet grass, and I cannot get any

Traction.

"Jodie, please!"

I have carried this blame for so long — it is unfair. I lost her too!

The crippling guilt over the last few months has been unbearable, like a dark cloud that I cannot shake. But this is too much. I do not deserve this!

She steps back into the darkness, and I know that this will now be my fate.

"I'm sorry," I plead as the tears stream down both cheeks.

"It's okay. It's nice down here," she says.

The eyes turn bright red as she slowly sinks into blackness. I am getting closer to the edge — soon I will be in the pit. I claw at the grass, but it does no good — this is how it will end for me. Perhaps this is what I deserve. The lid begins to come down as I slide towards the hole.

Perhaps Mum and Dad will be pleased to get rid of me. Maybe life will be easier for them without me — but who will they blame then? There is laughter from the darkness now; deep and other-worldly, and I begin to sob with fear. Halfway in — up to my waist, and I can see nothing below but the eyes — they float down into the darkness like falling embers. Up to my shoulders now, and the earthy smell of mud fills my nostrils.

This cannot be — Jodie didn't have an evil bone in her body. More laughter, and I am sure that this thing is not Jodie. I grip the edge of the pit with my hands. The lid is almost upon me now, and I will soon be in complete darkness — underground with whatever that is. I twist my head around in time to see the last of the mist disappearing, and the trees emerging in the distance.

It pulls me inside.

"This wasn't my fault!" I scream as loud as I can. "It wasn't my fucking fault!"

Then darkness, and silence.

I cannot breathe. I am slipping away — dizzy — swimming — the heavy smell of mud.

* * *

I can see my breath.

Shaking — freezing — where am I? The stars, I can see the stars!

Pushing myself up, I look around, trying to get my bearings. I am back on top of the hill, but there is no longer a ring of mist in the distance, just uneven brown ground and a scattering of trees that sway in the evening breeze. What the hell just happened? Did I fall asleep — was that a dream? I need to get out of here. How long have I been asleep?

As I fumble through my pocket, my fingers finally lock around the compass. I urgently yank it out, sending the scrunched-up candy wrapper flying into the air. It falls to the forest floor, landing next to my right foot. For a fleeting moment I think I hear a distant groan, but it might be just the wind blowing through the trees. I stare at the wrapper and think about picking it up, but she's gone.

She's gone.

I do not think we will ever find out what happened to her. She belongs to the soil now — damp, rotten and overwhelmed by darkness. Whatever I experienced was preying on my guilt, trying to lure me in — it nearly got me, but I will not carry the blame anymore. I will not. I do not think I will be hiking around here for a while. It's time to let go — find a different spot. This land feels bad now. I need to get home. Mum and Dad will be worried, hopefully.

MARK TOWSE
ABOUT THE AUTHOR

After a 30-year hiatus, Mark recently gave up a lucrative career in sales to pursue his dream of being a writer. His passion and belief have resulted in pieces in many prestigious magazines, including Flash Fiction Magazine, Raconteur, Books N' Pieces, Artpost, Colp, Antipodean SF, Page & Spine, Twenty-Two Twenty-Eight, and Montreal Writes. His work has also appeared twice on The No Sleep Podcast and also on The Grey Rooms. Nine anthologies to date include his stories, two of which are on the 2019 Horror Writers Association recommended list, and a further eight anthologies set for imminent release in 2020 also contain his work. His first collection, 'Face the Music' will shortly be released by All Things That Matter Press.

Mark resides in Melbourne, Australia with his wife and two children.

You can Follow Mark here:
https://twitter.com/MarkTowsey12
https://www.facebook.com/mark.towse.75
https://marktowsedarkfiction.wordpress.com/
https://www.amazon.com/Mark-Towse/e/
B07H8DBS31%3Fref=dbs_a_mng_rwt_scns_share

Seita
Thomas K.S. Wake

"**I** told you it was still alive. You missed, again."

The massive blood stain glistened on the moss where Steve had hit the bear. In the waning daylight it wasn't the easiest thing in the world to get a killshot, but he had been doing this for almost 25 years. Only if the animal hadn't moved at the last minute.

And Carl was right, Steve's aim had been off lately, ever since he got that letter from the doctor. Cancer by itself is a horrible, soul-crushing word, and when it's partnered with 'brains' and 'malignant tumor', it destroys all the hopes and dreams a person might have had.

"The fucker moved just when I released the arrow."

Carl spat on the ground and kneeled to get a closer look to see which direction the animal was headed. The tracks imprinted on the moist moss were lined with crimson streaks of splattered blood, like sanguine roses.

"Well, at least it's leaking pretty heavily. Shouldn't

get far. C'mon." Carl stood up and measured the gloomy thicket in front of them.

"Are you serious? I'm in no mood to go wading in the dark through the…"

"Well one: you should have taken a better aim then. Two: we can't let a wounded grizzly go wandering free; it's dangerous. And three, you're the one who got us this gig. In fact you insisted that we take this one. There's no fucking way you're bailing on us now."

Carl was right, and Steve hated it.

"Shit, you're right. I know, I know. I'm sorry, I'm just exhausted and my head hurts. And we haven't hunted on these grounds before."

"Of course I'm right. And don't be sorry, be a better shot. If you're feeling sick then maybe you should have thought about that before you agreed to do this. This is the only place where we could snag us a grizzly on such a short notice."

Without waiting for a reply Carl entered the thick woods, and Steve took one last look back at the clearing they had just crossed. The sun was sinking below the horizon, bathing the landscape in golden light as the bright orange stripes withdrew to reveal the dusk lurking underneath.

The last of the light drew away the night conquered the sky, and the moon took its place as the watcher of their dark world. The two poachers disappeared into the dense woods, and Steve was sure that nature itself was punishing them; as soon as they had crossed the treeline it began to rain. Not just any rain, it was the kind of downpour that made you feel like God had taken a holy pressure washer and was dead set on cleansing the Earth and everything on it.

They should have turned back, but there was a lot riding on finding this animal. Steve needed the money. He had no idea how much his treatment would cost, but he had a sense it would be a lot. He liked living, and was going to do whatever it took to keep doing the thing he liked.

Soon the dampness soaked through their clothes, and even though they had the proper wind-and-water resistant gear on it wasn't enough.

"This gear ain't meant for diving." Carl said, as if he had read Steve's thoughts. They settled under a pine with thick branches to get at least some kind of shelter, and Steve huddled next to him.

"I think we've lost the tracks."

"Oh ya think, do you? What makes you say that, genius? Maybe the fact that we're trying to track it under a pitch-black, goddamn waterfall in a forest we just now set our feet in for the first time?"

Steve knew his friend's temper, and it was better to not say anything in retort. Instead he reached into his sodden coat pocket, offering a bit of chewing tobacco to Carl. They never smoked when on the hunt, but still needed their nicotine fix, so it was the perfect solution. Without a word Carl took the lump and shoved it into his mouth.

"Of course it's mint, lame fucking flavor." He scoffed at the peace offering, but chewed down nonetheless.

"What the Hell is with you, seriously?" Steve erupted. "I know I messed up with the shot, but it's not like we haven't had to work for our fee in the past. And this isn't even the worst weather we've tracked something in, so what the Hell is grinding your anus?"

Carl chewed once more on the tobacco, then spat it on the ground. He took a moment to decide whether or not to tell Steve what had happened, but figured he may as well.

"Mackenzie left me, and she took the kids."

Steve paused. He felt his anger cool down as the rain ran down his back, and he took in what his friend had just said.

"Shit man, I am sorry. Can she do that?"

"I don't know. I suppose, especially since I haven't exactly been a model husband with the drinking and all. We had our ups and downs for sure, but I really did love 'em."

Steve recounted all the times Mackenzie had called him in panic from their bathroom when Carl was in one of his moods. He was usually trying to kick down the door while their two kids, Clara and James, were bawling their eyes out in the next room. At some point Steve had lost count of the number of calls, and of the number of times he had exchanged punches with his best friend when he was too drunk to listen to reason. All the same, Steve knew deep down that Carl was a good man.

"Maybe she's just a cunt like the rest of them."

Really, really deep down.

"Hey, not cool. That's my sister."

"Sorry."

"When was this?"

"Two, maybe two-and-a-half weeks ago."

Steve wasn't surprised that Mackenzie hadn't called him. She had always been ashamed that she ignored Carl's drunken fits, and she was ashamed that she had chosen a husband that was so much like their father had been.

He would call her first thing tomorrow.

Steve placed his hand reassuringly on his friend's shoulder, and they stood there in the cold, soggy darkness without saying a word as the rain pummeled down around them.

The poachers had gotten lucky with their rain-based misfortune, and they had been about three hours into the chase when they realized they were utterly lost. The tracks had gone pretty much in a straight line, but the darkness, plus relentless rain, had made navigation essentially im-possible.

As they stood under the tree they decided to call it quits, and instead prioritized finding their way out of the forest. While retracing their steps they heard labored breathing, and it was coming from not too far away in the blackness of the forest. By sheer luck they had somehow circled behind the bear, and Steve didn't plan on missing twice.

Carl prepped his rifle against his shoulder and went on point, following the sound. Steve took his position back and to the right of Carl, quietly placing an arrow on his SR6. Steve always hunted with a bow, even though lately his hands had been shaking more and more. Sometimes they felt like they weren't even his.

The huffing was moving away from them, but they were quickly gaining on the creature. Carl nodded and drew Steve's attention to the trunk of a tree. Even in the inky rain he could see the shine of blood on the bark as rivulets of water ran through it.

Closing in on the kill was always a very exciting moment. Steve's vision narrowed, and the sounds of the rain pounding on the ground and the foliage faded into the background. The labored sound of the bear's breathing heightened, and he didn't feel the cold or the wetness anymore. The clamminess of the inner layer of his clothes was not there anymore, and those things just didn't matter. He was in the zone, and he knew Carl was too.

They started to put their weight more carefully on each step, drilling their boots toe-first into the ground to avoid stepping on loose branches. They moved as quickly as they could, while still moving as silently as possible. The breathing was getting closer with every step, and it was clear that their quarry was slowing down.

The rain stopped almost as abruptly as it had come, water was slowly dripping off the branches as a biting wind began to pick up. The gusts seeped through their clothes and embedded a chill into the bones of the two poachers. Trying to subdue the shivers emanating from within they stepped out of the thicket, finding themselves in a small clearing. Almost on cue the clouds slowly drifted apart, and pale, blue moonlight fell upon the clearing.

The bear was standing there, breath steaming in the increasingly cold night. Carl raised his rifle and took aim as Steve drew his bow, but there was something peculiar about the behaviour of the animal. Bears can be viciously aggressive when wounded, and since the men had been on the chase for almost three hours they knew the wound wasn't fatal, but the bear just stood in the middle of the clearing. It was facing away from them, swaying back and forth like a baby being rocked to sleep. It didn't acknowledge them at all.

"What's it doing?" Steve asked in a whisper.

"Beats me. Maybe it's delirious from the loss of blood? Who knows, and I don't care. Easy kill."

Steve's eyes focused on a shape next to the bear that he hadn't noticed before. It was a six-foot-tall formation of piled stones. He didn't see the exact details, but the structure gave an impression of being deliberately created. It was there for a reason, and someone had constructed it. It was wider at the base, narrowing as it went. It was like a man-made stalagmite.

"What's that?"

Carl looked up to see what Steve was pointing at. He lowered his rifle and looked at the pile of stones. The bear was rubbing its injured shoulder against the mound, coloring them with its blood. It was a surprise that the structure took the bear's weight. The bear must have touched a sensitive spot, because it let out a booming wail of pain as it jerked away from the stones. Still huffing it turned around, dropping its swaying head as it scented the forest floor.

"Shit!"

The bear had gained focus, and it knew they were close. Its head shot up, and it rose to its hind legs. Popping its jaw it moaned and wuffed, clearly unhappy. There were about forty feet between the men and the animal, but that was nothing to a charging bear. It lunged forward, its front legs still in the air, as it moved towards its attackers.

Carl fired from the hip while raising the rifle to a proper aim position. The bullet penetrated the bear's left ear, shredding it to pieces, but the charging animal didn't slow down. It roared, gaining speed as its front legs touched the ground.

Steve released an arrow. The bow made a quiet thang as it propelled the carbon projectile towards its target.

The rifle was propped at Carl's shoulder, when the arrow hit. The jagged, hardened steel tip entered the bear's eye, effectively popping it. The tip pierced its skull, exiting from the back of its head, but the bear kept charging. A heartbeat later the bear's trajectory suddenly wavered, the brain no longer giving information to the legs.

Carl fired, but the spot between the shoulder blade and the neck he was aiming for wasn't there anymore as the massive animal hit the ground. The bullet swished just over the falling bear's back, ringing against the stone structure and ricocheting off of it with a sharp twang.

The forest fell completely silent. The night ambient faded away, no wind to be heard, not a single bird call or any other sound.

"What...the...fuck?" Steve's words sounded like they were coming from inside his head. The sound didn't carry further than a couple of inches. He lowered his bow, and he felt like they were in a sensory deprivation chamber.

He tried to hail Carl, but he couldn't seem to hear him. Finally Carl turned to him and shouted something, but Steve couldn't hear what.

He looked up and noticed that the clouds weren't moving. In fact, as he looked at the forest surrounding the clearing he realized that nothing was. Branches weren't swaying, the water wasn't dripping from the needles and the entire landscape had become a still image.

Steve made it to Carl and tried to talk to him, but he could barely hear Carl even when they were standing a foot from each other.

"What's happening?!" Steve shouted, sounding like he was screaming underwater.

"I don't know! Everything just went...off?" Carl shouted back.

In the confusion Steve was relieved, since he had initially thought it was the tumor that was affecting his hearing as it pressed against his brain. At least now he knew they were both experiencing this weirdness.

A low-pitched hum started to rise, emanating from the stone structure. The sound was barely audible, but it felt tangible. It crawled along the ground, over the bear's carcass and making the fur stand on end. It continued towards the poachers, the sound making the ground vibrate ever so slightly.

Steve picked up something in his peripheral vision, movement in the shade of the trees. Something was circling the clearing, something that was able to move despite the entire forest seeming to be in stasis. Carl saw it too. He prepared his rifle, and Steve put an arrow at the ready but didn't draw.

The shadows under the trees stirred. There was another figure speeding in the shade where the moonlight didn't quite reach, and this one was smaller than the one Steve saw. There was something uncanny about the second figure, but Steve couldn't put his finger on it

Seeing the shadows suddenly move made Steve feel unspeakable dread bubbling inside him. It slithered on the surface of his organs, constricting them, coiling its cold fingers around his bones and squeezing tight.

The surrounding forest sighed.

Carl followed the second figure through his sight, but he screamed when he looked at the bear.

It had risen to its hind legs without either him or Steve noticing it. The bear's face was a crimson mask; the black hole where Steve's arrow had pierced the eye looked at them with a blank, accusatory stare. The gore from the arrow's exit wound decorated the neck, and there is no way the animal should be alive.

"Holy fuck!" Carl shrieked, instinctively fired his weapon. The sound of the gunshot was suffocated at the barrel. The bullet hit the bear's torso, disappearing amids the fur, but it seemed to have no effect on the animal.

It growled, the sound shattering the silence. The stasis was lifted, and the world was running again.

Steve drew his bow and released. The arrow hit the bear in the belly with a dull thud, sinking in up to the nock. Steve readied another arrow and fired again, this time hitting the muzzle at a slight angle, tearing half of it off exposing tissue and part of the bear's gums.

The beast still did not drop, and it looked like it didn't even feel the torture the men were putting it through. It charged, targeting Steve.

Steve drew and released, the arrow swooshing through the air and hitting the bear in its side. The projectile penetrated the skin, sinking into the animal with no visible effect.

The crazed bear tried to paw off Steve's head, but he just barely made it out of the way of the deadly claws by rolling to his left. He ended up in a high-knee position. He raised his bow and sent another arrow to meet the bear that was turning back to claw him, roaring as it turned. The arrow entered the open maw with a loud crack, wedging into the palate as the tip poked through the skull.

The bear stopped charging, coughing and gagging, trying to vomit out the irritating projectile lodged in it's mouth. It backed up, head down, looking almost depressed as it wandered towards the stone pillar and collapsed. It finally remained motionless.

Steve sighed in relief and turned to Carl, who was fixated on the shadow standing on the edge of clearing just out of view.

"What's that?"

Carl shook his head, not taking his eyes off the figure. Steve drew his bow, taking aim at the humanoid shape.

"Who goes there!?" Steve tried to sound confident and strong, but failed. The shadow fidgeted, making Carl panic. He fired, missing the target and hitting a tree as the bullet sent bark flying.

Steve held his breath, centered the figure on the steel aim and was just about to release when the clearing behind them started stirring.

He spun around, and what he saw fractured his sanity; the bear was getting up again, but there was something different about it. Something otherworldly. It's movements were jerky and uncoordinated, and the ground beneath it was pulsating and undulating. Something was forcing its way inside the carcass of the grizzly as the re-animated beast turned to Steve.

The pale moonlight lit its torn up face, but there was no solace in seeing it, only more horror. The bear's flesh was already rotten and decomposed, hanging in saggy lumps on its sides like it had been dead for days. The skin on its face was peeled off, revealing the white bone underneath. The loose part of the muzzle looked shriveled, and the fur was covered in rancid moss. Maggots were raining from its torn, swollen belly. There was no way the animal was alive, yet there it was, speeding towards Steve on jiggly, desiccated legs. The one eye burned with rage, focusing on the man who had punctured the other. There was something squirming under it's skin, fueling the husk.

Steve let out a primal scream, drawing the string and releasing, but in his panic he had forgotten to put the arrow in the arrow rest. The string rang empty, and he dropped the bow as the grotesque creature rushed towards him.

Carl pulled his attention away from the shadows, managing to keep his cool. He fired twice, hitting the target with both shots, but they only caused clouds of puss to squirt from the entry wounds.

Steve was able to pull out his Bowie knife and take one swing at his assailant, cutting a massive gash in a shoulder before the animal collided with him, launching Steve into the air like a ragdoll. He tried to break his fall with his hands, but he caught the ground at an improper angle and his left wrist snapped with an audible crack. He tumbled over the broken hand, twisting it even more. He could feel the shattered bone fragments gnaw at his flesh, but somehow he managed to keep a hold of the knife.

Whimpering he started to crawl somewhere, not knowing or caring where, just away. He was now being driven by instincts, and they were soaked in fear.

Carl took aim and pulled the trigger, only to hear the sound of an empty rifle.

"Shit!"

He grabbed the barrel and attacked the bear, swinging as though he had a baseball bat. The rifle stock made dull thudding sounds with no visible effect. The bear turned, lightning-fast, and hit Carl with a massive foreleg.

It made the 220 pound man do a backflip, landing on his back hard. The wind was knocked right out of his lungs, and his eyes were filled with black dots as he struggled to breathe.

Steve turned to face the beast. It was standing there, about a foot from his face, measuring the man in front of it.

Steve was staring right into the judging eye of the bear. The animal tilted its head, curious about what Steve was going to do, almost taunting him. The dangling muzzle swayed back and forth, almost like it was laughing.

"What the Hell is this, man?"

It had to be the tumor. This wasn't happening.

The bear brought the decimated muzzle just an inch from Steve's face, blowing a puff of putrid air through the nostril that was still intact. Steve retched, nearly vomiting. The bear threw its head left and right a couple more times, then it turned and started to walk away. Steve was staring after it with a broken breath, fighting to keep himself collected.

His mind just could not process the situation. The bear stopped and slowly looked over its shoulder, as if it was having second thoughts about leaving. It turned around completely and started huffing, scrabbling at the ground.

Steve wanted to flee, but he couldn't even raise himself up on his elbows as the animal charged. He screamed, flailing at the air with his knife. He made contact, but couldn't tell where.

The bear twisted its head sideways and opened its mouth. Steve's head was encircled by teeth, and the inside of the creature stank of wet, decomposing soil. He screamed into the bear's throat, but it paid no mind. The animal stood up, Steve dangling from it like a marionette whose strings had been cut. His eyes rolled into his head. He knew he was dying as he tried in vain to pry his head out of the bear's mouth. He couldn't breath, and the world around him started to fade away.

"Steve…" Carl wheezed, but could do nothing else.

The sound of broken bone was followed by moist, soft squishing when the bear finally put Steve out of his misery and crushed his head.

The bear got back down on all fours, huffed a couple of times and wandered off to the woods, disappearing into the shadow of the trees.

"Fuuuuckk!" Carl cursed into the air, finally catching his breath. He crawled to the rifle, his legs still unable to carry him yet. He took the weapon and reloaded it,glancing over at his dead friend.

Steve's head was a lump of bone fragments and meat, and there was nothing Carl could do about it.

Using the rifle as a crutch he managed to get to his feet, just in time to hear the snap of a twig behind him. He turned around and saw someone standing on the edge of the shadows. The figure didn't move, yet Carl got a chill as it stared at him with unseen eyes.

There was a sudden stirring of leaves behind the figure, but it didn't move.

"Who the fuck are you?"

No answer. A smaller figure emerged from the depths of the forest and stood to the left side of the bigger one. Carl held his rifle stock on his shoulder, but the barrel was still pointing towards the ground.

"Say something!"

A third figure appeared from the trees. It was smaller than the first one, but bigger than the second one.

"Tell me who the fuck you're, or I swear to Christ I'll…"

"You'll do what, Carl? Educate me some more?"

In an instant Carl lost control of his bladder, his jeans soaking with urine.

"Mackenzie? It can't be. You're…"

"Dead? Oh yes, I am. We all are."

All three of them stepped into the clearing, and now it was Carl's time to scream. The left side of Mackenzie's face was caved in from the force of the hit that killed her, and there was no mistaking who he was seeing. They were his wife and two kids, Clara and James, but there was no way they could be here. It was impossible, because he had killed them and buried their bodies far from here.

"Are you going to hurt us again, Daddy?" Clara asked. She was wearing the pyjamas Carl had buried her in. They were covered in soil, just as most of Clara's face was.

"No! I…I didn't mean it…"

"Just like you didn't mean to backhand me so hard that I dislocated my jaw when I was four?"

James' face was distorted with the same expression of fear and disbelief that he had worn when Carl shot him. His voice was laced with anger, and the .375 entry wound was still wet on his chest. The guilt was crushing Carl from the inside, like he was being vacuum sealed. He gasped for air, his heart working on overdrive.

"You're not real!" He fired at his wife without aiming, her left hand exploding into a cloud of pus and grey, flaky flesh. She didn't even flinch.

"Remember our trip to Quebec, Carl? When Clara was just a baby? We went hiking in Taiga, and that was the last time you were a decent father and husband."

Carl remembered, his eyes filling with tears.

"You promised to teach me camping Daddy, when I grow up. You never did." The words dropped like mushy soil from Clara's mouth.

Carl started sobbing. He aimed the gun at Clara, but couldn't pull the trigger. Not again.

"And you promised to teach me how to hunt, how to shoot like you and Uncle Steve." James chimed in. As James grinned Carl could see worms wiggling inside his gums.

"In a way you did. Kind of hoped I wouldn't have been the target, but aim for the center mass, right Dad?"

"I'm sorry. I'm so, so sorry. Mackenzie, please... when you told me you would leave and take the kids, I..."

"Did what every normal man would do? Shot your children and smashed your wife's head in with a shovel, just because she came home from work early and caught you burying our children? What a man you are!"

The gruesome trio approached slowly. Carl couldn't move, not even when James took a step and his leg deteriorated under him. It turned to soil and he fell to his belly, but he continued to crawl towards Carl on his hands and knee.

"Look Daddy, I'm all broken up. Hold me Daddy!"

"Please...I'm sorry." Tears were streaming down Carl's face and they mixed into the snot running from his nose.

Clara's skin bulged and undulated. It tore open, and soil welled out. Clara emptied like a balloon, and soon she was just a heap of skin and dirt on the ground.

"See what you did, Carl? How're you going to make this right? You can't buy your way out of this with a bouquet, like you did after your nights of beer and battery."

Suddenly James grabbed Carl's leg. He recoiled, losing his balance and falling to the ground. James continued to crawl up his leg, and Mackenzie sat on Carl's chest.

"C'mon love, let me help you."

She grabbed the hand that was still holding the rifle and started to twist it towards Carl's jaw, trapping his fingers in her fist. It was impossible to get the barrel under his chin from that position, but that didn't stop Mackenzie from trying.

"Stop it, it doesn't bend that way!" Carl cried out.

Mackenzie laughed, and with a quick jerk she broke his forearm.

"Oh, look at that! It did bend after all." She placed

the barrel under Carl's jaw.

"James, dear, would you like to teach your father how to make a killshot?"

The boy reached for the trigger guard.

"James, please. I'm sorry. I love…"

The shot entered Carl's throat and exited from the neck, shattering his spine. He felt the immense pain in his head at the same time he lost the feeling in his legs. He was paralyzed, but he didn't die.

"That looks bad my love. Let me kiss it and make it all better."

Mackenzie's mouth opened wider than was naturally possible, and she started to regurgitate wet soil onto Carl. Among the soil there were twigs and rotten leaves, and as they piled on Carl's face he could feel something squirming inside the mixture.

He tried to scream, but his mouth was immediately filled with the putrid paste coming from his wife's mouth. Something crawled from the soil onto his cheek, and he felt a sting as whatever it was started to burrow into his flesh.

He tried to beg for his life, but his wriggling just allowed the thing to slip down his throat into his stomach. He was gagging, and the forest denied him the comfort of unconsciousness.

The stone structure was humming.

Carl felt the thing reach his belly. It was pushing out barbs along its entire length, punching holes into Carl's windpipe and stomach lining. He shook as his body went into shock, his insides filling with solid wetness. His limbs welled up like balloons, and as they burst they spewed out soil that burrowed thin, root-like tendrils onto the ground. He was decomposing, even as he was still alive.

He tried to scream, but could only muster a muffled wail. Even if he could have cried for help there was no one there to respond. He was all alone in the clearing, slowly dying next to an ancient stone structure which had been erected by God knows who.

THOMAS WAKE
ABOUT THE AUTHOR

Thomas was born into the harsh winters in the Nordic Finland. Tempered by the shamanic winds, thousand lakes with a thousand stories, the whispers of the birch filled forests, he fell in love with horror at the render age of 6 when he saw Re-Animator. That led him to search for the source story and that was it. Cosmic horror wrapped it's nebulous tentacles around his imagination and it has been feeding it ever since. Consuming book after book, he realized his dream; to be a writer. And that dream has guided him his entire life.

Twitter: https://twitter.com/ThomasWake12

Hollow Woods
Brian Duncan

"**E**mma Charles, if you don't get down here right now I'm not taking you to the park!"

Emma's head snapped around at the sound of her father's voice. She was elbow deep in LOL Dolls, trying to decide which would be the least baby one to bring with her. Truth be told she wasn't sure any of them would make the cut. Her open backpack next to her contained only her sunblock, a towel, and her phone. If girls in Florida were into dolls or makeup or anything like that she was going to be woefully lacking.

She threw two dolls into the bag, studied their baby-ish faces, and tossed them back into her closet. She should have asked what games they were going to play today.

"Emma!"

"I'm coming right down," she shouted. Her father would be standing at the bottom of the stairs, glaring upward toward her room, his keys in his hand. He was the most impatient person on Earth. It wasn't even his hangout.

Resigned to a doll-less afternoon, she zipped her bag closed.

"See," she said as she crested the second floor landing, "here I am. You don't have to yell."

"Yes I do, because if I don't yell for at least five minutes it will already be dark when we get in the car." Emma rolled her eyes, and her father's tone lightened. "You look beautiful today."

"Dad, knock it off," she said, rolling her eyes again.

"I can't help it. You're so cute."

"And you're a dork. Can we go? I'm waiting on you, you know." Smiling he bowed low, extending a hand to the front door. Emma smiled. She had been nervous about what to wear to a wilderness park that was also a beach (she thought her canvas shorts and denim top might be too dorky.) His compliment helped ease her mind, even if he was being a dork about it.

On the road her dad sang to old music he swore was from the best decade ever, even though it sounded like distortion and whining to her. Why did everyone from the best decade repeat the same lyrics over and over a hundred times?

Twenty minutes into the drive she turned to her dad. "How much longer is it?"

"At least fifteen minutes," he told her.

"You've got to be kidding me."

"Hey, your little friends are the ones that wanted to

have a day at a place way out of town called Nate's Hell."

"God Dad, you're so clueless. It's called Tate's Hell, not Nate's Hell." She dug through her backpack to reveal her phone.

"Tate's Hell? Oh, no, I think that's the other way," he teased. "We might have to turn around and drive another hour and a half."

"Very funny. Oh, crap."

"Don't say crap," he told her. "What's wrong?"

"My phone's going to die." She swiped through a spider web of cracks to scan her social media pages. When there weren't any updates she sent a group text to Kayla and Caroline. *15 min out. B there soon.*

"You know you can always call me to come get you if you get freaked out, right?" Her dad asked her.

"I'm not calling you, and I'm not getting freaked out." Her phone chimed as Kayla responded they were at marker 45 in a gazebo. Caroline didn't text in.

"I'm just saying that it's the first time out with your new friends, and it's perfectly okay to…"

"There it is! Turn here, you're going to miss it!" The car turned at a long sign built into the rocks which read Tate's Hell State Forest. "They're at marker 45, by the gazebo." They drove the winding road in silence. Emma stared all around her. There was nothing so dense and green in Arizona, and even her short time in Florida had not prepared her for this. The trees gave way to huge expanses of lake before swallowing up the scenery completely with moss, trees and high grass. A sign they passed read that there were Florida Black Bears in the woods, and that it was a crime to mess with them. Emma glanced uneasily at her father, hoping he had not noticed the sign.

The road finally found a flat, grassy clearing next to a swamp. "There! Stop, they're right there!" Emma bounced with anticipation as her father pulled into a parking spot near a huge wooden structure that held two tables. Two backpacks sat at one of the tables.

"Where are their parent's?" Her dad asked. Without really registering his question she shot out of the car before it had rolled to a complete stop. "Hey!" He shouted after her.

Kayla was sitting on the dock rubbing bug spray into her olive arms. Above her Caroline turned, smiling as Emma ran up, her footsteps echoing loudly on the sun bleached boards.

"There she is," Caroline said. She stepped forward and hugged a surprised Emma. The two had spent the last five weeks in English and Algebra 2 together, but they had never been close enough to hug. "We've been waiting for you." She looked over Emma's shoulder. "Oh, you brought your dad."

"Yeah, he drove me here."

From behind her Emma heard her dad approach on the walkway. "Ladies," he said. The three girls smiled up at him.

"Hello Mr. Charles, it's good to see you again," Caroline said.

"Hello Caroline. Where are your parents?"

"They dropped us off, like an hour ago. They're coming back around seven when the park closes, then Kayla is staying the night with me. Is it okay if Emma stays the night, too?"

Emma's dad looked around him at the small grass clearing with its gazebo, at the swampy terrain, at the three small girls standing on the boardwalk. "They just left you here? Without anyone to watch you?"

"Duh, they drop us here all the time," Caroline told him. "The rangers come by like every thirty minutes so there's always someone watching. Besides, they don't want to spend all day hiking with us. Mama says if she wanted to go marching through the swamp and fighting off mosquitoes she would move down to the Everglades and sell her car. So can she?"

"Can she what?"

Caroline rolled her eyes again. "Can Emma stay the night at my place? We're going to watch that old James Cauldron movie, the one about the serial killer stalker guy."

"I guess," he answered, "but she doesn't have any overnight clothes with her."

"That's okay, we'll take care of her."

"So, your parents just leave you girls out here?" He asked. He scratched the back of his neck, a mannerism Emma knew meant he was stalling a decision he didn't want to make. "I don't know if I'm comfortable with that."

"It's fine. Like I said, the rangers come by. Besides, we have phones. If anything bad happened it's not like we would be lost on the path or anything." Emma's dad watched Caroline for what seemed like minutes, and if she was uncomfortable by his scrutiny she didn't show it. In her short time at Pinebridge Prep she had seen this display many times with their shared teachers. Caroline didn't let the advantage of adulthood dissuade her holier-than-thou attitude.

It was one of the traits Emma liked most about her.

"Okay, I guess. If you girls are sure you'll be okay out here?" It came out as a question. Caroline nodded her head.

"We're going to be great. My folks will be back at seven, and then it's sleepover time!" She grabbed Emma by the shoulders and shook her playfully.

Emma, unaware she was going to be jostled, shrieked first in surprise, then in joy at the playfulness.

"Okay, okay." He looked into his daughter's smiling eyes. "If you need me, you call me. You understand?" Seeing his sincerity, the smile dropped from Emma's face. She nodded, somber.

"We're going to be fine. Now, if you'll excuse us, we want to make it to the lakeside to go swimming before there's too many tourists." Caroline pronounced the last word with the disgust most children reserved for the darker sufferings in life.

Emma's dad nodded, winking at his daughter. "Have fun!"

"I will," she said.

Then Emma was alone with Caroline and Kayla.

"So, what do you want to do first?" Emma asked. The other two girls exchanged a smile.

"We've got to get our bags, then we're going somewhere cool," Caroline told her.

"Where?"

"The dwarf palms!" Kayla barked. Caroline shot her a dark look.

"Dwarf palms? What are those? I thought we were going swimming," Emma asked.

"We can go swimming in the lake, if you like getting eaten by alligators," Kayla said as they pushed past her.

"There aren't alligators in the lake," Emma said, trying to sound more confident than she felt.

"This is Florida, there are alligators everywhere," Caroline corrected. "Basically if there's water there are snakes and alligators in it. Why do you think they built all these wood walkways over the wetlands?"

Emma's eyes scanned the high-grassed, swampy terrain.

"Well, let's get hiking," Caroline said, her backpack securely on her back. "We've got to get to the clearing before it gets too dark."

Without answering Emma followed the two girls onto the boardwalk, their footsteps sounding like drumbeats in the hot afternoon air. They passed two pairs of hikers before they came to the next grassy clearing in the wetlands, where two tables of young children were performing tests on water samples they had taken from the preserve. A dozen pairs of eyes watched them as they walked from one boardwalk to another.

"Can we stop for a minute?" Emma asked. She sighed heavily and sat at a bench built into the side of the boardwalk's railing. She couldn't be sure, but to her it seemed like they had been walking for at least an hour.

Caroline and Kayla stood over her, watching her wipe sweat from her brow and neck.

"Here, take this," Kayla said, holding out a bottle of water. Emma took it, smiled a thanks and drank deep. If she had known this was going to be a hike, instead of a swim in a lake, she would have brought her own water and snacks. As it was she was at the mercy of her friends.

"How much longer are we going?" Emma asked, looking around her. Even the water was green here, covered in a blanket of dense algae.

Caroline scanned the surrounding area as well. "Not far, I think. You're going to like what we found. It's, like, the coolest thing that's out here."

"What is it?"

"It's a-" Kayla started. Caroline elbowed her sharply in the ribs. "Ow!"

"It's a secret, you'll see," she said. "Just wait. It's killer."

They were moving again in no time. The boardwalk gave way to land again, and this time it didn't transition back. They walked on wet grass that squeaked under their sneakers. A clearing revealed a huge lake to their left, and Emma fought off her desire to jump in and cool off. Caroline's words about snakes and alligators came to her, and she squished the urge to run and jump.

They walked until the trees closed in, then the path they walked on curved sharply right. "This way," Caroline announced. Instead of following the path she stepped into the underbrush to the left. Kayla entered the tree cover with her, and the two were immediately thrown into shadow.

Emma didn't move. Her feet were glued to the white chalk of the path.

"Well, are you coming or not?" Caroline asked. There was the slightest hint of cruelty in her voice.

Emma thought of everything that could be in the knee-high grass. They had no terrain like this in Arizona, and an entire world of unseen fears hid in the ten inches of green below her.

"What about snakes?" Her voice quivered slightly, and she hoped that they wouldn't notice.

Caroline rolled her eyes dramatically. "If there were any snakes here do you think I would be stomping down here?" Emma still didn't move, and Caroline made a frustrated noise deep in her throat. She stomped her feet on the ground, making squishing noises. "Hey, snakes! Are there any snakes in here? Spiders? Gators? Anything that wants to eat Emma? Hey Bigfoot, you in there?"

The three girls stood, listening to the woods. "There, see? Nothing in here cares that you're walking through the woods. Now would you come on, before some tourist sees us walking off the path and finds out where we're going?"

Emma stood still for a minute longer, staring at the disappointed face of Caroline and the downcast face of Kayla. These were the first friends she had made since moving clear across the country, and she sure wasn't going to let them down because of her irrational fear of snakes.

She stepped off the path, into the gently sloping high grass. Below her Caroline smiled.

Walking through the woods was harder than walking along the path. For one thing there were roots and grass tangles that tried to trip her every few steps, and then there were the shadows. The trees overhead created a canopy that blocked out almost all of the sunlight, so they were walking in a gloom that was broken occasionally with solid beams of sunlight.

The worst was the disorientation. After only a dozen steps Emma couldn't see the trail behind her. A dozen more and even the woods seemed unrecognizable. The three girls would walk in a straight line for awhile, then turn to avoid a tree or tangle of thorny bushes in their way, and Emma wasn't sure if they corrected their direction. In the dense woods there was no way to know if they had been walking in a straight line or constantly changing direction.

Her legs, already tired from the hike to the woods, started to ache with weariness. She thought of Caroline's face, disappointed and impatient, and said nothing.

"Caroline, are you sure this was the way?" Kayla asked after some time.

Caroline high-stepped over a fallen, rotten trunk. "Yes…I know it was here. It was right over here." The girls continued walking.

The brush grew thicker. Long, sharp leaves reached out to scratch against Emma's arms and legs. The woods were closing in around them, and the girls continued to walk in single file until Caroline pushed through a wall of green, sharp leaves. They closed behind her, blocking her off from the other two. When Kayla and Emma pushed through the wall of green Caroline was not there.

"Caroline?" Kayla asked, her voice breathy.

"Caroline, wait up," Emma called through the trees. There was no answer. "You know where she's going? You know where this clearing is?"

Kayla shook her head. "It wasn't like this last time. Last time it was right off the path. Last time…" her voice trailed off as she looked around her with wide eyes, near panic.

"You mean we're lost in here?" Emma looked behind her. The way they had come was as dense as ever, and there was no trace of any sort of path.

"Kayla!" Caroline's call came from their left. *Far* to the left. "Hey, I found it! It's over here!"

The girls looked at each other before pushing through the foliage to the left, toward their friend's voice. They shoved through a green wall into a wide clearing. The outside was ringed with leaves that were crowned with sharp points, and the ground was a rotten mixture of leaves and pine needles. Caroline was standing next to a wooden, high-backed chair, the wood of which still looked wet. Animal bones littered the ground around it.

"Told you I knew where it was," Caroline said.

Kayla walked to it shakily. She took off her backpack and set it by the chair. Caroline stripped off her backpack and Emma, following the other girls, did the same. Her pack made a squelching noise as it hit the leaf strewn floor.

"What is this?" Emma asked.

"This is one of the most haunted places in all of Florida," Caroline told her. "This is where Tate came when he walked through here." When she saw Emma's expression she asked, "Do you know why they call this place Tate's Hell?"

"Caroline, I'm not sure-" Kayla started. Caroline silenced her with a look.

"It's called Tate's Hell because, like a hundred and fifty years ago, there was a man that lived here called Jebediah Tate. He had a son named Cete. They tried to make the land work, but they couldn't. They were going to lose everything, so you know what they did? They called on a medicine man to help them. Kayla, get ready." As Caroline said this Kayla started to rifle through her backpack.

"The medicine man said he was going to help old man Tate, but they would have to pay. They would give him their fattest, healthiest pig every year, and they would also give him the pine-tree forest on the land. Against Cete's objections Jebediah made the deal. 'Don't forget my pig,' the medicine man told them, 'and stay out of my pines.'

"Well, they got rich and happy after that for like four years, but Jebediah was an idiot and he forgot that they owed everything to the medicine man. When the next sacrifice was due he wouldn't give it up to the medicine man, so eventually the crops and the cattle both died. Jebediah and Cete were starving. They had more pigs than they could handle, but no one wanted them. They wanted beef and corn."

She paused for a moment, glancing around at the clearing.

"Eventually Jebediah died, leaving Cete alone with this failing farm. So he did the only thing he could think of: he took his old dog into the pine forest to hunt scrub cows." Behind Caroline Kayla was standing by the chair, watching the two avidly. Caroline was almost within arm's reach of Emma, who fought the urge to take a step back.

"You know what happened in those pines?" Caroline asked. "A panther got Cete's dog, and a rattlesnake bit him in the ankle. He got all lost and turned around, and he couldn't find his way out. For nine days he was stuck in these swamps. When he came out on the other side he was, like, fifty miles away. He said he had seen Hell, said he had seen the Devil and walked through his kingdom. He even said he sat in the Devil's throne." Emma and Caroline were very close now. Slowly Caroline reached out and took Emma's hand, then turned back to the chair in the clearing.

"See, he was half right. Xan is not the Devil," she turned to look deep into Emma's eyes, "but this is his chair."

"Zan?" Emma asked.

"Xan," Caroline corrected. "There are places in Florida, hidden far away from people, where little gods still have influence. This is one of those places. Xan took Cete, but kicked him out because he wasn't worthy."

Caroline pulled a hesitant Emma to where the chair and Kayla stood waiting.

"Not worthy?" Emma questioned. She was sure the two were playing a prank on her. This must be a special kind of Florida hazing that was designed to scare her senseless, and despite the cold spike of fear she felt in her chest she refused to let the other two see her fear.

"Xan told them - told both Tate men - that they had to give him a pig as a sacrifice every year, then they would be in his good graces. When Cete refused to give the pig up, just like his dad, he proved that he wasn't worthy. Now it's time to see if you're worthy."

Emma looked from one girl to the other. "Worthy of what?"

"To see Xan. All you have to do is sit in the chair." Emma looked to Kayla, who was examining the ground to the left of her and Caroline. "We both did it already, and I've got to tell you that it's gonna be cool!" Emma was standing in front of the high-backed chair, and with a hard push Caroline knocked her backwards. Her legs hit the wet seat, and she fell back into it. A small, disgusted cry escaped her lips, but before she could move Caroline's hands brought her arms to the moldy armrests and held them there. Caroline straddled Emma, holding her in place with her weight. Her bony knees dug into Emma's thighs.

"Ow, what the crap? Get off me!"

Caroline raised her head to the canopy over them. "Xan, we brought you the sacrifice. Accept this pig, and deem us worthy!" She looked at Kayla, still standing next to the chair, her eyes wide. To Emma it looked like Kayla was in shock. "Do it," Caroline told her.

Kayla didn't move.

"Do it!" Kayla looked from Emma to Caroline, but hesitated at the sharp command. When Emma looked at the girl on top of her she saw true madness in her face. Fear began to course through her then, stronger than before.

"Fucking do it, you stupid bitch!"

When Kayla looked at Emma her face was set with determination. The girl beside the chair raised her fist, a kitchen knife clutched in it. The blade was dull in the gloom, but it was almost the length of Kayla's forearm. It was the kind of knife Emma's dad had in their kitchen back home, the kind he called his 'do anything' knife.

Before Emma could react Kayla stabbed out with the knife.

At first there was no pain, just a pinch in her side. Then she could feel the blade slide into her, yet there was still no pain. Kayla held up the blade, now covered in a thick liquid which looked black in the shadows.

"You idiot, you're supposed to stab her in the heart!" Emma barely registered the words. Her side was wet, and starting to ache. With every second the pain became worse, and with each heartbeat her right side felt hotter and hotter.

In desperation Emma pitched herself forward. Caroline had been kneeling on top of her, and she pitched backwards at the movement. She landed on the moist ground with a harsh grunt. Emma turned to face Kayla, who was still holding the knife.

"Wh...what are you doing?" Caroline wheezed on the ground. "Kill her!"

The words seemed to snap Kayla out of her daze. Her eyes focused, and the grip on the knife hardened.

"Kayla, wait" Emma started, not knowing what to say next. Instead she pointed to a spot at the other end of the clearing. When Kayla turned to look Emma ran.

She didn't think about direction as she ran, only that she had to put distance between herself and the girls in the clearing. The barrier of green she hit at the edge of the clearing was like a wall, and she pushed hard against the wide, sharp leaves until they gave in and swallowed her. There was no visibility at all; the more she ran, the less she could see. There was green all around her, scratching, clawing, holding her, slowing her down. Her side was throbbing hard now, and a sharp needle of pain stabbed her whenever she put her right foot down.

Behind her were sounds of pursuit through the

woods.

Emma broke through the densest of the growth, vaguely noting that there were small cuts and scratches all over her arms and legs. Her face, and neck, stung from their own greenery-induced marks. Emma tried to run as soon as her feet hit clear ground, but her ankle twisted. She fell onto the ground hard, her side blossoming in a flower of pain.

Looking around she saw a root tangled twice around her ankle. *How the Hell?* The sound of her approaching attackers cut the thought off, and she tore at the green root until she could wiggle her foot out of the tendrils. As soon as she set her weight down she cried out, collapsing to her knees. The sounds of Kayla and Caroline stopped briefly as they heard her.

Emma looked to her swollen ankle. It was at least sprained, if not broken.

Her attackers started through the leaves again. Emma scrambled to a nearby tree, crawling to the far side and pulling her knees to her chest. She made herself as small as she could, knowing that if they saw her around the tree they would kill her. Emma wondered if they would try and drag her back to the chair before they stabbed her to death.

If they did she would fight them every step of the way.

The girls soon emerged from the wall of spikes and stood, panting on the other side of Emma's tree. Emma held her breath, her heart was beating so hard that she could feel it under her shirt. There was no way they couldn't hear it thundering through the woods.

"Where did she go?" Caroline spat from the other side of the tree. Her voice wasn't light and playful anymore. "I'm going to kill that little bitch." The girls shuffled in the leaves for a few seconds. Emma was sure they would come around the tree and see her, but their footsteps disappeared into the woods.

When Emma thought they were a decent distance away she rose, trying to run. Her right side and leg were wet and sticky. Her shirt was stuck to her side, the material tugging painfully every time she moved. Putting any weight at all on her left foot was like stepping on glass. She knew that she was hobbling through the unfamiliar woods more than running, but she couldn't stop.

"Emma," Caroline called from somewhere behind her. "Emma, where are you? We want to help you."

Emma rounded another tree and pressed her back firmly against it. She was having trouble pulling air into her lungs, and her head was swimming. As she bent over to catch her breath the woods started to fade to gray around her.

Oh no, don't you pass out now, she thought. *If I pass out here they'll kill me.*

"Emma!" Caroline's voice was closer, impossibly close. They were right behind her tree again as they circled back. Emma straightened, pressing herself hard against the scratchy bark of the tree. "Emma!" The next time Caroline called she was in front of Emma, only about a hundred feet or so away.

Emma scanned the trees, but couldn't see very far in the gloom. She looked up through the canopy above her, and her heart lurched in her chest. Between the branches the sky was a dark violet. Three small, brilliant stars watched her from above, which seemed impossible. It had been late afternoon when they stepped off the path, but they had been in the woods for maybe an hour tops. Had she really lost so much time?

When Caroline called out for her again, this time behind her tree and a little farther away, Emma took off in the direction she thought she had been going.

Her head swam. Her skin felt cold, but her side where Kayla had stabbed her was on fire. She tripped over a tangle of roots and fell, crying out in a symphony of pain, fear and frustration. "I heard her," Kayla said from somewhere to her left. Emma's blood ran cold. "She's over here!"

Emma was on her feet and moving as fast as she could. Somewhere ahead of her there was light, so without thinking she diverted in that direction. When she hit a wall of thick leaves she didn't slow, but plowed right into them. With her head down and her eyes closed she pushed on, and when the woods let her go again she fell back into the clearing. Looming above her was the chair, and in the middle of the clearing someone had built a small fire. Somehow she had made a complete circle to end up back where she started.

Emma felt her eyes sting. "No," she whispered, "No,

no, no..." A twig snapped across the clearing, and Emma flattened herself against the chair's tall back. It occurred to her that she was just another small animal, running from hiding spot to hiding spot to get away from some hungry predators.

There was no further sound in the clearing. Slowly she looked around the edge of the chair. The clearing was a confusion of shapes and shadows in the night, and any of the squat shapes could have been someone crouched in wait for her to come out. Or they could have been dwarf palms, their wide leaves reaching out with hungry, needled fingers.

Emma scanned the edges of the clearing. If she could find where they came in...

A shadow moved against a pale tree. Emma didn't move. She could barely breathe. She watched the shifting shadows caused by the campfire, thinking those were probably what she had seen in the first place. After what seemed like an eternity the figure against the tree moved again, and she could tell that it was tall and lanky. She couldn't see what was casting the shadow, only that it seemed to be patrolling around the far side of the clearing.

As she watched the thing seemed to turn toward her, and Emma let out an involuntary whimper. Against the pale trunks of the trees behind it the thing seemed completely made of void. Its outline shifted and changed, and it looked like the poorly-drawn cartoons she sometimes saw on YouTube. The two held each other's gaze - Emma's hurt and scared, and the shadow's dark and mysterious.

It bent over and, though nothing seemed to touch them, the wall of green leaves parted. Slowly Emma rose to her feet. Now, outside of her hiding place, she faced the thing straight on. It had no real body that she could see, and had she not paid attention it would have only been another shadow in the woods. It was holding the way for her, like a doorman.

"Are you..." Emma's voice cracked, and her throat hurt. She cleared her dry throat, swallowed a few times, and tried again. "Are you Cete Tate?" The shadow didn't answer. She took a step forward. "Are you…" she swallowed again, "Xan?" Again it didn't answer. She took another step. "Where does that go? Will that get me out, or does that lead to them? Caroline and Kayla, I mean." Again there was no response. A breeze blew through the clearing, and in it Emma thought she heard whispering behind her.

Did she trust this – whatever it was – to help her? Caroline seemed to think Xan was on her side, but this might be her only way out.

Emma shook her head. There really was no choice. She crept to where the leaves were parted, watching the shadow-thing all the time. It didn't move. Slowly she stepped into the greenery, glancing back every few steps until her view of the thing was lost. Before her the green departed, behind her it closed. No roots grabbed at her, and no leaves cut her. She was in her own pocket of protection.

She stepped out of the claustrophobic green and looked around. There were a dozen trees ahead of her, and through them was the sun-lit pathway they had come from. She walked to it, feeling relief and pain and weariness all weighing her down. When she stepped out of the trees she breathed deep.

The ground rose gradually above her, and she was back at the hill where they had first gotten off the trail. Emma fell to her knees and started to climb the grassy embankment. Her strength gave out halfway up, and she fell onto the grass. Though the ground was wet it was not the dead, rotten wet of the woods; this was the wet of fresh grass in the late afternoon.

The world began to grow gray again. Emma idly wondered if the girls were still chasing her. She wondered if they would find her here, laying in the grass, and decide this was close enough to the chair to kill her. Her eyes drooped, and it took all of her strength to open them again.

Far away she heard voices.

Her eyes closed a second time, and again she fought to open them.

"Oh my God," someone said from somewhere above her. "It's a little girl!"

She couldn't turn over, couldn't even raise her head. She was utterly spent.

"Call nine-one-one," the voice said in a panic. There were hands on her, but the world was swimming away. "She's alive, get an ambulance!"

She thought of the girls she had wanted to be her

friends luring her into the woods. She thought of the roots twisting themselves around her ankle. She thought of the shadow showing her the way out. The voice above her was asking something over and over, but she could barely make it out. She thought it was "Who did this to you?" but it could have been "Who saved you?"

She sighed, the word coming from her almost without effort. "Xan."

On the edge of unconsciousness, somewhere deep in the woods where she shouldn't have been able to hear, two girls started to scream.

Emma Charles passed out in the stranger's arms as the sound of a siren approached.

Brian Duncan
About the Author

Brian Duncan is a writer and artist in Florida where he resides with his wife and two sons, Ben and Michael. As a student of English and Journalism he explores many styles of writing, focusing mainly on suspenseful fantasy horror. When he is not writing he can be found sitting around a table playing board games or iceside at a Lightning game. Currently he is training for his first half marathon.

Brian can be contacted at the following:

www.Excessiveramblings.com

www.Facebook.com/authorBrianDuncan

www.Instagram.com/S.BrianDuncan

Don't Miss Out!

Looking for additional content?
Becoming an exclusive Patreon member gives you
a chance to be a part of the action as well as giving you
creative content every single month, no matter the tier.
Vote on upcoming themes, extra author interview
questions, get free eBooks and in the higher tiers get
paperbacks sent to your home before they are even
released.

Here at Eerie River Publishing, we are focused on
providing paid writing opportunities for all indie authors.
Outside of our limited drabble collections we put out
each year, every single written piece that we publish
-including short stories featured in this collection have
been paid for.
https://www.patreon.com/EerieRiverPub

Sign up for Eerie River Publishing's monthly newsletter
to get all the up to date information on new releases,
author interviews, book giveaways and so much more.
Sign up for our newsletter here.
https://mailchi.mp/71e45b6d5880/welcomebook